for B, E, and BLT

HOW A WOMAN BECOMES A LAKE

ALSO BY MARJORIE CELONA

Y

JANUARY 1986

CHAPTER ONE

Lewis

He found the car in the second parking lot at Squire Point, doors splayed, engine on. It was a fancy car—something Lewis Côté could never dream of owning. He climbed into the driver's seat, scanned the expensive leather, ran his hands over the plush black steering wheel, and took the keys out of the ignition. Through the car's open doors, the snow fell around him, landed on his thighs, and blew into his hair. Someone had drawn a pattern in the condensation on the passenger side window—crosshatches, as if to play tic-tac-toe. Lewis rooted through the glove compartment, checked under the seats, spun around. The back seat was covered in grey and white dog hair, so Lewis whistled and clapped, and after a few minutes a nice-looking dog—a husky, perhaps—emerged from the woods, its fur caked with snow.

"Hey, boy," Lewis said, patting the dog's head and letting it lick his hands. "Help me out here."

They walked together, Lewis having fashioned a makeshift leash from a rope he had in the trunk of his patrol car. The trail was icy and Lewis's boots slid out from under him. He walked like a duck to keep his balance. The cold air slivered his lungs. There was no reason to draw his gun, but his free hand hovered by his hip, in case.

An hour ago, a woman named Vera Gusev had called the station from the Squire Point pay phone, saying that she had found a little boy. She was at the second parking lot, she said, the boy keeping warm in her car. He had been separated from his father in the woods and was cold but fine—and that was all she said. The sound of her dropping the receiver, it clanging off the side of the phone booth, a muffled cry that could have been "hey" or "wait," then nothing. Lewis had driven cautiously to the scene, the roads slick. New Year's Day was a quiet one on the job, everyone asleep, hung over, or in jail from whatever nonsense they'd gotten up to the night before. He cursed himself now for taking his time.

When had it ever been this cold? The blizzard had come at the end of November, blanketing the whole region, and then the temperature had plunged. All anyone could talk about was the weather. Not in eighty years had so much snow fallen. Most people in Whale Bay didn't even own proper winter coats. Usually it snowed once or twice a year, an inch or two, and melted by the morning. The blizzard was fun at first. School cancelled; everyone out walking. The army was called in to salt the roads. No plows—there wasn't money for that. Anyone from the East Coast—or the Midwest, as was the case with Lewis—thought this was a non-event, silly even. The high comedy of shovelling a driveway with a cookie sheet, a casserole dish, the lid of a garbage can. The snow was so high that children knocked down foot-long icicles from the street lights and used them as swords.

Only one death so far: a man whose car had filled with carbon monoxide as he waited for his windshield to defrost, the tailpipe clogged with snow. There wasn't much sympathy for him. Should've known better. Maybe suicide then. A homeless man had almost died of hypothermia, but was fine—had been interviewed by the local news while eating a dish of ice cream in his hospital bed.

Of course, the requisite traffic accidents and power outages. A fist fight in a grocery store over the last carton of milk. Some looting. A collapsed roof, a destroyed greenhouse. Mostly, though, the eerie silence that accompanies so much snow, and the inevitable camaraderie from enduring an out-of-the-ordinary event. A return to kindness, Lewis thought. The simplicity of survival. He had missed the snow.

He was twenty-four, attractive yet baby-faced, unmarried and without children—still a boy in some ways, even though he carried a baton and a gun. He got a little thrill when he told people what he did for a living. "So young!" they said and he wanted to say, "Do you think I haven't paid my dues? Do you think I don't deserve it?" He wondered when he would stop being young. When he would cease to be the baby of the department. When all the joshing, the incessant joking around about his boyish looks, would stop. He felt himself to be a deeply earnest person. A good person. Even as a boy, he had a knack for reading people, a skill he attributed to his father, who was crazy in an invisible, functional way, so that Lewis had spent much of his life trying to piece together what had made his childhood so fraught, and why as a child he had been so nervous and unhappy. His mother had died so long ago that he had almost no memories of her, but there was an uncle he planned to contact someday, who he hoped could provide answers. But Lewis hadn't gotten around to it yet. It seemed like such a huge undertaking: to go after the truth like that.

It was snowing again. It had been snowing all day and the forest was silent except for Lewis's footfalls and the heavy panting of the dog. The dog pulled hard on the leash and Lewis had to brace himself on a tree trunk so he wouldn't spill forward.

"Whoa, boy," he said, then again more forcefully, snapping the leash a bit. But the dog was unrelenting and led him off the trail and into the woods. The snow fogged his glasses and Lewis could taste it on his lips, metallic and cold. He hoped he wasn't about to uncover some grisly scene, though he did feel something bubbling up within him, something like excitement. He looked behind him, trying to memorize his way back to the trail. Squire Point was a confusing place. There were two parking lots with trailheads—both led to a large reservoir with a swimming hole that locals called "the lake"; the second trail cut through a small campground. The trails were unmarked and it was easy to go in circles. People often got lost, but all were usually found within a few hours. There were only so many ways a person could go.

"Vera Gusev? Hello?"

Why come out here in such bad conditions? Why not stay home? The dog leapt over a fallen tree and Lewis scrambled over it, caught his pant leg on a branch. He felt the snow creep into his socks, cold water between his toes. His hands burned. He passed the abandoned campground, and then he and the dog were standing at the edge of the lake, frozen over and covered with a dusting of snow. The dog whined and pulled against the leash, wanting to go out onto the ice.

"No, no," he said to the dog. "Bad idea."

Although the snow was falling fast, Lewis thought he could make out a trail of footprints on the ice. He squinted, snow in his eyelashes. Nothing. The footprints were gone. He hoped Vera and the boy hadn't wandered onto the ice. People thought frozen lakes were stable, and they walked out onto them. People did this sort of thing all the time. They drove snowmobiles and trucks onto lakes! Lewis had done this as a boy every winter, in his father's red pickup truck, on Lake Mendota. Even there, two or three people fell in every year, fishermen mostly, their bodies pulled out—sometimes alive, sometimes not—covered in icicles. That was the trouble with frozen lakes. There was no way to tell the thickness of the ice, nor the depth of the water beneath.

"Okay, boy," Lewis said to the dog, and the dog sat, obediently, by Lewis's side. The snow stopped, as if someone had flicked a switch. Now that the sky had cleared, Lewis could see the great iced-over expanse of the lake, a pale blue colour like a wolf's eye, and the bright swatches of beach sand that lay below the ice, looking almost tropical despite the cold. A bird loitered on a branch, repeating its song. Lewis put his hand on top of the dog's warm head. His hand seemed to mould perfectly to the shape of the dog's head, as if it was meant to be there, meant to fill the emptiness of his hand. How did anyone get through life without a dog? He'd had a border terrier when he was a boy, and perhaps that was why he was largely okay, despite what he had been through with his father. Someone had to love you unconditionally in order for you to survive. Someone had to love you as much as you needed to be loved.

He scanned the lake, but there was no one. No signs of anyone having fallen through. He looked at the dog, tongue out, expectant. He heard the rumble of an airplane overhead. What can you see that I can't see? What do you know that I don't know? If Vera Gusev and the lost boy were out there, in the forest or under the ice, the lake, the dog, the plane, the sky—they gave away nothing.

CHAPTER TWO

Jesse

The paper boats were difficult to make, and Jesse's hands were clumsy from the cold. It was New Year's Day, and his father had brought him and his brother to Squire Point. They were supposed to write their wishes for the New Year on the paper boats, then set them on the surface of the frozen lake and wait for spring. When the ice melted, their father said, their wishes would come true.

Jesse was ten, and Dmitri, six. They sat in the back seat of their father's car with the heat on high, each with a sheet of pale blue paper and a black felt pen. Theirs was the only car in the parking lot. Their father told them that most people preferred to go to malls. They had gone to the mall once, but the crying babies had upset their father and he had been short with his sons, annoyed. What was there to do with your children when you didn't live with them anymore? And, so, they drove around.

On these long drives, they listened to the marine forecast. Their father had a transistor radio that bleated small-craft advisories, swells, wind waves, and knots. It was always on, though their father hadn't gone sailing in years. Something he had done in a previous life—that was how he put it—when he still lived in San Garcia, a two-days' drive away.

Their father had driven them out to Squire Point slowly, the roads unplowed. The car hit a pothole and their father swore. The Pineapple Express, their father said, and Jesse thought he was talking nonsense again. Their father talked of spiritual things sometimes—the universe and reincarnation; ghosts, spirits, telepathy—and he began to do so now. Squire Point was a magical place, their father said, a sacred place. It wasn't all crazy talk, like their mother, Evelina, said. Jesse felt that Squire Point was indeed sacred; he felt it in his bones. He knew Dmitri would feel it soon, too. You had to be old enough to feel things like that.

They pulled onto the highway and their father told the boys about his old days in San Garcia, about his new girlfriend, and about his ex-girlfriends, an impressive list. He farted. He farted again and again. He sang and they made up songs. He hollered at a woman in a bus shelter, called her "chicky-poo." He lit a cigarette but did not roll the window down. He didn't wear a seat belt, though the boys were buckled in tight. It seemed to Jesse that it was a very long drive out to Squire Point, but time slowed when he was with his father—whether because he savoured the few afternoons they spent together, or dreaded them, he couldn't tell.

Their father's name was Leo, short for Galileo, though hardly anyone knew that. He was muscular, though too thin, with a curved neck like a heron's and a big nose. Jesse knew he looked like his father—olive skin, so dark in summer it was almost black; the same dark hair; that same nose. *Remarkable* was the word people used—it's remarkable how much you look like your father, they said. At first glance his father was a handsome man. The closer Jesse looked at his father, though, the less handsome he became. His eyes darkened when he drank: glassy and black, sunken into his face. He'd been born with a club foot and it had been corrected with surgery, but an ugly scar ran across his ankle that to Jesse looked like the face of a monster. His left foot and leg were smaller than his right—another thing hardly anyone knew. Who would notice such a thing? Most people didn't notice much—even at ten, Jesse knew that to be true.

But Jesse noticed everything. His father kept a little bottle of tequila in the glove compartment and a slice of lemon in a plastic bag, smoked hand-rolled cigarettes from butts he'd picked off the ground. Their mother had kicked him out six months ago. Before he left, they all lived in an old house with a giant monkey-puzzle tree in the front yard. Now the boys lived with their mother in a small white beach house, and their father lived in a one-room apartment in what was said to be the seedy part of town. He slept on a foam mattress, with a travel pillow and a navy-blue sleeping bag, an extra blanket wadded in the closet for the boys. Nothing on the walls. A suitcase in the corner. No washer or dryer. A red toothbrush beside the kitchen sink. Nothing in the fridge except a half-empty bottle of wine. Jesse sensed that other people didn't live this way. His father's clean-shaven face, the medicinal smell of his aftershave, the specks of blood on his chin stopped up with toilet paper. The sight of him, the sound of his voice, made Jesse feel as if his whole body might shatter. Every time he'd seen his father these past six months—once a week was their current arrangement—his mother asked whether he'd had a nice time. He understood that he had to say yes. He knew, on some primal level, that it was better to have a bit of a father than no father at all.

Besides, his father was smiling and telling Dmitri a joke about a football-playing centipede. He pulled into the first parking lot at Squire Point, reached into his jacket, downed a can of beer in three gulps, then threw the empty can out the window and into the snow. "So the coach says to the centipede," his father said, "'Where were *you* during the first half?'"

Jesse watched his father glance at Dmitri, pause, pause some more, then, when the silence had become almost unbearable, his father erupted: "And the centipede says, 'I was putting on my shoes!'"

He seemed to be in a good mood. He told his sons that after they made the paper boats, he would let them shoot his rifle. They were not to tell their mother this, though they could—they *should*—tell her about the paper boats.

"You hear me?" he said, and Jesse nodded, remembering not to act too excited—their father was easily irritated, and the day could darken. That was the problem with his father, his mother had told him—he was neither good nor bad, but rather half of one and half of the other.

Outside the fogged-up windows of the car, the spindly birch trees, encased in ice, looked as though they were made of glass. Jesse wrote his wish on one side of the paper, turned it over, folded it, made a crease, and brought the edges together to form a V. The next part was difficult, and his father spoke in a slow, loud voice, holding up his piece of paper to demonstrate how, with the right folds, it could become a little hat that could then be flattened into a diamond.

Dmitri looked bewildered, and Jesse's fingers shook, but soon the diamonds became little triangles, and then even smaller hats, and when the boys pinched the edges of their pieces of paper and pulled them apart, two small blue boats emerged in their hands.

"Put a penny in the bottom to weigh it down," their father said, and passed each of his sons a coin. "Helps the wishes come true."

Last weekend, Jesse had met his father's new girlfriend. She was shorter than his mother, as thin and muscular as a dancer. Her name was Holly, and she had wild blond hair and wore no makeup. She answered the door in a long white gauzy dress, black leggings, and beat-up running shoes without socks. On the drive over, his father told the boys that she ran a harbourfront art gallery, with a studio in the back where she slept and an easel for her own work.

Jesse could tell she was pretty, but like his father, she seemed off. For instance, her studio had no bathroom or kitchen. She kept a bucket in the closet with a roll of toilet paper beside it, and in the same closet she stored cereal, peanut butter, soup cans, a hot plate, and a camping stove. When they had first arrived, their father presented her with, as he put it, a "windfall": three half-used rolls of toilet paper, a tube of toothpaste, a large bag of beef jerky, and a bottle of multivitamins. Then, of course, out came the cans of beer.

She was an artist, sold her greeting cards and calendars to tourists. His father said the word *artist* with some reverence. Jesse thought the greeting cards were dumb. Watercolour paintings of flowers and fishing boats, so boring. Why not take a picture? Still, his father seemed lighter in her presence, and Jesse felt a tinge of guilt for he realized that he, too, was having a good time. Holly told him and Dmitri to look up, and when they did, they saw that the ceiling was covered in hundreds of origami birds. She put on some kind of tribal music and danced with her arms over her head. Jesse saw that she did not shave her underarms. It was thrilling to see the wild tufts of dark hair, as thick as his father's, sprouting from those bone-thin white arms.

"Let me draw your boy," she said. She stood behind a butcher-block table and sketched Jesse, then handed him a piece of paper with a charcoal portrait of his face. He could see his father beaming at this gesture, this bond between them. It *was* flattering to be drawn, and Jesse blushed.

When he got home, he hid the drawing under his bed where his mother would never think of looking. But she must have seen the piece of heavy construction paper while she was vacuuming. She presented him with it the next day: a charcoal rendition of his big eyes and sunken cheeks, his look of alarm, his bangs parted evenly down the centre of his forehead.

"He shouldn't make you spend time with his girlfriends," she said. Her tone was sharp, like when Dmitri was first born and she would get so frustrated that she would stop the car, reach over Jesse's body, unbuckle his seat belt, push open the car door, push him out.

After his mother went into her bedroom for the night, Jesse climbed into Dmitri's bed and fell asleep with his hand on his brother's back. He watched his brother's little sleeping body breathe in and out beside him. He had torn the drawing into pieces to show his mother that it meant nothing.

It was Jesse's idea to run back onto the lake and steal a look at his father's wish. His father had left his cigarettes in the car and was stomping away from the boys, calling over his shoulder at them to stay on the trail.

Jesse wondered what he wanted his father's paper boat to say: *I want to come back. I miss Jesse. I miss my family.* Once his father was out of sight, he grabbed Dmitri by the hand, told him to be quiet, and the two of them sprinted to the edge of the lake, then inched out carefully, testing each step to make sure the ice could support their weight. The lake was covered in a fine layer of snow, and they held each other's hands tight. Jesse figured he had about five minutes before his father returned.

He thought that a frozen lake would look something like a mirror, and that when he looked down, he would see his reflection. But the ice beneath his feet was covered in snow, and there was nothing to see within it.

Dmitri saw the bear tracks first and pointed at the imprint. They were only a few feet out on the lake and the tracks were hard to make out, could even be a big dog's. The bear had come out about ten feet onto the lake, then circled back. Jesse told Dmitri not to worry, for already his brother's face was breaking into a cry, and if his father returned and found his youngest son upset, Jesse knew he would be punished; it didn't matter why or what had happened. His father got angry. He got so angry Jesse thought he was going to kill them, smash every glass in the house and bust out every window with his fist and kick over the chairs and pound the table with a hammer until it crashed into a million pieces on the floor. He'd be looking at the coffee pot and the next minute it was being whipped across the room, not for any reason, even when everything else was right—bills paid, waffles on the table, the radio on. The night their mother kicked him out, he got so angry he ripped out a handful of her hair.

Jesse's hands began to shake from the memory, and he tried to figure out how long it had been since his father had left to get his cigarettes. Two, three minutes? Not long. But for how long had he looked at the bear tracks? Jesse pinched Dmitri's arm and told him to shut up—"Shut up, you *wimp*!"—and pushed his brother ahead of him. "Get going," he said. "Dad will be back soon. Hurry up, let's go." A few puddles had formed in the snow ahead of them but Jesse continued, his hand gripping the back of his brother's coat for stability. Neither boy was dressed right. The wind ran through Jesse's jacket and he felt the ice through the soles of his rubber boots. He wished he had on another pair of socks. He wished that he were home with his mother, that he was anywhere but here, on this frozen lake, miles from his house, with a damned bear and his crying brother and the long day ahead of him in the cold with his father. He was ashamed that he hadn't been able to think of something better to write on his paper boat—he should have wished for his family to be together again, for his father to be sweet like he was before Dmitri was born. Instead he'd been so nervous to finish his boat before his father got impatient that he scribbled *I want a dog* even though there was no point in wishing for something like that. He would either get a dog or he wouldn't, and luck had nothing to do with it.

"What did you wish for, Dmitri?" he asked but his brother didn't answer. He didn't have to. Jesse knew that Dmitri wanted only for his father to come home. Dmitri, the favourite. Dmitri, the good. Dmitri, with the wavy hair of his mother. Dmitri, with the innocent face full of freckles.

The boys walked along the ice until they saw the blue paper boats ahead of them, sodden, half-submerged in an inch of snow. One had begun to unravel and lay on its side. The thaw would not carry them to the reservoir. They would be buried in the snow, destroyed, forgotten. Jesse felt a horrible ache in his chest.

Dmitri stood shivering, his head down and tears in his eyes, while Jesse knelt and unfolded the sturdiest-looking boat, removed the penny and set it on the ice. His father wrote in uneven capital letters, much of it already wet and illegible. It was surprisingly long—almost a full page. He must have written it before he picked them up.

I WANT TO HAVE A REAL, SINCERE TALK WITH EVELINA AND TELL HER I'M GETTING REMARRIED.

The ice shifted underneath his feet, and Jesse snapped his head up, grabbed Dmitri so he wouldn't fall. Their father should not have left them out here, not even for five minutes. "Don't make me angry," Jesse muttered. It was something his father said and he found himself saying the same words—Don't make me angry, you don't want to make me angry. He felt the burn of rage spreading through his chest and into his throat and behind his eyes. It was time, Jesse thought, to teach his father a lesson.

CHAPTER THREE

Denny

Denny Gusev heard the knock at the door and ignored it. It was late afternoon, but he hadn't gotten out of bed, hadn't bathed, hadn't had a cup of coffee. His wife had been gone all day. She'd taken Scout to Squire Point as she did every morning, probably stopped at the store afterwards, they were out of milk, couldn't hurt to pick up a few things. Maybe she had an appointment today—he couldn't remember.

He got up wearily, pulled on his bathrobe, and headed for the front door. He'd been lost in some sort of daydream about an ex-girlfriend, how he used to ride a bicycle. He checked the wall clock as he passed the kitchen: almost four. UPS guy maybe; too early for Mormons. A summons? Oh, to be an early riser and go-getter like his wife; to be ready for the world by 6 A.M. He would never be that person. Guilt began the moment he woke and saw Vera's half of the bed already made. Guilt as he rubbed the sleep from his eyes in the bathroom mirror, knowing he was rising only because Vera was up, knowing if it were up to him—his lazy, slovenly self—he would sleep until noon. Guilt when he walked into the kitchen to see her coffee cup and breakfast dishes washed and drying on the bamboo rack, Scout's leash missing from the hook by the back door, traces of kibble in his bowl, his water dish refilled. Guilt at his hand resting so comfortably on his belly as he perused the misty morning from the kitchen window, the ocean obscured. Guilt that some bird was pecking around on the snow-covered deck and the feeder was empty. Guilt that he needed to start his day, shovel his way out to the studio, finally finish the engagement ring he'd promised a client weeks ago. Guilt at anything, at everything, oh, and now the guilt that the knocking at the door was getting louder, the person impatient, knowing somehow that this lazy man had scrambled back into the bedroom to find some clothes. Guilt at his clothes left in a heap, the fabric cold and sort of slimy feeling from being on the floor, one foot slipped into one pant leg, the knocking so much louder, my god, man, it's only a UPS package for heaven's sake; guilt that the shirt he pulled over his head had a smear of grease from last night's buttery popcorn, painfully visible over the sad expanse of his stomach. He opened the door and saw a policeman—and sitting beside this policeman was his own dog.

He led the policeman into his dark living room, cleared the pile of *Time* magazines off the couch, and invited him to sit down. The policeman untied the makeshift leash and Scout bounded into the kitchen and began loudly lapping water. An empty bottle of bourbon sat on the coffee table from the night before, and Denny and the policeman looked at it, then up at each other. He felt suddenly ashamed of the opulence of the living room—the modern halogen ceiling lights, the grey velvet couch, the built-in bookshelves with blown-glass vases and expensive books about art and design. Vera liked nice things, showy things. Everything had to be grey, white, or black. Who do you think is going to stop by—*Architectural Digest*? It was meant as a joke, but he had hurt her feelings.

The policeman told him about the call Vera had made from the Squire Point pay phone. She had found a little boy in the woods, and had told the dispatcher that they were waiting in her car at the second parking lot. But when the policeman arrived, she and the little boy were nowhere to be found. Her car was idling, the doors wide open. The dog, running loose in the woods. Maybe, the policeman said, they had for some reason left the parking lot and gotten lost on the trails? Maybe the dog had run off and they had followed?

"I'm sorry," Denny said. He rose to his feet. "I don't understand. Why would she leave the car on—the doors open—"

"What time did she leave to walk the dog?"

"I don't know. Later than usual. After lunch? She goes to Squire every day," Denny said. "I slept in and when I woke, she was gone, Scout's leash was gone. She usually goes before work—"

"To the woods by herself?"

"It's not a dangerous place, as far as I know," said Denny, and his voice was frantic, high-pitched. He sat and buried his head in his hands. He looked at the latest issue of *Time* beside him on the couch, with its big cover story about Halley's comet about to pass by. "I used to go with her—I should have gone with her—she loves going for these long walks." He paused, collected himself. "I, well," he patted his belly, "am not so diligent." A joke at a time like this? What was he doing?

The policeman tilted his head. "You weren't worried when she didn't come home?"

"I thought maybe she ran some errands—or had an appointment I'd forgotten about. We don't really check up on each other, if you know what I mean."

We don't really check up on each other. Why? Why hadn't he called out to her as she left and asked when she would be home? Was it possible that he hadn't wanted her to return? Hadn't wanted to face the moment when she came through the door and saw that, yet again, he'd done nothing with his day? That this year would be the same as the last?

Sometimes when he heard Vera's car, he'd scramble out the back door and into the studio, pretend he'd been in there for hours. He sensed she never fell for it. And, well, he could tell by the way she'd slammed the front door when she left for Squire Point that she was still mad at him. He had wanted to stay up and watch the fireworks last night, that was all—it was New Year's Eve! He wanted to have a few drinks at the house, then walk to the harbour, celebrate with the crowd. He didn't want to be stuck in the house. Was that such a crime? Apparently it was. His drinking! His socializing! His lateness coming to bed! Vera with her goddamned routines—in bed by nine, up at six. Never a deviation. Her rigidity was maddening, especially on a night like New Year's Eve. Why couldn't they go watch the fireworks like normal people? Or—if she didn't want to go, why couldn't he go alone? No. She wanted him to stay home, eat dinner with her, talk with her in the living room, go to bed with her at nine.

But by nine they were shouting at each other. She stomped outside, furiously smoked a cigarette, stormed back into the house and into the bedroom, pushed her earplugs into her ears and turned off the light, leaving him with his bourbon in the living room. He drank and listened to the revelry outside. Craned his neck out the window to get a look at the fireworks. Counted down in a whisper, checking his watch. Then, with a boldness that astonished him, he left. He snuck out like a teenager, watched the fireworks over the harbour, then slunk back home. Another year. He wept, soundlessly, mouth open, in the studio before finally trudging into the house. He had trouble not catastrophizing. Every time they fought, he feared the marriage was over.

"An appointment seems unlikely," said the policeman. "Everything is closed."

"Do you think she was kidnapped?" Denny asked.

"No, no, I think she's lost, but—"

"Then shouldn't you be searching for her? It will be dark soon. What if my wife is out there? And we are, we are—"

"There's a search and rescue team being assembled as we speak, Mr. Gusev—what I am trying to determine now is if there's anywhere else she could be."

"No," said Denny.

"How old is your wife?" the policeman asked.

"Thirty," said Denny.

"Younger than—"

"Yes."

"Do you have children?" the policeman asked, and Denny watched him scan the living room for pictures, the floor, what he could make out of the bedroom.

"We're planning to, despite—despite—listen, is my wife missing? Is that what you're telling me now?"

"I'm trying to determine that. There are other possibilities."

"Other possibilities?"

The policeman took out a small notepad and began writing something down. "Is there anyone who can confirm that you were here all day?"

"No, I don't think so, I mean I was asleep." He felt the guilt, again, spreading over him like sweat.

Until this moment, his life had been relatively easy: his father's apprentice since he was twelve; supporting himself as a custom jeweller by the time he was twenty. He was a lucky person, an exceptional person. Even his arthritis diagnosis had seemed beside the point at first—a little pain in his hands, in his knees, now and again. Big deal.

He was an artist. He loved the process of ring-making—the magic of it. The moment the plaster cast exploded in the water and revealed the ring inside.

"Asleep all day?" said Lewis.

"I mean, more like napping. My car—my car's been in the driveway—maybe one of the neighbours?"

"Okay, we'll ask. Is there anyone Vera might be with right now? Anyone you can call?"

Denny picked up the bottle of bourbon, then set it down. "No. What is happening?"

"Gusev—is that a Polish name?"

"Russian," said Denny. "It means goose. Funny, yes?"

"Does your wife ever go to Squire Point with a friend, a companion?" The dog had trundled back into the room and put his muzzle on the policeman's knee.

"Scout," said Denny. "Scout, come here." He patted his leg and Scout slunk over and sat on Denny's feet. "I don't know what to say right now. No."

Denny felt a knot of pain forming in his chest, and, unable to fight it, let a few tears drop from his chin onto his pants. "I love my wife," he said to the floor. "Please, I don't know what is happening."

"What do you do for a living, Mr. Goose?"

"Gusev."

"Gusev, I'm sorry."

"I'm a goldsmith."

"A goldsmith, Mr. Gusev?"

"Jewellery—I'm a custom jeweller. I have a studio at the back—where I do my work—I—listen, I'll level with you. I should have been in my studio all day. I'm on this deadline. Lately I can't make myself go out there until the evening—I don't know why—I enjoy my work—"

"What have you been doing all day?"

Denny shook his head. "Nothing. I slept until around noon. I read the newspaper. I went to sleep again. I'm sorry, I'm trying to be honest, pathetic as it sounds." He nodded at the bottle of bourbon on the table. "I overdid it last night. Doesn't happen often. I don't know—it's been a waste of a day."

"Are you all right, Mr. Gusev?"

"Maybe, I don't know. Vera asked me that very thing last night."

"You argued?"

"No, that's not what I meant. It was simply a discussion."

A discussion. He glanced at the floor to see if the picture she had thrown at him was still there, glass in shards, but she had cleaned it up. The photograph was resting on top of the bookshelf. It was their wedding picture. He would get it reframed as soon as this nonsense was over.

"And you make a living from your work?"

"I do."

"And what does your wife do? Does she work, too?"

Ah, that question would irk Vera. He raised his voice a bit. "Vera is a professor. Cinematography."

"A filmmaker?"

"Experimental films," said Denny. "I mean, if you're about to ask whether you've seen her work—"

The policeman gestured out the picture window, and it took Denny a minute to figure out that he was pointing at his car. His Mercedes. "You do well for yourselves."

"I inherited when my parents died. We bought nice cars."

"What brought you to Whale Bay?"

"Vera's position," said Denny. "I mean, who lives here, right? It's beautiful. Affordable. Ocean views. We talk about moving to the city. She could commute. We talk about being more normal. You know."

"Life insurance?"

"What? I mean, I'm not sure. Vera might have taken out a policy when she was first hired. I'm sorry, I don't know."

"You don't know."

"I don't know."

"Was she a drug user?"

"Excuse me? No."

"Suicidal?"

"No."

"Tattoos, piercings, or birthmarks?" said the policeman.

"What? No. Her ears. But her rings—she'll be wearing three rings I made her—one is extremely valuable, an alexandrite gemstone—"

"Artificial limbs?"

"No. No. Listen, the rings, the rings are distinctive—particularly the alexandrite—I can show you a picture—I made them for her—"

"Her doctor's name?"

"What? I think she goes to someone at the clinic downtown. The rings—"

"Are you all right, Mr. Gusev?"

"I—you keep asking me that. I—" God, he was out of breath. He was panting like a rabid animal. He couldn't feel his hands. "I need to tell you about her rings."

"I'll need access to her dental and medical records. And a few photographs."

"All right," Denny said. "Let me look. She—"

The policeman stood and picked up a photo of Vera from the fireplace mantel. "Does she still look like this?"

Denny looked at the picture. Her hair, as long and black as it ever was, her glasses, her formidable build. She wore a red blazer with shoulder pads, the French Riviera in the background. She wasn't smiling but she was proud. "Yes," Denny said. She was in her late twenties in the picture and looked essentially the same. Such a perfect square jaw. "You can take it, if you want."

"I'll need another. One in which she's smiling. Okay?"

"I am a good man."

"I didn't say you weren't, Mr. Gusev," said the policeman. "Smiling. With teeth."

"Teeth?"

"Teeth," said the policeman.

"May I ask why?" said Denny.

"You really want to know?"

"I do."

The policeman moved toward the front door and, with one finger raised to indicate that Denny should stay seated, opened it to reveal the snow-lit sky. "So—worst-case scenario—she can be identified by her skull."

CHAPTER FOUR

Evelina

Evelina Lucchi walked toward her small house, snow crunching beneath her boots. She could hear the foghorn and the ocean, and she wondered where Leo and her boys were, what road they were driving down; she wondered if he missed their life together, if he regretted his actions, if he ever thought about anything in a deep way, and whether he was serious about this woman, this *Holly*.

It was only four o'clock—not late enough to panic, though it was getting dark already—and she let herself have the stupid thought that Leo had kidnapped her sons, taken them down to San Garcia to start a new life. But he was too selfish. He wouldn't want the responsibility.

Despite the cold, she sat on the front steps of her little beach house, waiting for Leo and the boys to return from Squire Point. She tucked her long skirt underneath the soles of her boots and buttoned her jacket up to her chin. After she'd kicked Leo out, she'd cut her hair, then dyed it a shimmering auburn that looked purple in the light. Leo had not said a word to her about it. She'd started wearing earrings again, too, long pendants that reached her shoulders—costume jewellery, Leo had said about the peacock feather ones that she was wearing now—and the occasional smear of red lipstick.

Entering our "goddess" years, are we? she imagined him saying, for that was how most of their conversations happened these days: in her head.

She tucked her earrings into her pocket, then produced the scratch-and-win card she'd bought at the corner store and rubbed off the numbers with the edge of a dime. After a few minutes, the card revealed she'd won five dollars. She was ashamed of her habit—though she could hardly call it gambling. She felt her mood grow lighter, tucked the winning card into her pocket, and pulled out the next one. A dud.

She'd been a cook on a fishing boat before her sons were born. That was how she met Leo. A Christmas party at one of the captains' houses. Beer bottles all over the coffee table, half-empty bowls of chips. Evelina was in a relationship—an on-again, off-again thing with another cook—but couldn't stop herself from flirting with Leo. He cornered her in the kitchen, slipped his hand around her waist before she knew his name.

"Stop," she whispered. "I'm with someone."

"Oh, shut up," he said. And they laughed.

She wasn't beautiful—he told her that on their first date. But up close, Leo said, her features were difficult to reconcile, and that's what made her fascinating. He could look at her face for hours and never understand it, he said. Something about her bone structure, its lack of symmetry. From every angle, she looked like a different person.

"For instance," he said, taking her face in his hands on their first night together, "if I tilt your head this way, I can see you're sort of old-fashioned. This is your serious side, the side of you that's mad at me for being better-looking than your boyfriend."

"I am not," Evelina said, but she was.

"Now look at me straight-on." He scanned her eyes. "Here's your vulnerability. Here's your sad-little-person face." He pushed her chin down toward her chest. "From this angle, you are the most beautiful."

"When I'm not looking at you?"

In those days, she felt wildly out of control, like a ripped-open sofa cushion, the exposed springs bouncing around like a Slinky. She liked Leo's matter-of-factness. She liked that he claimed to know her better than she knew herself. She liked that he was taller than she was. Often, when she was around other women, she felt like a giant or a man in drag.

Leo pressed his mouth to hers, lifted himself on top of her and pushed her legs apart. "Open sesame," he said, and she knew she would have to forget that line, to bury it somewhere deep within her mind.

A weirdo. A weird person. Leo had grown up in San Garcia, a coastal city twelve hundred miles south of Whale Bay. Was estranged from his family and wouldn't say why. Didn't speak to Evelina for a week when his brother died because he felt she hadn't comforted him in the right way. That was his signature move—to not speak to her if something was bothering him. It made Evelina crazy.

But how she loved being seen with him in those early days, his broad shoulders in his green military jacket, his square jaw, the way he nodded at strangers to say hello. The way he always held onto her in some way—his hand on the back of her neck, his hand slipped up the back of her shirt, his hand in hers, his hand on her leg. Sometimes the only way she knew he was mad was if they were out in public and he wasn't touching her.

She was a weirdo like him. A misfit. A depressed teenager, high-school dropout. Lived here all her life, unlike her sister, who had left for the city the minute she'd gotten her high-school diploma. Evelina spent her summers tree planting until she found steady work on a fishing boat. Paid well. Hard work but long stretches of time off. Felt happiest out on the water, especially once the shore disappeared. Didn't feel much like a woman. More like a fish. Or a water bird. She'd never met a woman like herself before. She'd never seen herself in a book, or in a movie. Was more comfortable around men because then she didn't have to talk.

The first boat she worked on was a heavy wooden seiner, about forty feet. Just Evelina, the captain, and another deckhand. She learned how much food to purchase and how to cook easy, hearty things. She made ten thousand dollars in her first three months. It seemed like a fortune then.

She never thought she'd get married. Never thought she'd have children. Thought she'd be on the deck of a steel trawler forever, even as an old woman, white hair down to her waist, maybe own a fleet someday. There was one woman she knew who was a captain. She was large and wild, and Evelina used to think she'd end up like her: oblivious to sexist remarks, insensitive, ready to pull out a gun and shoot a seal if it got caught in the net. Ready to shoot another boat if it got too close to hers. All the boats had guns.

But then she met Leo at that Christmas party, and right away he started talking about wanting to have a baby. When they made love he would put his hand on her belly and close his eyes.

Now here she was, on the cusp of becoming his ex-wife. With two boys. She spent her days inside now—had gotten her GED and a job as a bookkeeper for the Whale Bay Operatic Society. A steady pay-cheque, but dull. It was why she was addicted to the cards—that little rush, seeing if she'd won big. Such a pale comparison to the feeling of walking the docks, her pockets stuffed with cash, the wind in her hair, only nineteen years old.

Today she'd bought two cards—she had a strict two-a-day

limit—and she fidgeted with the dud card, then went inside to wait for her sons. She'd left the kitchen window open—stupid, so stupid, the heating bill—and the counter was damp with a dusting of snow. She washed out three soup bowls and made the table lovely for her boys—two nubby candles, her old tobacco-leaf placemats, paper towels folded diagonally, even a wine carafe filled with yellow dahlias she'd bought the day before, as round and alien-looking as sea anemones.

She dug at the dirt underneath her fingernails and felt her anger bloom—Leo, who'd gotten so angry when she'd confronted him about Holly; Leo, who held her against the wall, his hand on her neck, when he suspected once—falsely—that *she* was having an affair.

Of course, all she could think of were his bad qualities. She had read somewhere that after a separation a parent should not speak ill of the other parent. So she tried to reminisce, as much as she could with the boys, about Leo's good qualities. How he used to take them to feed the ducks on Saturday afternoons. Drawing with them at the kitchen table. Long games of tag, leaping around the yard, letting the boys tackle him, their little knees digging into his sides.

By filling their minds with the sweet things, she hoped she could block out the things she wanted them to forget.

The relationship was still all tangled up in her mind. Sometimes she felt she couldn't trust herself or her version of things. For instance, sex. How could the same reality feel so different? Sometimes it felt as though her insides were coated in plastic and Leo's penis was a dry pink pencil eraser. Or it hurt. Worse, sometimes she felt nothing at all. A kind of horror seized her in the moments before they made love. She hated Leo during sex if she was honest, his penis as durable as only the hardest part of her was—her elbow, for instance, her knee. The waterfall of pleasure that rushed over him. All that gasping. What had ever felt that rapturous to her? Nothing. Nothing at all.

He worked odd jobs, never staying at any place very long. Had big plans for his life, he said, though he never told her specifically what those plans were. There was a type of person in this world who could work a job, get married, have children, live in a house, mow the lawn on weekends, try out new chicken recipes, discuss what colour to paint the nursery. There was another type of person who could do half of those things well but lived in secret misery, and so squeaked out and gambled or had affairs—this type of person was Evelina. Then there was another type of person who didn't have it in them to do any of those things at all. Some of these people were homeless. Some—if they had money—travelled the world. Some, like Leo, pretended, forced themselves to do it anyway. A person like that could kill you. You could spend your whole life trying to get them to be someone they weren't.

He hadn't wanted to marry her, even after she got pregnant, even after Jesse and Dmitri were born. *It's not really my thing.* But they had married eventually at city hall; Dmitri, a newborn in her arms, and Jesse, four years old, already having ruined the day, Leo said, by wetting the bed that morning. Leo was better with the new baby than he had been with Jesse, changed his diapers, got up with him in the night. He seemed, like so many men, to be softening with age. Evelina felt hopeful. He got a steady job at the bottle depot.

She wasn't sure whether he was still working there now. Holly ran that touristy gallery at the harbour. He was probably sponging off her.

She supposed their life together had been okay before Leo had turned on Jesse. There had been a short period of time, even, during Dmitri's infancy, when the four of them had functioned as a family unit—Dmitri and Jesse sleeping between them, little hands balled into fists. Dmitri was so much smaller than Jesse had been. She had forgotten how small newborns were. She held him against her shoulder. He was like a baby squirrel.

It happened the first time a few months after he was born. She set

Dmitri's little sleeping body into the bassinet and slipped down the hall into the bath. He was such an easier baby than Jesse, who would have woken the second he hit the tiny oval mattress, screaming. She remembered when taking a bath had been so sacred to her. Now she was lucky if she bathed twice a week. She shaved her legs, scrubbed between her toes, ignored the obscene roll of fat that spilled out over her stomach so that she couldn't see the tops of her thighs. She hoped it would be gone soon. She was combing out her hair with her fingers when she had the thought that something was wrong, that she needed to get out of the bath. She fought it at first. Paranoia. Her inability to do something nice for herself.

It was the sound of glass breaking that finally got her out of the tub. She grabbed a towel off the floor and threw it around herself, ran toward the nursery, her wet footprints sinking into the carpet—and there was Dmitri, wailing in his bassinet. And there was Jesse, sitting on a stool in front of the bassinet. And there was a hole the size of a baseball in the lower-left-hand corner of the window, shards of glass on the carpet below. She asked Jesse what had happened but he didn't respond. Careful not to cut her feet, she walked to the window and peered out, searching for whatever had made the hole.

"A bird," Jesse said.

Had the bird flown in or out? What?

She walked toward her sons, Dmitri taking shallow, almost gasp-like breaths as he cried. Jesse was playing with something in his pocket—at first she thought he was playing with himself, something he did when he had to go to the bathroom.

"Show me your hands," she said, taking Dmitri into her arms.

Jesse took out his hands and showed her what he was playing with: a mud-covered rock. She looked into Dmitri's bassinet and saw that there was a small pile of rocks in there, too, near where Dmitri's head had been.

"Did you break the window?" she asked her son but he insisted, *no*, it was a bird. "Were you throwing rocks in here?"

When Leo got home, she told him what had happened, and he braced himself in the doorway of the nursery and held Jesse up with one hand as he hit him with the other. He hit Jesse until he admitted that he had dug up rocks from the garden and then thrown one at the window. But Leo couldn't get him to say why. He hit him until Evelina made him stop. Her son flailed back and forth, his arm almost wrenched out of its socket.

This is the kind of thing that happens when you have children before you've done all you've set out to do, she thought. She knew in that moment that Leo was starting to hate Jesse, and possibly her, too—that for some men having a family had a dangerous side, that marriage and children could create a counterblast of sorrow, of disappointment, of rage.

He promised it wouldn't happen again, and it didn't, as far as she knew, for a time. But then one afternoon Dmitri walked into their bedroom complaining of an earache and the next thing Evelina knew, Leo was rushing toward Jesse, yanking his arm over his head, hitting him with those long, wild swings. She sensed, too, that there were other beatings she didn't know about.

And so it went in their house, year after year: Jesse the bad, Dmitri the good.

It's just a spanking, Leo said.

Was that what it was? Her own parents had hit her with a wooden spoon.

One night she took a wooden spoon from a drawer in the kitchen and, as an experiment, not really knowing her intentions, slapped it down upon the flesh of her upper thigh. She waited until the heat of the slap subsided, then did it again, harder, with force. A few moments of burning, the pain spreading then dissipating. If she were angry, though, wouldn't she hit harder? What if she were really angry? What if she were *in a rage*? She glanced at her thigh, then at the kitchen counter, and down the spoon came, as hard as she could muster, on the plastic laminate. There it was. The force with which a parent would hit their child. And who ever hit a child once? She brought the spoon down on her own thigh, to a count of ten.

The next time it happened, she sensed a meanness coming from Leo that hadn't been there before. By then she suspected he was seeing someone else. He hadn't touched her in such a long time. She rushed to Jesse, wedged her body between him and Leo. *Get out, get out,* she yelled, and when he didn't move she dragged him into the bedroom, threw his clothes into his arms, told her she would kill him if he didn't leave.

She sat in the empty kitchen and felt the silence of the house close in on her. It was a beach house, supposed to be a summer rental. Really not much of a home. Too small. Poorly insulated. She should move inland, away from the relentless wind. But, wait, there was a sound. She held her breath. Was the water running? She checked the toilet, which sometimes ran, but it was silent. She put the toilet seat down— a point of contention between her and her sons—and headed back to the kitchen. Was the leak coming from under the sink? Her life felt so absurd in that moment, racing to check the toilet, sticking her head under the sink, the water bill escalating in her mind.

She caught herself—she was going down the rabbit hole of despair—and laughed. There was no leak, no running water anywhere. Just the drip of an icicle melting outside the kitchen window. Her anger softened into sadness, and she closed her eyes. But where were her sons?

Surely they would be home soon. What would she do if they weren't? Call the police?

Of course Leo hadn't kidnapped them. They'd been in a car accident. That made more sense. A fender-bender, no one harmed. Well,
then, all she had to do was call the hospital. The boys would be fine.
Her husband arrested for drunk driving and put in jail. What a
delight! What a way to start the year! She rifled through the phone
book until she came to the number.

Her fingers were thin from the cold and her wedding ring slipped
to the top of her knuckle when she reached for the phone. It was stupid to still wear it. Leo had never worn his.

There had been no car accidents involving children that day. She
called the hospital twenty minutes outside of town in case they'd gone
to that one, but there had been no accidents there either. Did that
mean they were in a ditch somewhere? Waiting for the police and
ambulance by the side of the road?

Had Leo taken them for dinner and forgotten to mention that
was part of his plan? She usually asked him when he'd be bringing the
boys back, but today she hadn't—he'd given her *that look* when she
asked, as if she were his mother. She hadn't felt strong enough to deal
with that look today.

She walked into the boys' bedroom and tried to pass the time
by tidying up their toys. She put their Smurfs and He-Man action
figures back in the toy box. She picked up their shared Walkman
off the floor and put it on top of the dresser. She put Dmitri's
stuffed bear, Brownie, back on his bed. Jesse's *Ghostbusters* poster
was coming free from the wall and she taped it back into place.
In the trash can was a robot drawing Leo had done for Dmitri.
Jesse had torn it up, like he'd torn up the picture Holly had drawn
of him.

Maybe she'd drive around, see if she could find them. Leo would
take them to McDonald's or Marco Polo's Pizza. She hated moments
like this—when there was, in fact, a right and a wrong thing to do. If

she left and they came back and she wasn't here, Leo would be forced to keep the boys with him.

She could leave a note on the door, though, saying she'd be back by six. That might be okay. She wrote in capital letters with a black felt pen, then added a little drawing of a smiling dinosaur to make it look as if she wasn't in agony—*BACK AT SIX, PLEASE WAIT HERE WITH THE BOYS*—and taped it to the front door.

Billy's Burgers, McDonald's, Marco Polo's. No sign of Leo or her sons. She sat in her car in front of the house, running the engine to keep the windows defrosted, rubbing her hands against her thighs to keep warm. She fingered the winning lottery ticket in her pocket. That would kill some time. She turned off the car and jogged up the street to the corner store, carefully, so she wouldn't slip on the ice. The snow stopped and the sky cleared. The clerk cashed in her ticket and sold her two more, and she stood at the counter scratching off the numbers because there was no one else in the store and she knew the clerk had a crush on her and she didn't want to be alone.

"If it were me I might call the police," the clerk said to her. He was a nice-seeming man. She could tell he cared about her. "What's stopping you?"

"I don't want to do the wrong thing," she said.

"No harm in it," he said and passed her the store's phone.

But she didn't want to call the police, not yet. First she would go back to the house to see if Leo and her sons were there.

The clerk offered to go with her but she didn't want the additional complication of Leo seeing her with another man. She didn't want to make Leo angry. She even felt a kind of yearning. She wanted to see Leo and the boys so badly she felt crazy. She wanted Leo to tell her one of his stupid jokes. He wasn't all bad—he had never been *all* bad. There was a sweetness, a vulnerability, an unusualness. Something special, childlike even. Playful. That was what had drawn her to him. He was not like other people. He was not an evil man.

"My boys," she practised saying in her empty living room when she got home, one hand on the phone. "They spent the day with their father and never came home."

CHAPTER FIVE

Leo

Leo Lucchi wasn't a hunter, but he'd picked up a thing or two from his father, and felt obligated to pass these skills on to his sons. Even more so since he'd left them. He wanted them to remember this day. He imagined them as men, telling their friends, or wives, or children, about the time their father had taught them how to shoot a rifle on New Year's Day.

But right now the need for a cigarette was like a stone in his chest. He cursed. He'd left his cigarettes in the car. He could drag the boys back with him, but it would take forever with them in tow, slipping every second in their rubber boots. And so he left his sons on the path—*I won't be long; I need you to stay right here; we've got such a fun day ahead of us*—and hiked the quarter-mile back to the parking lot, his rifle over his shoulder, taking big steps until he could feel the burn in his hamstrings and in his calves.

When he reached the parking lot, he leaned the rifle against the car and allowed himself to enjoy his cigarette. His boys would be fine for another minute or two. He closed his eyes and felt pleasantly, surprisingly, happy. There was no one in the parking lot except him.

A new year. The first day of the year. The first day of a new year. He
felt the snow landing softly on his shoulders and in his hair. He could
do this. He was enjoying himself. So much of the time, he didn't enjoy
his sons. He loved them—that wasn't it—but the *grind* of it: washing
their sticky hands after they'd eaten something, getting their jackets on,
finding their socks, making sure they had snacks—it exhausted him. It
was tedious. He longed for them to be older—teenagers, and then
men—people he could talk to, have a drink with. People who could
pour their own juice without spilling the fucking stuff. People who
didn't need to be monitored so closely every minute of the day, always
on the verge of disaster, always hitting their heads. But right now he felt
a lightness. Maybe it was being inside that bothered him. Maybe from
now on he should only take his boys here, Squire Point, or the beach.
Maybe it was being cooped up with their whininess and their neediness
that irked him. Maybe he could finally really love them, and be good to
them—to Jesse—if they stayed outside.

He smoked his cigarette down to the filter, crushed it under his
boot, and set off for the place where he had left his boys, the rifle over
his shoulder. As he walked toward the lake, he went over the first
exercise he would give them, the first thing his own father had taught
him about how to shoot.

*First, you have to determine your dominant eye. This is easy. Pick
something specific, a bird's nest, for example, and point at it with both
eyes open. Without moving your finger, close your left eye. Is your finger
still pointing at the target? Now open your left eye and close your right
eye. Has your finger shifted? Your dominant eye is the one that is still
pointing at the target when your other eye is closed. Get it?*

His old Remington was too heavy for the boys, but he figured
they could watch at first. He would buy them BB guns once he got
some money together and they could go out every Sunday. He would

do this at the start of next month, set a little money aside, maybe one gun for them to share at first, see how they took to it. He'd seen guns on sale somewhere, the hardware store maybe—a cheap one would do. His boys wouldn't know the difference. They could spend the spring and summer shooting at foam targets; by next winter, he would have saved enough—and they would be good enough—to buy them each a real rifle. What else was he supposed to do? Take them bowling? He could hear Evelina's voice of disapproval in his head.

Oh, what the fuck. He was who he was. No, that wasn't true. Every day was an opportunity to become a better person. And today was the first day of the year.

It is a sin in hunting to wound an animal. At some point, you will shoot something and it will not die. It will escape to suffer. To hunt is to have an intimate knowledge of life and death—

He tried to remember the words of his father's lecture so many years ago, but he found himself thinking of the Swami's lectures instead. Holly had given him one of the Swami's tapes on consciousness, which had sat untouched in his glove compartment until the night Evelina kicked him out. He'd driven to a lookout, put the tape in the stereo, and pressed play.

Leo had worried that the Swami would be boring but he sank easily into the Swami's words. The Swami said each person must reach the source of his thoughts in order to achieve self-realization. Where did his thoughts come from? Leo wondered, alone in his parked car, a can of beer in his hand. And how come his thoughts seemed to come from a place outside of himself? And how come he couldn't control them? If they were *his* thoughts, surely he should be able to control them. Surely, he ought to be the source of them. Whose thoughts were they then? And how come he never ran out of them? They were like tidal waves crashing upon him, and within him, and it was ceaseless.

The brain is a chaotic place, the Swami said, filled with thoughts of the past. Yes, yes it is, Leo wanted to shout, yes! And how can I stop it from being this way? Tell me, please.

After listening to the tape, he wanted, more than anything, to see the Swami in person. He imagined the Swami picking him out from the crowd as a kind of chosen one, and then travelling the world. Leo knew in his heart that he was special. He was not like other people. He would not die, for instance, in some sort of freak accident—a car crash or avalanche. He was on this earth for a reason. In the car, after listening to the Swami's words, this conviction deepened. He knew he had to see the Swami one on one; he had to be really *seen* by him. He had to be elevated from this basic life.

Little things, said Holly. Start with little things, little changes. Don't try to change yourself all at once. It was her idea to make the paper boats with the boys. She told him that they should write down their resolutions—call them *wishes*, Holly suggested, every child knows what a wish is—and set them on the frozen lake at Squire Point. Leo believed in things like this—in writing down what you wanted, in visualization. *Visualize a better future.* Write it down. He shut his eyes and imagined his life after he married Holly and devoted himself to the teachings of the Swami. He was such a finer version of himself in this vision. A man in linen slacks, with a leather wallet. A soft-spoken, patient man. A wise man. He straightened his back and slicked his hair behind his ears.

Sure, he had flaws, but he'd never done anything horrible. Nothing really wrong. He'd only been arrested once, and even that was a misunderstanding—he meant to pay for the watch but had just forgotten. And he hadn't actually ripped out some of Evelina's hair the night he left. She'd been screaming at him—for Christ's sake, her goddamn anger—with her fists up like a boxer, and before she could hit him he grabbed her arm and twisted her away from him, and some of her hair got caught on the button of his coat.

Jesse and Dmitri had come into the room afterwards, when Evelina was standing with her back against the wall, wailing, a few strands of hair in her hands. A few strands of hair! Calling him a monster. Telling him to leave and never come back. There wasn't time to explain to his sons what had happened, and everything he had tried to say since—*You know, you think you saw something, but*—came out like a lie. Evelina was so hysterical when they fought. He was never that angry—just got his feelings hurt easily and needed some space for a few days—but she'd storm into whatever room he was in, foaming at the mouth.

He didn't mean to be so tough on Jesse. Besides, he wasn't a quarter as tough on Jesse as his own father had been on him. That had to count for something. It was easier with Dmitri—he was so small, sweet, affectionate. His needs were simple. Love me, hold me, feed me. Fine-boned, goofy-looking. He loved drawing. He loved it when Leo drew robots. He had the little robot drawings taped up all over his bedroom walls.

"Can you draw me a robot, too?" Jesse would ask. But that wasn't what he was asking. Can you love me as much as you love Dmitri? That was the question behind every question.

He did love Jesse. It wasn't that he didn't. A few weeks ago, he'd drawn them each a robot, and told them to tape the drawings to their bedroom walls, something to look at when they missed their dad. What was he supposed to do when he came back inside after a cigarette to find the drawing of Dmitri's robot ripped to shreds? What was he supposed to do, Evelina?

———

The trail shot out in front of him, empty and white. He was out of breath, and he couldn't see his boys in the distance. He whistled, told himself that they were behind a tree, for some no-good reason invisible to him at this moment. There was no need to be angry, no reason to panic. He would not let his mood ruin the day. He would not let his anger seep into this day, the first day of the year.

"God damn it, god damn it," he said, trying to shake off his mood. Why should he be angry? Why should he be afraid? He had felt so light a few minutes ago, before he'd started thinking about Evelina and the boys. The Swami said that when he felt himself about to lose control, he should imagine floating upward, high above the clouds, until the earth was the size of a marble. Now look down, the Swami said. Look down at the marble and see how little your panic matters. Now zoom out even further, to the edge of the universe, where the marble is no longer visible, where it is smaller than a single grain of sand.

But that wasn't helpful, at least not at this moment. Even at the very edge of the universe, Leo wanted to know where his boys were. He whistled again, called out their names, stopped walking so he could listen for signs of them. Hadn't he told them to wait right here, under this tree? Not to travel more than two feet from this point? He called out their names again, angrier this time, he couldn't help it. He felt the sweat on his neck, the anger at himself for leaving them, the anger at Evelina, the anger at the boys for walking off, the anger at them for being improperly dressed, their stupid rubber boots.

He closed his eyes and tried to quiet his mind, his anxious thoughts.

But, wait. There was a voice to his left, a soft voice, but a voice nonetheless. Leo snapped his eyes open and stomped toward the voice, through the deep snow and toward the lake, which he could see now through the trees.

What—what was that—

Jesse was in the middle of the lake, Jesse was hunched over and pawing at something—where was Dmitri?

"Jesse!" It startled him how hard it was to speak—to scream. "Jesse!"

He dropped his rifle and broke into a run over the ice, his feet catching and slipping out from under him, every muscle in his body willing him toward the middle of the lake—"I told you not to move—"

Jesse sat on his knees pounding furiously at a puddle of water in a patch of broken ice, his eyes full of fear. "It's Dmitri," he was saying, "it's Dmitri, Dad, do something, help, Dad, Dad please, he fell in, please, Dad, please."

In an instant, Leo broke through the thin layer of ice with his fists, crashed against the frozen lake with all his weight until cool black water bubbled up beneath the surface and spilled out under his knees. He unzipped his heavy jacket, threw it behind him and reached frantically into the water, gripped the sides of the ice and dunked his head, brought it up, sputtered and choked, then braced his feet on either side of himself, his arms searching helplessly under the frozen water for his son. He dunked his head in again. His eyes burned with cold, his legs scrambled—and he wrenched his head out of the dark water to take a breath, a sensation that burned his lungs, and he plunged underneath again, scanning the blackness.

What was he supposed to do? Should he dive in? The hole was not big enough for his body. It was not big enough, even, for Dmitri's body. Could his boy have slipped through, like a mouse through a crack in the wall? He felt the hot sting of tears and the awful panic of not knowing what to do, and he plunged his head in again, coming up only to scream, a howling wail, then plunged down into the ice once more.

CHAPTER SIX

Jesse

Jesse backed away from his father, his hands in his pockets. From a safe distance, he watched his father break the surrounding ice with his fists and plunge his head in again and again. He stared at the tendons in his father's neck, so well defined that they were grotesque. Was his father actually this upset or was he acting? His father's reaction—this crazed desperation—was unlike anything he had ever seen before. He felt embarrassed. He felt numb. He felt nothing.

"Dad," he said softly, in a voice he knew was too quiet to be heard. His father had made a hole in the ice, big enough now for a body.

If his father died—one push, it would only take one push—he would be gone from their lives forever. No more fear. Could he even imagine it? His father had not hit him since he had moved out, but it was always there, between them, those moments, his arm wrenched out of its socket. The look on his face before it would happen.

He stepped toward his father, but could not make himself raise his hand.

Maybe Dmitri, then.

After all, it did feel good to inflict pain on Dmitri. He got a little rush out of it—a quick pinch, a shove—even when he knew what the consequences would be. With Dmitri gone, his father might see Jesse as he truly was, not as a shadow over his brother, a dark figure looming over his brother's head, but as a boy, a brave boy, a good boy. He prayed for the lake to swallow one of them—even himself—for the earth to rip open and carry one of them down to hell.

When his father came up yet again for air he moaned, and Jesse felt a deep, sick feeling in the pit of his stomach that what he was doing was not only wrong but also evil. It was an awful sound his father was making. It made Jesse think of men in medieval dungeons, wrists shackled, awaiting execution.

"Dad," Jesse said. "Stop." But his father dove his head and shoulders again beneath the ice, searching frantically, his legs splayed.

"Stop," Jesse said, but his father had surfaced again and was punching the ice to make more room for his body, and his hands were bloodying the surrounding snow.

"Dad. Please." He rushed toward his father and grabbed one of his legs and pulled him with all his might. There was still a chance for happiness, Jesse thought, even now. Everything is temporary. Everything has an end.

"Stop, Dad," he said again.

But his father continued to punch the ice, to make room to dive under the water. His face had turned a shade of purple, so dark it was almost black. His fingers were shaking from the cold.

"Stop," Jesse said, louder this time. "It's a joke."

He let go of his father and scanned the trees. "It's a joke," he said again, but it was as if his father had entered a different dimension and could not be brought back.

Whatever he had been unable to feel before, he felt now—a real sense of panic, tears forming in his eyes, a desire to reach up and peel back the sky to reveal some other universe, some other possibility. "Please, Dad, I'm sorry," he yelled, tugging on his father's leg again, but his father was preparing to dive under the ice. He raised his arms over his head.

"Stop," Jesse said again. "It's only a joke." He scanned the forest frantically, and at last caught eyes with Dmitri, who was crouched behind a row of white birch trees at the edge of the lake, out of sight, and he nodded at his brother that it was finally time to stand up, to run over, to put an end to this horrible game.

There was still a way to recover from this, Jesse thought. If only he—but before he could complete the thought, Dmitri sprinted over the ice to their father, leapt onto his back and shrieked, "Daddy, I'm behind you. Daddy, it's a game, I'm behind you."

And Jesse watched his father spin on the ice, his lips blue from cold. He watched his father turn to see Dmitri. He watched his father throw back his fist and bloody Dmitri's nose with one quick punch.

CHAPTER SEVEN

Denny

There would be an extensive search. Divers would cut through the ice and search the lake for bodies. If nothing turned up, they would have to wait for the spring thaw—a sad, morbid fact. But death wasn't the only option. She could have fled. People did. She could have been kidnapped. People were.

Denny set his wife's diary down and turned to face Officer Lewis Côté and one of the detectives, who was removing long strands of Vera's black hair from a boar-bristle brush. The three men stood in the bedroom, while Scout nosed at their feet. A second detective was outside, under the night sky, talking to the neighbours.

"I've never violated her privacy like this before," Denny said and passed Lewis the diary. It was a dream journal, and as much as he tried, he couldn't find anything in it that pertained to reality—to Vera's reality. She dreamed often, it seemed, of birds. Of tending to birds. There were some notes about films she wanted to make, things to say in upcoming lectures. Reprimands to herself about quitting smoking.

His friends thought she was boring, despite her impressive accolades. Denny was outgoing—*gregarious* was the word people used—full of stories, always the one to host poker night, ready to laugh. He felt as though he were the only person on earth who knew Vera. Her parents kept in close contact with her, called every few days, but she didn't like them as much as they liked her. They weighed on her, even though she was sweet with them on the phone (they hadn't heard from her either—he tried to downplay the fact that there was a policeman watching him as he spoke to them over the phone—and the last thing he wanted was for them to show up, though he knew they would come immediately). He *knew* Vera, though. He knew she was secretly as funny as he was—and ten times as smart. She could have made a living as a filmmaker, though she was happy enough at her university job. Already, at thirty, an assistant professor at the expensive private liberal arts college down the road, envied by and more successful than her colleagues. Right after he'd met her, her film *Mirror* had screened at Cannes.

"Was she taking any medication?" the detective asked, but he was already rooting through her bedside table. Denny couldn't remember whether the detective had asked permission to do this, but what did it matter? He wanted his wife to be found. They could ransack anything, he supposed. The detective held up a blister package containing white pills. "Clomid?" he asked.

"She was having trouble getting pregnant," Denny said.

"Uh-huh," said the detective.

The blister package was unopened. His head felt heavy. He thought she'd been taking it. She was taking pills for anxiety, too, but they were hidden in her makeup kit. He fought the urge to hit the detective hard, in the face, for putting his hands on her pills.

The detective was a short man with a bland, forgettable face—there was something too soft about it to contain any intelligence. Lewis, on the other hand, seemed more capable. Lewis was young and handsome—he wore an interesting watch, European maybe, and

stylish glasses with black frames. A person Denny might have gone
to the bar with in another life. What was a person like that doing as
a small-town cop? He was too handsome for this place. People who
looked like Lewis didn't live here.

"We'll need another photo," said the bland detective.

That old familiar stab of guilt. The policeman had asked him to
do this over an hour ago. And what had he done but sit on his stupid
velvet couch and cry?

"Is she actually missing?" Denny said, though his voice seemed to
be coming from outside the room, or under it, perhaps from the basement. "Has it been long enough to—I mean, what if she—"

"This is a missing persons investigation," said the detective.
"There's a child involved."

"I'm sorry," said Denny. "I'm so sorry." He turned to Vera's dresser
and studied the wedding portrait.

"Something more natural?" said the detective. "More like how she
looks every day?"

Denny fought the urge to apologize again. Of course. She never
wore her hair up, like it was in the photo. She certainly never wore
a red flower in her hair! Flowers in people's hair! What a thing.
"Okay," he said. He found their photo albums in the living room,
flicked on the overhead light, and flipped through the images. She
was usually the one behind the camera. But there was one of her on
the couch, a snapshot, Scout curled in her lap like a baby. She
looked like herself, her dark hair cascading over her shoulders and
pooling at her waist. She looked happy, if not a little tired. He
couldn't remember when he'd taken the photo. What they'd done
before, or what they'd done after.

"I'll need to know what she was wearing when she left the house."

"I was asleep," said Denny. He didn't have a mental inventory of
her entire wardrobe. He couldn't very well go through it all, then

announce, via a process of elimination, what she had on. "I don't know—" He pushed past the men and studied the contents of the hall closet. "Maybe her parka? It's cold. Her parka isn't here. She has a green parka." Was it even green? He was failing her. "She wears boots when she goes to Squire Point. Hiking boots." He scanned the floor for them but they were gone. "I think?"

"A hat?" said the detective, joining him in the living room.

"I don't know."

"Any defining characteristics on the jacket?"

"No. I don't know." He couldn't even remember what the jacket looked like. "If she's out there, in the woods, she's going to get cold—"

"The boots? Brand?"

"Brand?"

"What kind of boots, what size."

"I'm sorry?"

"Your wife's shoe size."

"Seven? Eight."

The detective nodded to the photo in Denny's hand, and Denny passed him the photo of Vera.

"Teeth," said the detective. "One with teeth."

The air in the room had an awful quality to it: a stale, dead quality. Denny took a gulp of it and gagged. The living room was full of pictures of him and Vera and he made a sweeping gesture with his arm. "Pick one?" He didn't mean it to come out so exasperated.

"Height and weight correct on her driver's licence?" the policeman asked.

"Yes," said Denny, though he didn't know. How would he know? Why wouldn't they be?

"Hair colour?"

"Dark brown. Almost black. It's very long. To her waist."

"Eyes?"

"They're brown."

"Eyeglasses?"

"Yes." He imagined her, without her glasses in the woods. She could hardly see without them, and he pictured her with her arms outstretched, groping in the dark, in all that snow.

He couldn't remember Vera's middle name.

What was the matter with him? Was something wrong with his brain?

"Has she recently travelled internationally?" said Lewis.

"Not since our honeymoon."

"Health problems?"

"No."

He was shaking his head when the second detective came through the front door, tapping his notepad with a ballpoint pen. He asked Denny to sit down.

"I don't want to sit down," said Denny. "I want to run. I want to go to Squire Point and find Vera. I don't think I can sit down right now."

"Hey," said Lewis. He put his hand on Denny's shoulder. "It's all right."

Was he acting flustered? Why was Lewis's hand so forcefully on his shoulder? Denny stared at the well-manicured hand, its lack of wedding ring, its buffed nails with big white half moons. It was an unusually beautiful hand. Did he need to be comforted? He tried to soften his face. Or was acting flustered a good thing? Did a guilty man act flustered or calm? How about an innocent one?

"Last night," said the second detective. "Can you tell us about last night?"

"Last night?"

"One of the neighbours claimed he heard shouting. Saw you leave the house around midnight. Can you tell us where you were going?"

"I went to watch the fireworks," said Denny. "That's all. Vera didn't want to go with me. We argued about it. We certainly weren't shouting—"

"The broken glass in your garbage can—was that from last night?"

"She—what I'm trying to say—Vera broke it. You see, it wasn't like that. We were arguing, yes. It got maybe more heated than it should have. It's just a broken picture frame."

The detective raised his eyebrows. "When was the last time you hit your wife, Mr. Gusev?"

"I have not. No. Never."

"Did you strike your wife last night, Mr. Gusev?"

"I told you—I have never—"

"Around what time did you come home from watching the fireworks?"

"Right after," said Denny. "I was only gone an hour." He could feel the heat of Lewis's hand on his shoulder, and wanted to shrug it off. Years ago he'd read a book about a man falsely accused and imprisoned for thirty years before finally being released. Was this how it started? Was this the beginning? The moment life took a wrong turn?

He put his hand on top of Lewis's, gently, tentatively. "Please," he said to Lewis, and Lewis removed his hand. He hoped that would be the end of it, but the second detective began firing more questions at him.

"And did you come back to the house?"

"I went to my studio for a while." He closed his eyes, trying to remember the night before. In his mind, he saw his hand reaching for the door to the studio, opening it, the bottle of bourbon in his other hand. Then what?

"And this was before or after you and Vera fought in the yard?"

"In the yard? Excuse me? I don't recall—"

"The neighbours said it was quite a show," said the second detective.

"In the yard? Like animals? I assure you, we did no such thing."

"You like to drink?"

"Excuse me?"

"The bottles in your studio—"

"I take a drink from time to time, yes," said Denny. His hands were tingling, and he took a deep breath, cracked his wrists, then his knuckles, willing the blood to return to them. The oak tree. His neighbour must still be mad about that. How else to explain these false accusations? Fighting in the yard? He hadn't meant to kill the neighbour's tree last year. And so what, anyway. The goddamned thing was half-dead. This was a hell of a way to get revenge. "We never fought in the yard," he said.

"Sounds like you did last night," said the second detective. "Look, a number of your neighbours told me about it."

"I don't remember any such thing," said Denny. He searched his mind. What? When? What time? What did he say? What did Vera say? "Listen, my neighbours are—how should I put this—assholes? There was this oak tree—"

"An oak tree," said Lewis.

"A Garry oak. You know, they have a society—about the trees. My neighbour is a member and, you see, a Garry oak was right on the border of our properties and it was dead already—a hazard—"

"Hey," Lewis said. He shook his head. "Let's sort this tree stuff out later. The important thing is we need to better understand what happened between you and Vera last night." He reached out his hand, as if he was going to place it, once more, on Denny's shoulder.

Things were coming back to Denny, horrible things, about the fight they'd had in the yard. Yes, in the yard, like animals. He could remember it now. He had told her she was awful, that she was smothering him. He had called her a controlling monster. An awful monster.

"We had a fight," said Denny, ducking his body so Lewis's hand would not touch him again. "Look, I'm so tired right now. I can barely keep my eyes open. I am so worried and I am so goddamned tired."

"Tell you what," Lewis said to Denny. "Let's go down to the station and get this sorted out. We'll get you some coffee, let your head clear. You can tell us more about Vera."

"But who is looking for her? What is anyone doing right now to find Vera?"

"Denny," said Lewis. "I really do need you to calm down."

But how could he calm down? How could he explain his marriage—or the fight last night—to hostile people who thought he had done something wrong? All marriages had dark corners. He was trying to be honest, but what was honesty anyway? What was the *honest* answer to why they didn't have children yet, to why Vera had an unopened package of fertility pills? How could a person be honest about ambiguity, about contradiction, about how one minute, children seemed like the perfect and natural solution to their failing marriage, and the next, they seemed like something that happened only to other people—happy people. What was the honest answer to why he hadn't been worried when she'd been gone all day? He couldn't explain even the simplest of his choices, let alone why he had told her she was a monster.

Leave me alone. It had been the last thing he'd said to her. And she had. He was alone.

Maybe if they hadn't fought, she wouldn't have taken Scout for a walk. Maybe they would have had breakfast together. Oh, for Christ's sake. They wouldn't have done that, even if they hadn't fought.

"Denny," Lewis was saying. "Come on, Denny."

Gently, as if he were a child, or a drunk, Lewis linked his arm through one of Denny's and the bland-faced detective did the same on the other side, and they led him out of the house.

Under the snowy sky, a man no older than twenty walked toward them. He stopped and fished a camera out of his messenger bag, pointed it at Denny and clicked. And that was the picture that appeared in the paper the next day: Denny's hunched-over body, escorted by the Whale Bay Police Department, getting into a patrol car in front of his house. It landed on the stoop of every house in Whale Bay with a thump.

CHAPTER EIGHT

Dmitri

The passenger seat was reserved for Jesse—*oldest gets to sit in the front*—but right now things were different. Dmitri searched for himself in the side mirror, and once he found his little face, he tried to see if he looked different now that his father had hit him. His nose had stopped bleeding but his face was sore. He could feel it swelling under the skin. Did he look older than six? He jutted his chin. He sneered. Despite feeling something in his chest that was either nervousness or fear, he wanted to ask his father if he could sit on his lap, like he used to do, and take the steering wheel, ducking down if his father saw a police car.

"I'll quit for you, Dmitri, I will, I will," Leo said and pushed his cigarette into the metal ashtray. He pulled out of the parking lot, and they left Squire Point. It was starting to snow more heavily. The birch trees looked as though they'd been dusted with icing sugar, and Dmitri wanted to lick them.

His father glanced at him as he drove, ruffled his hair, patted his knee. He frowned and pulled over, fetched an old washcloth from the trunk and filled it with snow. "Hold this to your face," he said to Dmitri. "You'll be all right."

He asked his father when they would come back for Jesse, and Leo said that Jesse needed to be punished, and they would return when the time was right.

Northwest wind ten to twenty knots becoming north five to fifteen knots after midnight.

His father switched off the transistor radio.

Dmitri pressed the washcloth to his face, the snow melting and running through his hands. His face was numb but he couldn't tell whether it was from the cold or his father's fist. The seat of his pants had soaked through from crouching in the snow for so long, and his fingertips tingled and stung. Jesse had said it would be a fun game. His eyes had narrowed after he'd unfolded the blue paper boat and read his father's wish. *What does it say, Jesse? What does it say?* Jesse told him it was too wet to read, that the ink was smudged. He said they had to play a game so their father wouldn't be angry at them for coming out here and reading his wish. *But how will he know we read it?* he asked Jesse. *He just will.* Jesse told Dmitri to crouch in the bushes by the edge of the lake and not move a muscle, and not say a word. *Don't ruin it*, Jesse said. Dmitri wanted to ask more questions but his brother's face was fierce. So he agreed to Jesse's game and slid over to the edge of the lake, Jesse shouting at him to crouch lower, to move to the left a bit, no the right, no the other way you idiot, until he was completely out of sight. It didn't matter. Their father would be back soon and put an end to the silly game.

Jesse banished for the time being—*Stay right here and think about what you've done*—his father drove to the lookout and he and Dmitri looked over the town and beyond to the ocean. His father pulled out a flask and took a swig. He seemed to always have a drink within arm's reach, a can of beer or flask in his pocket, the glove-compartment tequila. The snow-covered woods of Squire Point were visible to the left, Jesse somewhere within, out of sight.

Leo tapped his cigarette against the window. His eyes were watering and red. He looked at Dmitri. "You all right?"

"I'm okay." Dmitri bit his lip. He couldn't tell whether his father was drunk. He often wanted his brother to be punished, but now, thinking of Jesse, cold and shivering by some lousy tree, he felt a sort of sorrow. Maybe Jesse will freeze to death, he thought, and then dug his nails into his palms to punish himself for such an ugly thought.

"We'll go back for him in a bit," Leo said. "Let me cool off first." He took another swig from his flask then held it upside down and shook his head.

They drove through the snow to the liquor store, and Leo bought a little bottle of something and some peanuts for Dmitri. He asked a woman in a red coat if he could buy her a cup of coffee and when she turned away, Leo made his hand into a gun and shot at her butt. They got back into the car and Dmitri found his face again in the side mirror. It looked okay; he looked okay. He could tell everyone at school he'd been punched. He could say Jesse had done it.

"Jesse should live with Mom and I should live with you," he said to his father after they'd been on the road for a while. He was proud of his idea, which seemed so clever. But his father's voice came out harsh.

"Don't talk like that," he said. His jaw was clenched and Dmitri cowered a bit, wondering if his father was going to hit him again.

"Heading down south in April," his father said instead, his voice lighter. "You remember Holly? Well. Be gone a few days is all."

He knew that when his father talked about going "down south," he meant San Garcia, where he was from. Dmitri wanted to see it more than anything. But he had asked his father for things like that before—day trips, even an hour with just the two of them—and his father had said no. Dmitri sensed, too, that any demands placed on his father right now would backfire. It was better to stay small, to keep quiet.

"I wanted to tell you boys something today but—" His father stopped speaking. He held his hand out in front of him, stared at the back of it as he drove. "I'm going to marry Holly," he said to Dmitri.

Dmitri did not know what to say. Maybe he had misheard him; maybe his father was going to a place called Merry Holly.

"It doesn't mean I don't love your mother," his father said.

"Okay," said Dmitri.

His father kept looking at him and so he nodded vigorously, like, Yes, yes, it's all right, Dad, it's all right, Dad.

"Wasn't so bad leaving him out there, was it?" his father was saying, the car picking up speed, headed down the snow-covered country road that led to Squire Point. "Leave him out there for no more than an hour—couldn't have been thirty minutes. Think it over. Sort it out in his head. Right?" He turned to Dmitri. "Right?"

"Right."

"I did a good thing just now. Could've gotten real angry at him. Could've made a real mess of it."

Dmitri bit his lip again.

"Could've let him have it," said Leo. "This way is better."

His father was slurring his words and Dmitri wondered how much he'd had to drink, and why he kept lighting one cigarette after the other, even after he'd told Dmitri he was going to quit.

"I did the right thing back there. I did the right thing."

"You did, Daddy."

His father was making strange, gasp-like sounds and wiping his eyes. Perhaps his father was crying, but Dmitri had never seen anyone cry like that before.

"Your nose okay?" his father asked.

"Yeah."

"You know I didn't mean it, right? So don't go telling your mother."

"I won't."

"That's my boy."

Up ahead, the sign for Squire Point appeared, then the turnoff for the first parking lot. An inch of snow had fallen since they'd left, covering their tire tracks, the place they'd parked before. The car slid a bit.

"Shit," his father said. "Hate this stupid crap." The car slid again and he put his hand over Dmitri's chest to keep him from falling forward. "There we go. No problem now. Okay."

His father took another swig, wiped his eyes once more, and turned to face Dmitri. "You stay here. I'm serious this time. When I tell you boys to stay somewhere, I mean it."

"Okay, Daddy."

"I'm going to have a talk with him, then I'll take you both home, all right?"

Dmitri nodded, and watched his father disappear down the trail and into the woods. His father had left the engine on, but the air coming out of the vents was cold. Dmitri swished his body back and forth against the seat for friction. He was crying before he knew it, then angry at himself for crying, for being a baby. Despite the cold, his face felt hot to the touch and he pressed his fingertips to it, then sucked them for warmth.

"Please," he said. "Please come back."

He watched the dashboard clock. Five, ten, fifteen minutes. What was taking so long? He prayed for his father and brother to return. *Dear God, please, I'll do anything you want me to do.* Finally, the backseat door opened and Dmitri swivelled his body to see Jesse climbing into the car. His brother's face was white, and Dmitri wondered if the snow had gotten into his veins.

He watched his father lean over the seat and fasten Jesse's seat belt, tug it a little afterwards to make sure it was secure before closing the door. "Watch your hands," his father said.

"Did you get a whooping?" Dmitri asked in a whisper so his father wouldn't hear. "Did you, Jesse?" His brother was silent, save for a scratching sound he was making, running his fingernails over the back seat. "What took you so long, huh?"

But his brother wouldn't answer him. He was shivering, and little icicles were in his hair, making him look older than his ten years.

"Huh, Jesse?"

Dmitri turned away from his brother and looked out the window. His father was on his knees, combing through the snow with his hands—then he stood, scanned the parking lot, moved to a new spot, crouched again and moved his hands through the snow. Finally, on the fourth try, Dmitri watched him pick up a beer can and put it in his pocket.

His father started the car, but the tires spun out, and so he reversed, stopped, went forward, reversed, bunny-hopping the car. Dmitri felt his body jerk back and forth against the seat belt, as if he were riding a mechanical bull. He hopped in his seat a bit, enjoying the motion.

"That's okay," his father said. "We'll get out of here. Have to get the tires to catch is all. No problem. Don't worry."

The birch trees covered in snow. The empty parking lot, the snow falling in little clumps, all different sizes. The footprints from his father and Jesse filled in until they were invisible. The sky darkened, it seemed, with every breath Dmitri took. The windshield misted over until it was white, and his father rubbed a patch in it so that he could see. His brother's fingernails continued to scratch the back seat. The tires caught, finally, and the car sped free. Dmitri could smell the booze on his father's breath, and even his father's mouthwash, his deodorant, his cologne. "This did not happen, it has never happened," his father said. His voice was gentle, almost a whisper, and as they began the long drive back into town, he told his boys that this day had never happened, this day had never been.

CHAPTER NINE

Evelina

She sat in a play area for children at the hospital. Her chair was slippery, and she spent the first few minutes figuring out how to anchor herself. A poinsettia was on the table beside her. Jesse fiddled with his cuticles. Dmitri sat cross-legged on the floor, assembling a jigsaw puzzle. They were the only family in the waiting area, and Evelina wished desperately for some other family to join them. She put her hand over Jesse's.

"Stop," she said. "Stop fidgeting."

Just as she had been about to call the police and report her sons missing, Leo and the boys had returned, pale-faced and weird-acting, all of them. Leo said it was an accident, that Dmitri had slipped on the ice and fallen face down. Jesse nodded, corroborating. She had put the boys to bed after Leo left, but Dmitri had woken an hour later, crying, holding his little face.

"Tell me what happened," she said but Dmitri shook his head.

"We were playing a game," Jesse said to her. "It got out of hand. Dmitri slipped." His voice was quiet. She could detect a note of terror in his tone.

"Is that all?" She looked at her son's face, his big dark eyes, his high cheekbones.

"He fell on the ice. That's all." His voice trembled and Evelina saw he was fighting something, an outburst of anger, or maybe tears.

A nurse appeared at last, and they were ushered into an examination room. Evelina told Jesse to sit quietly, and helped Dmitri up onto the hospital bed. "My boy," she said to him, and kissed his forehead. His face was puffy from the blow, his nostrils crusty with blood.

It was a small room. Linoleum floor. The smell of burnt coffee. The ceiling too low. The walls water-stained. She wondered—she had often wondered this about anyone who worked indoors—how they survived each day in such a depressing setting. She needed to see beautiful things. It's why she had done well on the fishing boats. No matter how hard the work was, she could look up and see the ocean. She should quit her bookkeeping job and get back on the water, where she belonged.

The doctor was a woman in her forties. She prodded Dmitri's nose, apologized when she hurt him, and told him that his nose was not broken and that he would be fine in a couple of days. She gave him a sticker of a golden retriever.

"There will be bruising," she said to Evelina. "He'll need to sleep with his head elevated. And come in if his nose starts to bleed and you can't stop it." She gave Dmitri a tiny ice pack tucked into a fleece pouch. "Of course I have to ask," she said to Evelina, her voice soft, her hand on Evelina's shoulder, "whether you want to press charges."

"Against whom?" Evelina said. Dmitri had taken the ice pack out of the pouch and was squishing it between his hands.

"They don't stop," said the doctor. She raised her eyebrows at Evelina. "It isn't easy, I know."

————

After the boys were in bed, she drank a beer, quickly, embarrassing herself. She was not a drinker. She wouldn't buy dahlias again. They had wilted instantly, sad yellow husks of themselves. Once she was sure the boys were asleep, she slipped out the door, her coat buttoned to the neck so the store clerk wouldn't see that she was in her pyjamas. The clerk was wearing a V-necked sweater and a ball cap (to hide his baldness, she knew), his face covered in ashy stubble. He looked more like a bookstore owner than a man who worked at a corner store. He was the owner, of course, she reminded herself when she considered whether they might have a future together.

When he saw her, he slipped a couple of scratch-and-win cards out from under the counter and held them up for her to choose.

"Oh, all of them," she laughed. "And a couple of those Pac-Man ones, too."

He gestured to the stool he kept at the end of the counter, where she sometimes sat and scratched the cards. "I could make us tea," he said, after she had told him that her boys were finally home.

"Oh, no, thank you," Evelina said.

The store was brightly lit and Evelina felt revealed, as though every thought was visible beneath her skin. The smell of licorice—those red licorice cigars—was bothering her, making her feel sick.

"Take a couple of treats for your boys," he said and plucked two lollipops from a rotating stand. "So glad they're home safe."

"Yes," she said. "Just out a bit late with their dad. I overreacted."

"No matter," the clerk said. "You know, I'm always here if you need to talk."

A good man. Possibly a little too old for her, but a good man. How to transition to a good man after she'd been with Leo? She worried that the clerk would bore her. And not after a few years—rather, she worried that he would bore her the second she reciprocated his interest. What a shallow person she was. The clerk had a bulbous nose, which she inspected too closely in the fluorescent light, trying to convince herself to leave. She wanted to feel something for someone again. She wanted someone to take her mind off Dmitri's face. Could Leo have done it? It seemed too brutal an act, even for a man who she had seen being brutal.

She tried to figure out how tall the clerk was. He was elevated behind the counter, but by how many inches she couldn't tell. She had only ever seen the top half of him. He was the kind of man who would cook her dinner. Do the dishes afterwards, too. The kind of man who would take her sons to the museum. Buy them books. Be patient with them. Kind. A family man. Or a man who wanted a family. She wasn't sure, of course, of his situation.

In the distance, the sound of sirens. "Uh-oh," said the clerk, gesturing out the window, where a police car went speeding by, lights flashing. "They're coming for me."

She tried to laugh but all she wanted to do was cry.

"I've been meaning to ask," the clerk began. He leaned on the counter and looked at her.

"Yes?"

"I'm a member of the church around the corner. We have a weekly potluck. Of course, anyone is welcome. I wondered whether you might—"

"Oh," she said.

"That's all right, no matter," said the clerk. He rang up the lottery cards, his cheeks flushed. "I hope I haven't offended you."

"No, no, no," she said, wishing she were a different sort of person, a person who would love to go to a church potluck. "It's—"

"No need to explain," he said.

———

The next morning, she sat at the kitchen table and pulled the scratch-and-win cards from her pocket. A church potluck. She imagined herself in a high-collared blouse, a Jell-O salad in her hands, in the basement of some community church. Nope, not a weirdo fish like her. She turned on the radio and tried to make herself pay attention to the news.

A woman was missing. Her car had been found at Squire Point yesterday afternoon, abandoned, engine running. Before she'd gone missing, she'd placed a call to the Whale Bay Police Department about having found a little boy. Helicopters and a canine unit were searching the woods of Squire Point.

Squire Point. Where Leo had been yesterday with the boys. She felt furious with herself that she had let them go into the woods with their father in such bad weather. What kind of a mother—what kind of a parent—

"Oh, god," she said to her empty kitchen, thinking of this poor woman, lost in the snow, with someone's lost child. Someone's poor, dear child.

"Mom?" It was Jesse, in the doorway, in his plaid flannel pyjamas and bare feet. "A policeman called last night while you were gone," he said. He handed her a scrap of paper where he had scribbled a phone number. "I told him you were asleep. He wants you to call him."

"That doctor," said Evelina. "Oh for heaven's sake. You'd tell me if your father hit your brother, wouldn't you?"

CHAPTER TEN

Denny

The sky was a pale colour, neither blue nor white nor grey, and it took Denny until Lewis was pulling into his driveway to realize that it was dawn and he'd been at the police station all night. He let himself into the house and bent down to hug Scout. Miraculously, his wonderful dog had held his bladder, and Denny praised him and apologized, then stood in the backyard under the awful sky while Scout peed in the snow.

The dresser drawers were open in the bedroom, the bedclothes thrown to the floor. He walked from room to room, shutting drawers and cabinets, picking up clothing, books, shoes. Had he done this or had the police been here in the night?

He made the bed and got into it, and held his dog. He leapt up and turned on the heat, then rushed into bed again, his breath visible in the frigid air.

A few miles from where he lay, a search team was trying to locate his wife. He should be there, too, searching. The detectives obviously thought he had killed Vera. What a thought! Imagine him going out to Squire Point with Vera and—then what—murdering her? Burying her body in the snow? To what end, he asked the detectives. Why would I do that? Marital problems, they said. Fertility problems. Infidelity. Life insurance policy.

They would investigate every aspect of his life and marriage, the detectives told him. They would turn him inside out. He lay on his back and replayed the interrogation over and over, each time answering their questions better, differently, more honestly, more deviously. He imagined an action scene from a movie: jumping from his chair, overpowering the detectives, fleeing the station. His hands began to ache and he held them to his body. He didn't want to examine the thought, but there it was, floating in his mind. Maybe she hadn't disappeared at all. Maybe he had driven her away. Maybe he had driven her to suicide. *Leave me alone.*

He was relieved his parents were dead so they wouldn't be dragged into this. Vera's parents were driving up to Whale Bay, would be here tomorrow. Or was that today? It was already seven in the morning. A bird that he called the "whistle bird," for lack of knowing what it was, began its morning whistling. When he and Vera had first moved into the house, he'd spent hours researching bird calls. So many different kinds of finches. It had put him in a bad mood and he had given up.

The pounding on the door startled him awake and he jumped from the bed and ran into the living room, where Scout was pawing the door with his big feet.

It was Lewis, in plainclothes. Stylish jeans and a black parka, black leather boots with blue laces. He wore tortoiseshell sunglasses. Denny regarded him as if for the first time. He hadn't considered until this moment that Lewis was a real person. But here he was, holding two cups of coffee and a bag of pastries, the bottom heavy with grease. "My shift doesn't start for another few hours," Lewis said.

"May I?" said Lewis, and Denny nodded and led him into the living room. They sat on the velvet couch and ate in silence and Lewis gave the last bite of his pastry to Scout. The dog looked back and forth between the men.

"Scout and Vera are inseparable," said Denny. "He's nervous without her."

"A husky?" asked Lewis.

"Mixed with something else, too, we think," said Denny. "Lab or collie or shepherd."

"Heinz 57 variety then," said Lewis.

"Guess so."

"I had a border terrier when I was a boy," said Lewis.

Denny closed his eyes and felt the heaviness in his head, his heart, his hands. "You haven't found her," he said finally.

"We haven't."

"Well. Thank you for telling me, Officer Côté," Denny said.

"My name is Lewis," Lewis said. "I mean, it's okay to call me Lewis."

"I want you to know," said Denny, "though I'm sure everyone says this, but I need to say it anyway. I don't know where my wife is. And all I want is for her to come home."

"I believe you," said Lewis. "I listened to what you said last night. And I believe you."

Outside, a rattling, a garbage can being knocked over. "Shit," said Denny. He raced to the back door and into the yard, Lewis close behind him. A raccoon or possum, he couldn't be sure, skittered away. "During the day? Really?" He bent down and righted the garbage can. Two trash bags sat a few feet away, ripped open, their contents spilled onto the pavement. "Oh, come on," said Denny. He turned to Lewis. "You people are welcome to ransack whatever you want of mine if it will help you find my wife. But please." He dragged the trash bags back into the garbage can and wiped the tears that were falling fast down his face with the back of his hand. "Please don't destroy my property in the meantime."

"Let me help you." Lewis gathered the remaining trash and scooped it into the garbage can. One of the bags had torn and the ground was littered with cigarette butts.

"You a smoker?" said Lewis.

"It's Vera. She's going to quit. She's down to two a day."

"Looks like a lot more than two," said Lewis.

"Well," said Denny. "She was trying."

The men tossed the butts into the garbage can in silence, then returned inside and took turns washing their hands.

"Listen," said Lewis. "Why I'm here. There was a call placed on the Squire Point pay phone a few minutes before Vera called the police. We think Vera may have made this call."

"Okay?" said Denny. His eyes were heavy from lack of sleep.

Lewis told him that someone—maybe Vera—had called a woman named Evelina Lucchi but the call had not gone through.

"I don't know anyone with that name," Denny said. "As far as I know, Vera didn't either."

"They're about the same age. Maybe Vera had friends you didn't know about?"

"I don't think so," said Denny. "Look, I'm not that out of touch."

"We don't know for sure that Vera placed the call. But we're going to interview the woman to see if she knew your wife."

Who knows. Maybe Vera did have friends he didn't know about. A secret life. He almost liked the idea. It was a better reality than the one in which he had driven his wife to flee him, or to kill herself. Some other friend. A secret romance. He smiled. Vera the lesbian. Why not?

"What about the little boy?" said Denny.

"We have no new information." Lewis took off his sunglasses, and Denny saw that his eyes were red-rimmed, exhausted. "No one has reported him missing, and the search team has found nothing."

Denny felt himself softening toward this man, who seemed so genuinely worried about his wife, him, even his dog. "Well, I hope the little boy is okay. Whoever he is."

The pastries had awakened a kind of deep hunger in Denny, and he knew if Lewis left he would eat a dozen eggs, then a whole box of cereal, and who knows what else.

"I was going to make some eggs," Denny said, not looking at Lewis but at Scout, who was lying on his side, panting slightly. Denny watched as Lewis knelt and patted Scout's head, scratched him behind the ears.

"Sounds nice," said Lewis.

They ate in the kitchen, standing up, not speaking much, while Scout nosed around in the snow outside. Denny dipped his toast into his egg yolk and raised it to his mouth. The food had perked him up a bit. He felt more rational and less guilty—more convinced that Vera was only lost in the woods somewhere and would soon be found. She was resourceful. She could build a lean-to, a shelter. He thought of her on her hands and knees, rubbing two sticks together.

"A lean-to," he said aloud, not meaning to, and Lewis raised his eyebrows but didn't respond.

The men looked at the ocean, visible between the snow-covered trees. Lewis gestured out the window toward Scout. "He's got big paws, hasn't he?"

"We thought he'd be a lot bigger. Never did grow into his feet."

"Like me," Lewis said, wagging his foot at Denny. "Twelves. And I'm not even six feet."

"Like flippers," said Denny, and the policeman laughed.

The sound of laughter disturbed him. What if Vera was dead and could hear them laughing? "You know," he said to Lewis, "she's a wonderful filmmaker—her eye—she meant to make a living that way, to really pursue it, instead of teaching it. This kind of thing—when it happens—you realize you have to do the things you meant to do. Do you know what I'm saying?"

Lewis set his plate on the counter and looked at Denny. "I think so. Maybe." He gestured toward the wedding ring on Denny's finger. "Did you make that?"

"Yeah," said Denny. "It's meant to match Vera's—the alexandrite."

"What is alexander—"

"Alexandrite. It changes colour depending on the light—red to green. They call it nature's magic trick." He tried to keep speaking but felt something in his chest, in his throat. "I can't—"

"Hey," said Lewis. "She's going to come home."

Was she? He looked at Lewis. "I think I'm going crazy, you know? Could we get out of here, take a walk with Scout?"

"Sure, sure."

"I think I'm bored. I mean, bored out of my mind with worry. I need something to happen. I need something to happen besides what has already happened."

"I get that," said Lewis.

Denny whistled for Scout and the dog trotted into the kitchen and sat at his feet. The two men left the house. There was an owl somewhere in one of the Garry oak trees and Lewis and Denny stopped a minute to listen.

"A barred owl," said Denny. "This one I know. He's here a lot. The neighbourhood is full of birds."

"Is that so," said Lewis.

They trudged through the snow, past the other houses, some still lit up with Christmas lights. Professors', accountants', doctors' houses. Denny imagined his neighbours rushing to their windows, watching him walk past. The Hill, the neighbourhood was called. The only way to walk was downhill, toward the town, and Denny felt an ache in his knees as he and Lewis navigated the slippery sidewalk.

He thought of Vera stumbling through snowbanks, trying to find the road. Sticking out her thumb. Or waving wildly at a passing car. "I think I'm done walking. I don't want to be out if she comes home."

"I should get going anyway," Lewis said. "But, listen, if you remember anything, anything at all, or anything Vera said, call us."

They trudged back up the hill, and Denny watched the policeman drive off. And then he and Scout went back into the silent, empty house. He looked at the ceiling. He looked out the window.

Who did he have left? Who was there to talk to? Who could he tell about his day if Vera never returned? What he wanted to do was tell Vera about all of this. "Vera! Vera, you'll never guess what happened!" he wanted to say. "You disappeared!"

CHAPTER ELEVEN

Evelina

The bruises unfolded over Dmitri's face like butterfly wings. The white light of the early morning came in through the slits in the blinds and Evelina watched her son play with the stripes of light on the floor. He ran to the window, hearing something. He told her there were two taxicabs outside and so she went to the window to see what was happening. "No," she said, her hand resting on top of Dmitri's head. "Those are police cars."

A woman named Vera Gusev had gone missing at Squire Point on New Year's Day. She didn't know anyone by that name. She sat at the kitchen table with two detectives and a police officer—nice men, gentle men, snow in their hair—her sons in their bedroom with the door closed. She was wearing the peacock feather earrings, something Leo would have chastised her for had he been there. His voice was in her head. She offered the men coffee.

"This woman called my house?" she asked. She picked up a dime she kept on the table for her scratch cards and fiddled with it. "A wrong number?" she asked. "I don't know anyone named Vera Gusev. And my boys—well, neither of them is missing. They're in their bedroom."

She felt a kind of ticking in her brain, like a fire crackling, something about to ignite. She held her coffee cup to her face and looked at the detectives, at the policeman, who, she noticed, had a beautiful jaw.

"Can you explain your phone activity on New Year's Day?" one of the detectives said.

"My phone activity?"

"You placed two calls to local hospitals."

"I—" The ticking was getting louder in her mind, so loud it must be audible to the men. She took a loud sip of her coffee, hoping to muffle the sound.

"We'd also like you to tell us about that evening, when you brought your boy in to be treated for bruising."

"I—"

"We're trying to piece together what has happened."

"My boys spent New Year's Day with their father," she said carefully. Her heart was pounding as loudly as the ticking sound in her head. She pressed the soles of her feet to the floor. She felt she might float away from the table and through the kitchen window, get sucked out to sea by the wind. Surely Leo couldn't have had anything to do with this. "They were late getting home. I got worried. Paranoid. I called the hospitals, to see, to see if there had been any accidents—"

She looked at the men, but their heads were bowed; they were writing things down.

"—but they came home shortly after. My youngest—Dmitri—hurt himself while he was with his dad. He fell on the ice. That's why I took him to the hospital. Anyway, it's just bruising. There's really nothing more I can tell you."

"But the boys, and your husband, you can confirm they were at Squire Point on New Year's Day?"

"Yes," she said. "They were. It's a large—"

"It's a big park, yes," said the handsome policeman. "We know. We've been there."

When they left, Evelina bolted the door. Her legs were shaking. She felt the caffeine in her bones, behind her eyes. She felt the weight of what the detectives had asked her deep in her abdomen.

"They're gone," she said to the empty kitchen and seconds later Jesse was beside her. She decided to make a big breakfast to distract herself—boiled eggs, toast, potatoes, bacon, and fried tomatoes—and she put on music while she cooked. Her sons sat at the table. They listened to Al Green, then Sam Cooke. Dmitri was drawing a picture of Jesse. She kept reminding herself that everything was okay. They were eating breakfast together in their pyjamas. They were safe and warm. Dmitri's face would heal. Jesse would turn eleven this year. They would be her boys forever. She did not know this woman named Vera Gusev who had called her home and then vanished. A coincidence. An anomaly. Also a coincidence that Leo and her boys had been at Squire Point that day.

Still, she found herself unable to think of anything else.

Why had the boys been so late getting home? Why had Leo seemed so sad when he dropped them off? Why had his clothes been wet?

"Did you," she began, her sons shovelling the breakfast into their mouths unceremoniously, "meet a woman out at Squire Point?"

She watched for it—a conspiratorial glance between them, a swift kick to a shin—but the boys continued to eat, elbows on the table, mouths open as they chewed, forks in their hands like spears. They shook their heads.

"You are such animals," she said. "Sit up. Mouths closed. For heaven's sake."

When they were done, her sons sat in front of their empty plates. They were still as statues. They could sense her mood, she could tell. They were waiting, she realized, for her to pick up a glass and smash it into the sink. To slam her bedroom door, to not come out for hours. To leave the house in a fury. She had done all of these things before. She stood in front of her sons, her fingers in her mouth to keep from screaming.

She felt her heart, too large, in her chest. Her sweet boys. Dmitri, who had cried on Christmas Day when she suggested throwing out his stuffed bear to make room for his new toys. "I thought you might be embarrassed by it now," she had rushed to say, hoping the words would stop his tears. "Of course we'll keep Brownie. Of course."

"Got some new ones in today. Winter Wonderland," the clerk said, holding up the silver cards. "Twenty-five thousand."

"I'll take two." Evelina handed a five-dollar bill to the clerk and hesitated a moment, waiting for him to gesture to the stool at the end of the counter.

"Tea, Evelina?"

Oh, thank god. "Herbal, if you have it."

"I do."

"Thanks."

The clerk came around the counter and Evelina saw that he was taller than she had expected—at least a full head taller. He handed her a coin for the scratch-and-win cards and disappeared into the back of the store. She heard the kettle. When the clerk returned, she told him that the cards were duds. She fought the urge to buy two more.

"Ah well," he said. He handed her a red mug full of tea. He took the cards from her and tossed them into the trash. For the first time, the counter was not between them. Evelina sipped her tea and stared into the clerk's familiar face. Still, she could not imagine accompanying him to a church potluck. She wished religious people would wear signs, or hats—something to identify them, so she would know. She was too much of a misfit to get involved with someone who believed in God.

"I can't remember the last time I was so obsessed with the news," the clerk said. "This woman, Vera Gusev—"

"Yes," said Evelina. "I've been following it, too."

"Some kind of filmmaker," said the clerk. "They showed a clip from one of her movies last night, but I didn't think much of it. Endless shots of trains."

"Trains," Evelina repeated.

"What a thing," said the clerk. "So horrible to think about. I mean, the possibilities. I hate not knowing."

"Yes," she said. "Horrible."

"Is she out there, walking around in the snow? Lost? Stuck in a snowdrift somewhere? Maybe she fell into one of those tree wells and couldn't escape?"

"I don't know. I should go, get home to my sons."

"I'm going out there tonight," said the clerk. "I'm going to help them search. There's a boy—there's a child out there. Weird thing, though, that no one has reported him missing. Weird, yes? I just think no one's doing enough."

She nodded her head, her teeth clenched. She wanted to tell the clerk about the policeman and the detectives who had visited her, and their questions about the phone call from Vera Gusev, and about how she felt she couldn't trust Leo, though she didn't think, of course, that he could be guilty of such a thing—murder?—but she wanted to talk it out nonetheless. There was no one for her to talk to anymore. No one in her life. She wanted to bury her head in the clerk's sweater—wanted someone, anyone, to take her in their arms.

"Yes, it is weird, yes," she said. It was indeed weird that Leo and her boys had been at Squire Point that day, too. Her son's bruises. Her sons' silence. Why had Vera Gusev called her house?

She hurried out of the store, her tea still steaming on the counter. Her face was soaked with tears by the time she reached her house. The trouble was that she'd let her friendships lapse after she'd gotten involved with Leo. She could call her sister, or her parents, sure, but they had been so disapproving of Leo from the beginning and Evelina didn't want to deal with any smugness. And what was she supposed to say anyway?

On the answering machine, a message from one of the detectives who had been in her house.

"We'd like to bring you and your boys in for further questioning," he said, his tone so friendly and exuberant it sounded as if she'd won a prize.

"Why?" she said to the answering machine. "What do you want now?"

She shoved herself next to Jesse on the couch, moulded herself to his body, slid her hand under his pyjama top and pressed it flat against his warm back. He smelled like baby detergent. She still used it, even though it was expensive. She wanted to remember the smell of her boys as babies. She breathed him in.

"Don't," he said. He wiggled his body away until she removed her hand.

"What happened on New Year's Day?" she whispered. She glanced at Dmitri but he was completely absorbed in the television.

"I can't tell you," Jesse said.

"You have to," she said. "You have to tell me."

She took him by the shoulders. She stared at her son.

"Stop," said Jesse. "Let me go."

But years of working on fish boats had given her a kind of super-human strength and she channelled it, pressed her thumbs into her son's flesh. She thought of the cold and the wet and the eighteen-hour days, four in a row, how the net would go out and then come back in, over and over until it was time to run downstairs and cook.

In front of her was not the ocean, though—it was her son's beautiful face, and she saw that her son was about to break apart in her arms. She was hurting him. "I'm sorry," she said. She put her hands over her eyes. "I don't know what to do here." Should she scream at him? Threaten to gather up everything he loved in a black garbage bag and drag it outside until he told her the truth?

"Okay," he said. He moved toward her, speaking softly so that Dmitri wouldn't hear. "But you can't tell anyone."

They left Dmitri in the living room and she locked the door to the bathroom. She sat on the edge of the bathtub, and took her son's hands in hers. "The only person you need to tell is me."

When he finished speaking, she leapt for her coat and the car keys. She would drive over to Leo's apartment and she would kill him. Her son was begging her not to tell his father that he had told her what had happened, but she was so angry that she couldn't hear his words. She found herself racing through the streets of Whale Bay toward Leo's apartment. The cars parted for her. The red lights turned green. She sped through the town as if in a dream.

Away from the ocean, across the train tracks, past the industrial part of town, the street lights fewer and fewer, a corner store, a liquor store, some kind of seedy-looking bar, and then the row of depressing apartment buildings, the stucco discoloured and water-stained, none more than three storeys high. By the time she reached Leo's building, it was too late. A patrol car was pulling away from the curb, the unmistakable shape of the back of Leo's head in the back seat.

CHAPTER TWELVE

Lewis

The pained look on Evelina's face troubled him. It could be the look of someone who was lying. Regardless, Lewis excused himself to use the bathroom so that he could snoop around. She couldn't have lived in the beach house for long. There were unopened boxes in the living room, and her envelopes bore the yellow stickers of forwarded mail. The house was old and wind-battered, in need of a renovation. Probably had been a tourist rental for decades. Creaky floors. Ornate moulding on the large windows, dark wooden picture rails. Presumably gorgeous hardwood under this cheap carpet. The house smelled of food and dust and mould.

Everything in Whale Bay stank of mould to Lewis, who was unaccustomed to such constant dampness. He felt spores might be growing on his lungs. He'd been here three years now, had just stopped working nights. A small department: the chief and six officers, including Lewis. He hadn't expected it to be so boring; sometimes weeks would go by without an interesting call. The town wasn't altogether bad. Some would say it was a step up from Wisconsin, but the kinds of people who said that had never been to Wisconsin, couldn't tell the difference between Iowa and Idaho. Here he was, on the West Coast, in a small fishing town a stone's throw from Canada. From his apartment's roof deck, he could see across the Strait of Juan de Fuca. A peaceful place, the harbour crowded with tourists in the summer, deserted in winter, half the sky obscured by the Olympic Mountains. His Wisconsin friends talked unseriously of visiting. He hoped he would meet someone. He didn't want to admit, young and ambitious as he was, that he was lonely here.

The bathroom in Evelina's house had two doors—one for access from the hallway and one for access from a bedroom. Lewis ran the water and opened the second door—a peek, he told himself. He liked to see how people lived. Maybe he would apply to be a detective next year. He didn't think much of the guys he was working with on the Gusev case. Surely he could do a better job. For instance, what he was doing now, while they sat at Evelina's kitchen table, drinking coffee like lumps.

"Hi there," he whispered.

The boys were sitting cross-legged on their beds. The older boy had dark hair and a darker complexion than his mother but the younger one looked just like her. The younger one was drawing with crayons. The older boy was staring out the window and didn't look up when Lewis came in. Their room was unsurprisingly a disaster—clothing, books, stuffed animals, toys everywhere. Come to think of it, the kitchen had been kind of a sty as well. It was the chestnuts in the corner that caught Lewis's eye, however. His own father had done that: put chestnuts in the corners of his bedroom at night, to ward off spiders. He hadn't thought of it in such a long time. Little lines of cinnamon on the windowsills, too, to keep out the ants.

But now was not the time to be haunted by thoughts of his father. He shook off the memory of the chestnuts and the cinnamon and looked at the two little boys sitting on their beds.

The younger one's face had a spread of bruises, fresh ones, purple-blue. The boys were in their pyjamas. "Oh," Lewis said, looking at the little boy's face. "Oh." He had read the hospital report before they had driven to Evelina's house, but to see the little boy's face with his own eyes was another thing.

"He fell on the ice," the older boy said. "It was my fault."

The little one hopped off his bed and walked to Lewis. He wanted to inspect his badge. Lewis knelt and let the little boy run his hands over it. The boy didn't ask to see his gun and Lewis felt relieved.

"When did this happen?" said Lewis, though he knew the answer from the hospital report. The detectives had found a mug shot of a younger Leo Lucchi, arrested for shoplifting, his lips curled in a faint smile. He and Evelina were supposedly separated.

"New Year's Day," said the older boy.

The boy was staring at his hands. *A rich inner life.* It was a phrase that had been used to mock Lewis as a boy and it haunted him sometimes. *Bet you have a rich inner life, don't you?* Lewis knew—with the logical side of his brain—that it was harder in this world to be a girl than a boy. There was no disproving it. And yet deep down, Lewis felt that in fact there was nothing worse than being a sensitive boy. A sensitive boy who would grow into a sensitive man. It was worse than being a girl but no one could ever say it. Still, he wanted to find a way to tell the boy this.

"Anybody else live here?" he said to the older boy. "Your father?"

"No," said the boy. "No, sir."

The boy's hands were shaking slightly but his voice was clear. He was looking at Lewis from his perch on the bed, and the younger one joined him there. The older one put his arm around the younger one and they stared at Lewis that way, bodies together. What a thing it must be to have a sibling. Whatever had happened or was happening in the boys' lives, they had each other. What he wouldn't give to be able to call someone who was related to him—a brother or sister, preferably one who was older, one who could help him make sense of his father, of his childhood, and one who could help him make sense of his father's death. What would Lewis have done if a police officer had shown up at his house when he was ten years old?

"Our dad's getting married again," said the younger boy.

"Is that so?" said Lewis. He walked toward the boys and sat on the opposite bed. For some reason he held out his hand, though he didn't expect the boys to take it. "Can you tell me what you got up to New Year's Day?"

The boys looked at each other, then down at Lewis's hand, but didn't say anything. The younger boy was chewing his lip.

"It's okay," said Lewis. "I can ask your mom." He began to get up, but the older boy moved toward him.

"We went to Squire Point," the older boy said. "With our dad. It's a sacred place."

"Sacred?" Lewis asked. He thought about standing at the edge of the frozen lake with the dog, the wind through the snow-covered trees, the dog wanting him to step out onto the ice. "Is it haunted?"

"No," said the boy. "I don't think that's what my dad means."

A rich inner life. The boy reminded him so much of his own young self that he could hardly stand it. But surely this boy was not dealing with as much pain as Lewis had. This boy had a mother who seemed capable and kind. A sensitive mother, at least at first glance. And yet if a police officer had appeared in Lewis's childhood bedroom, he knew his young self would have been as polite and helpful as this boy in front of him was being. And if the police officer had asked, his young self would have said that everything was fine.

"Is—" Lewis started. "Is everything all right?"

The younger boy looked up at his brother, who hadn't taken his eyes off Lewis.

"Yes," said the older boy. "He fell on the ice is all."

"That's not what I meant," said Lewis, though he wasn't sure what he did mean. "I mean, are you both doing all right?"

The little one looked up at his brother again. "Are we all right, Jesse?" he asked.

"We're fine," said the older boy. He turned away from Lewis and his brother and went back to whatever he had been watching out of his bedroom window, which, Lewis could see now, was the white-capped and roiling ocean.

"Well, it's nice to meet you both," Lewis said. He backed away from the boys and disappeared back into the bathroom.

A pink canister of shaving cream and a pink disposable razor lay on the counter. Women's deodorant. Child-sized toothbrushes and bubble-gum-flavoured toothpaste, comic books on the back of the toilet and old copies of *Redbook* and *Vogue*. The toilet and bathtub were both pink. The tile was pink. No sign of a man. No pictures, no mail with his name on it, no men's shoes by the front door. Lewis turned off the water. He thought again of the little boy's face, and the way the older boy had looked at him.

When he returned to the kitchen, the detectives were thanking Evelina for speaking to them, for the coffee. Now what? They were going to leave? This Vera woman needed to be found. He felt something slimy in the pit of his stomach. What if they never found her? No matter how smart he felt himself to be, he felt the limitations of his own knowledge so strongly it was almost unbearable. The detectives had brushed Vera's car for fingerprints and he hoped the results were back, and that something would come of it.

Of course it had to be Denny, right? The husband was *always* guilty! Lewis couldn't quite believe it. He liked Denny. But anyone, even affable Denny, could make a death look accidental. All day and all night, news vans sat parked in front of Denny's house, as if waiting for him to burst forth from the door and offer his confession. And what to make of the phone call? Why had Vera called Evelina? This clue was far more interesting to Lewis than the broken picture frame in Denny's garbage can. It was too much of a coincidence that Evelina's sons had been at Squire Point that day, the little one's face all busted up like that.

He lingered a moment in the doorway, surveying the house one more time, and then Evelina. Her peacock earrings caught the light coming in from the open door, and Lewis saw they were many shades of dazzling blue. Something about her face—how it caught the light—made him hope he would see her and her boys again. He hoped this wasn't the end.

"Thanks again," he said to her, and then they were out the door.

When he got back to the station late that night, a group of men were waiting, grinning. It was after midnight. The men's clothes were wet, their noses and fingers bright red. They were old men, and some of them held steaming cups of coffee. Some had unlit cigarettes dangling from their mouths.

The oldest among them stood. He had something cradled in his arms, wrapped in a blanket, so that at first Lewis thought he was being handed a baby.

He stumbled back, not wanting to take it. He'd never held a baby before, let alone a dead one.

The old man frowned and turned to one of the detectives instead. "I found this," the old man said, his arms outstretched, "buried in the snow out at Squire Point."

The detective took the bundle from the old man. He opened the blanket bit by bit, and Lewis looked over the detective's shoulder.

"Oh," said the detective. "This is a beaut." He opened the blanket and looked at Lewis. "Look at that mahogany."

Lewis looked down at the mahogany stock, the nickel-plated receiver and gold inlay. He supposed anything could be beautiful, if made by the right hands.

"It's an old Remington," the detective said to Lewis, and the old men nodded at them, beaming.

CHAPTER THIRTEEN

Leo

He couldn't remember how to walk. How to swing his arms. Whether he took long strides or short ones. He thought an interrogation room would have a two-way mirror, like on television, but there was only a metal table and two chairs. Concrete walls, a fluorescent light overhead. He sat, and the detective sat across from him, a stack of files on the table. The detective tapped out a cigarette and offered it to Leo.

"Thank you." He put it between his lips and leaned into the flame of the detective's lighter. The detective slid a black plastic ashtray toward him and sat back in his chair.

Evelina had told Leo once that he was made of stone, impossible to hurt, that nothing she could ever say or do would hurt him. It wasn't true. Nothing had ever made him feel as bleak as this: the reality that Jesse hated him so much that he had pretended Dmitri had drowned. And now this detective, saying he wanted to speak to him, though he wasn't entirely sure why. He assumed Evelina was pressing charges against him for Dmitri.

He took a deep drag of the cigarette. "Well, look," he said. "Let me tell the story from the beginning."

Dad. Dad, it's Dmitri. Do something.

He hadn't meant to hit Dmitri so hard. Surely the detective would understand, once he had told him the full story. "I was trying to break through the ice," he said. "I have these bruises." He put the cigarette in his mouth and pushed up his shirt sleeves to reveal his beat-up forearms. He showed the detective his scabbed-up hands.

The detective stared at Leo's wounds for a moment, then sifted through the file folders on the table. "This your rifle?" he said, and slid a picture of Leo's old Remington across the table.

Leo felt the smoke from the cigarette catch in his throat. He must have dropped the rifle in the snow. He couldn't remember putting it down, or even the last time he had held it. He could only remember the ice, and the pain that radiated from his forearms as he tried to bust through it. He'd been so careful to pick up his beer cans. He couldn't believe it—he'd left the goddamn rifle out at Squire Point. His most prized possession.

The detective reached for his pen and looked up at Leo. "It's a real beaut. That mahogany, it's really something."

"It was my father's," said Leo. He blew smoke out into the room and ashed the cigarette. He took another drag and looked at the detective.

"Well then," said the detective. "Now that we've established it's yours, why don't you walk me through what happened on New Year's Day."

What was the worst thing that could happen—he might have to take parenting classes? Evelina wouldn't be cruel enough to try to keep him away from his sons. She didn't have that kind of spite in her. And, besides, he hadn't meant to hit Dmitri. It had all been such a terrible accident. He would tell the story plainly to the detective, and surely he would understand. The rifle had nothing to do with anything.

"We made these paper boats, see," he began, then set the cigarette down and walked the detective through the little folds. "It was a way of starting fresh—new resolutions. Getting it right this time," he said. But he'd left his cigarettes in the car. He left the boys on the trail, and when he returned Jesse was pounding on a little patch of thin ice in the middle of the lake, yelling that his brother had fallen through. But he hadn't. It was a prank. An awful prank. Leo couldn't understand it. The cruelty of it. Dmitri had jumped on his back and he had hit him, he told the detective, as a reflex. An unintended action.

"I didn't mean to hit him so hard. I was out of my mind. I take full responsibility for that. I am truly sorry about that."

"I might have killed my kid, had he pulled that on me," said the detective. He then produced a piece of paper and thrust it on the table: the hospital report with a description of Dmitri's injuries.

"I told you I was angry," said Leo. "I was. But I didn't mean to hurt him like this."

A reflex. That's what it was. He hadn't been in control of his own hand. Besides, the punch had been meant for Jesse. But he couldn't say that now.

"I think what happened was you snapped," said the detective. "And that poor woman saw you do it."

That poor woman. His cigarette was smouldering in the ashtray and the detective reached over and stubbed it out.

"What woman?" said Leo. "I thought this was about my son."

The detective held up his hand to silence him. He put a photograph of a dark-haired woman down on the table. She sat on a grey velvet couch, her arms wrapped around a big dog. "She's been missing since New Year's Day," said the detective.

"I don't know this woman," said Leo. He pushed the photograph away from him. His voice was quiet and low. "I promise you, I've never seen her before." He said it again: "I have never seen her before. My son—isn't that what this is about?"

"This woman called the police from the Squire Point pay phone on New Year's Day, saying she found a little boy," said the detective.

"What little boy?" said Leo. He leaned toward the detective. He was lost. He raised his hands. He didn't know what was happening anymore. The woman had called the police? When? Why?

"One of your sons?" asked the detective.

"I don't know what you're talking about," said Leo, but his hands had begun to shake. He put them down by his sides, out of sight.

"Okay," said the detective. "She also called your ex-wife."

"Evelina?"

"Back to the rifle—so you were shooting, doing some kind of target practice? Maybe you shot the woman by accident?"

"No," said Leo. He could feel spit forming on the sides of his mouth and he wiped it with his sleeve, fought the urge to grab the detective by the lapels and beat his face. "I was going to teach the boys to shoot. My dad did that with me, you know? I was trying to do something like that for the boys." He leaned across the table until he was inches from the detective's face. "I never fired the rifle—I told you what happened already, with Dmitri. I needed to get away from Jesse is all. I needed to get away from him. I left him so I could calm down. I left for maybe twenty, thirty minutes. Dmitri and I drove around. Then we returned to Squire Point, got Jesse, and I drove the boys home to their mother."

"Okay," said the detective. "Take a breath and calm down." He offered his pen to Leo and continued: "It would help me to be able to visualize this. Can you show me"—at this the detective unfolded a map of Squire Point, the lake in its centre, the two parking lots both leading to it—"where you were, precisely? Retrace your steps for me, show me on the map."

"Which steps?"

"All of them," said the detective. "From the moment you arrived to the moment you left."

"Okay." He paused a minute, considering where to start, what to say. "I parked here, in this parking lot," said Leo. He tapped the picture of the first parking lot with the pen. "We walked here, on this trail, with the paper boats." He dragged the pen along the map, showing the detective his route to the lake. "Then I walked back to the parking lot to get my cigarettes, then back to the lake. That's when I saw Jesse in the middle of the lake. Do you follow? Okay, then I left Jesse on the trail and Dmitri and I walked back to the car and we left for a while."

"And when did you encounter Vera Gusev?"

"Who? No, I never met her. I have never met her, I said. I drove around with Dmitri—then I parked where I'd parked before. Jesse was waiting for me. I simply took the boys home." He removed the pen from the map and stared at the detective. "There's nothing else to say. I don't know this woman."

The detective clicked his tongue.

"I don't know this woman," he said again, louder this time.

The detective nodded. "So you've never met her. And you never fired your rifle. And you don't remember dropping it in the snow."

"That's correct, yes."

"What about her car? Do you remember Vera Gusev's car in the parking lot?"

"I'm sorry, I don't. I was—as I said, I was upset, I'd had a drink—"

"I'm thinking," said the detective, "that Vera must have found Jesse in the woods when you left him." He leaned back, capped the pen, and slipped it into his pocket. "And maybe she was calling the police when you and Dmitri returned to Squire Point. And when she saw that you had hurt your other son—perhaps she—perhaps she accused you of child abuse—"

"No, that is not—"

"And then, as I said before, you snapped."

"No," said Leo, "that isn't what happened at all."

The detective made a snorting sound. "Okay, well, you might, though—you might try to help me understand something then."

"Understand what?"

"Why Jesse's fingerprints were found in Vera Gusev's car."

Leo looked at the table, at the photo of the woman and her dog. He stared into her eyes. What a mess this was. What a monstrous mess.

"His fingerprints?" he whispered. He wasn't sure he could speak, even if he had to. Something had happened to his voice.

"Indeed."

"What?"

"It's as I said," said the detective. "We found Jesse's fingerprints in Vera Gusev's car."

CHAPTER FOURTEEN

Jesse

"Yes," Jesse was saying to the other detective, his mother and Dmitri by his side. "Yes, I was in the woman's car."

It had been three days, but the leathery smell of her fancy car was still bright in his memory. And the dull scent of her cigarettes, like in his father's car.

He looked at the detective, then at his hands. What came out of his mouth next was a mixture of the truth and something he had rehearsed with his mother until it had felt true. He could feel the bruises forming underneath the skin on his shoulders, where his mother's fingers had been.

"It's okay," said the detective. "I'm listening."

Jesse saw a lollipop in the detective's front pocket and wondered whether the detective would give it to him when all of this was over, as if he were a baby. It was a red lollipop. Dmitri was looking at it, too.

"You can tell him," said his mother.

It was a very brightly lit room. So bright it hurt Jesse's eyes. He knew his father was in the room next to him. *Your story is the one that matters*, his mother had told him. *They won't believe your father anyway, no matter what he says. It's you who they will trust.*

And so Jesse took a deep breath and told the detective that his father had left him in the woods after he pretended his brother had fallen through the ice. That was true but it was difficult to say because of the shame he felt. He then said he met the woman on the trail. She had thought he was lost. That was true as well; she did think that.

"We walked to her car. We drove to the other parking lot to look for my dad. She called my mom, and then she called the police."

He looked at the detective and then at his mother. The detective was writing down everything he said, nodding at him to continue. His mother was holding Dmitri's hand and he wished she would hold his hand, too.

He said the next bit in a monotone, his eyes cast downward, his foot tapping the floor. "I got scared and opened the door, and her dog jumped out and ran into the woods. She ran after the dog and I never saw her again after that. My father came back and he drove us home."

Another man entered the room, and Jesse saw that it was the policeman who had come into his bedroom. The one who had let Dmitri feel his badge. The one who had looked at him with kind eyes. Who had asked if he was okay.

He wasn't sure anyone had ever asked him that before.

The policeman whispered something to the detective, then took a seat. Jesse saw that the policeman was staring at his mother. His mother straightened her back, crossed her legs at the ankles. She pushed her hair behind her ears. There was some small change in her mouth, in her voice.

"I'm sorry we can't be more helpful," his mother said, looking at the policeman and then the detective. "This is really all he knows."

He thought again of his mother's hands digging into his shoulders. His mother was so strong she could pull a drowning man out of the sea. She was so strong that she had pushed his father out of the house.

"Why didn't he say anything before?" said the detective. "About being in the woman's car."

"What was he supposed to say?" said his mother. "He didn't realize the woman he met was the same woman on the news. He is only a little boy."

"Yes, but why didn't he say something to his father? Why didn't he tell his father about meeting the woman?"

"I don't know," said his mother. "He was scared." She looked at Jesse, and he nodded. Yes, yes, he was scared. That much was also true.

The detective squinted at his mother. "Surely his father would have noticed a car idling in the parking lot when he returned, presumably with his son sitting in it. Yes?" The detective turned to Jesse. "No?"

"I got out of the car," Jesse said, and that part was also true. "After she went after the dog. I got out of the car and I waited."

Besides, he didn't know what his father did or didn't see in the parking lot. It seemed impossible that the detective was asking him to comment on something he couldn't possibly know. "I don't know what my father saw," he said.

"Okay, so walk us through it one more time," said the policeman. "The woman called the police while you waited in her car, and then what happened?"

Was this the moment that would divide his life into two? What would happen if Jesse told the truth right now? What would happen to him and his father? He imagined his father's neck snapping as he fell from the gallows. He imagined being next in line, the noose slipping over his head, the roughness of the rope.

But it was easy enough to lie. Play pretend, his mother had said. You can do this, she had said.

This day has never happened. This day has never been.

Pretend you're in a movie, his mother said. Pretend you're in a play. It's a role, she said. It's okay to mumble. It's okay to act scared. It's okay to correct yourself, to have to start again. Don't worry, she said, they will believe you. It's all going to be okay.

And so Jesse spoke in a low voice, slowly, as his mother had told him to do. The detective and the policeman leaned in when he started to speak, even though he had told them these things already. He wondered how many times he would have to repeat himself. "She called the police and I got scared and opened the door, and her dog jumped out of the car," he said.

"What were you scared of?" asked the policeman.

"I was scared," said Jesse, "I was scared of my father." Also true. Always had been true. Still, why was it hard to say? Why were his eyes filling with tears?

"And you didn't see the woman after that?"

"No. She ran after her dog." He hung his head and watched his tears land on his pant legs. "After a while my father came back. I got in his car and we drove back to my mother's house."

"Your father," said the policeman, "why didn't he go after her?"

"No," Jesse said again, though at this point the lies were burning through him like battery acid. He reached for his mother's hand under the table and it was right there, waiting for him. "He didn't see her. She was gone by the time he came back." He squeezed his mother's hand.

"It has been such a long day," his mother said, "and we are so very tired."

CHAPTER FIFTEEN

Leo

That night, Leo did not join Holly at her studio, and he did not call her. He sensed that it was better if they spent some time apart. He pressed his face into the cold fabric of his pillow, and it smelled like peppermint—like Holly's hair. He looked around the room, grateful that he was not in jail. He opened a can of tomato soup, not because he was hungry, but because he could.

Evelina knocked on his door at one in the morning, in her winter coat. She kicked off her boots and said the boys were sleeping, would never know that she was gone. She scanned the wall for a place to hang her coat, then dropped it on the floor. She looked as if she were about to take a dance class. A *leotard*, that's what it was called. And jogging pants. He'd almost forgotten how muscular her arms were, and he fought the urge to squeeze her biceps, which looked like they were made of steel. She looked strong and she looked furious, but she also looked tired. There was something funny she was doing with her mouth. She took off her hat and shook out her hair, which was shorter now, dyed and cut to her collarbone. He preferred it long.

"Is Holly here?"

"No," he said. He moved toward her. He watched her take in the single, airless room: its barren white walls, his foam mattress and navy-blue sleeping bag, the kitchenette. The bathroom, which had only a toilet. A single bulb hanging from the ceiling. The one window barred, impossible to open. Nowhere to sit down, which hadn't bothered him until this very moment when it seemed like the only thing to do was say, Will you sit down?

She stood in front of him and folded her arms across her chest. He watched her skin prickle in the cold. "Jesse told me what happened," she said. She stepped toward him, so close that he could smell the toothpaste on her breath.

"Everything?" he asked.

"Everything," she said.

He thought of his blue paper boat sitting in the middle of the frozen lake. He thought of the letter—his resolution, his wish—that he had written on New Year's Eve, Holly by his side. It could have been discovered by the search and rescue team as they looked for the woman. It could have fallen through the ice. Picked up by a curious bird. Shredded and stuffed into a nest by a squirrel.

"What did you tell the police?" she asked. It was horrible to be this close to her and to see the hatred she had for him in her eyes.

"Nothing," he said, shaking his head. "Nothing, Evelina. What did you tell them?"

"That Jesse met the woman after you left him alone—"

"Jesus Christ—"

"But that her dog jumped out of the car and she went after him. And Jesse never saw her again. And you didn't see her either."

"Okay." He put his hands on his knees. He had to catch his breath. He could live with that story, with that version of things. "Okay," he said again. "Look, I didn't know Jesse had been in the woman's car."

"You couldn't have known that," she said, her voice rising. "You left our son alone out there—"

"And I am sorry for that, Evelina."

"I think, Leo," she said, "I might kill you. I might kill you right here in this grubby apartment."

She leaned into him, her fists raised, and he felt a familiar flicker in his chest, a small pilot light of anger.

"Look, Evelina," he started. He took her fists in his hands. "I'm not all bad."

He looked down the length of Evelina's body and let go of her hands. She could hit him right now, and he would deserve it. He would let it happen. He would let her hit him, if that's what she needed to do. He waited for the blows.

But instead she looked around, as if the room might be bugged, and he saw the seriousness in her expression—that she was, in fact, worried someone might be listening. "The important thing is that you say nothing further," she said. "To anyone."

She pressed herself even closer to him, until they were almost embracing.

"I will keep your secret," she whispered.

"Why?"

"Because I think it's the right thing to do."

He could feel Evelina's heart. He could feel the space above her breast quiver, the rhythm of it. He wanted to touch her but instead he took a step back, turned away.

"Is Dmitri okay?" he asked. He wanted to know, for instance, whether she knew that he had hit Dmitri, or if Jesse was sticking to *their* plan—*their* story—about Dmitri falling on the ice. How much did Evelina really know? "I mean, his face."

"It's okay," she said. "It's healing."

He turned back to her and looked in her eyes, but there was no way of knowing what she knew. He fumbled in his back pocket for a cigarette but there was only a pack of matches.

"What about Jesse?" he said. He looked at his feet.

"I don't know, Leo," she said. "I don't know if he's okay."

He moved toward Evelina again until he was inches from her face.

The question, of course, was whether the two of them had a right to be happy. Given what had happened. But there didn't seem to be any way to ask that question.

Her skin looked as soft as velvet. He thought about what it would be like to kiss her. "If I do one thing right in my life," he said, "I want it to be this thing."

But she moved away from him and started rummaging through the sad offerings in his little kitchen. He watched her open and shut his cupboards, and he wondered why she didn't tell him what she was looking for—or why he didn't ask. It seemed to both thrill and annoy her, to rifle through his kitchen. She picked through his meagre cutlery until she found a teaspoon, then began inspecting his mugs. Eventually she settled on his favourite mug, and he wondered if she did this to be irritating. His tomato soup sat on the counter, cold now and untouched. Beside it, five empty cans of beer. She filled a little pot with water and set it on the stove.

"Jesus, Leo," she said. "If I wasn't so angry right now, I'd feel sorry for you."

He was surprised she had found a teabag somewhere. Maybe she had brought her own. He wanted her to leave, but he knew he still had to talk to her about Holly. The wedding. And how he wanted the boys to be there. It was the right thing to do. The boys should see the Swami and be blessed. Have their pain washed away by the Swami's words. How could he get remarried without his boys?

"This may not be the right time," he started. "But there's something I wanted to say."

"Then say it," she said.

The headlights of a passing car appeared on the ceiling, and he watched the light with her as it crossed the room. Sounds from above, despite the hour: the clicking of high heels across a hardwood floor, water moving through pipes, the muted mumble of someone watching the news.

"Holly and I are," he said, "making arrangements." It seemed to take him a long time to get the word *arrangements* out, but finally he said it, and he waited for her response. The water bubbled in the pot and she took it to the sink and sloshed it into the mug.

"We're not even divorced," she said and turned to him. She held the mug of tea in both hands.

"That's a paperwork thing," he said. "That can be done."

"Then do it," she said.

"The boys," he said, "should be present for the wedding."

"No," she said. "I don't think so. Not given what happened."

"In April," he said. "During spring break. I'll drive them down, drive them back up."

"No," she said.

"I'm not asking," he said. He felt the pilot light of rage flicker in him again. "I'm not asking for your permission."

She set down the tea and stumbled into her boots and coat. Her mouth was tight.

"They're my sons too, Evelina," he said.

"And if I say no?"

He shrugged. "Think about it." He supposed the trip would be easier without the boys. Him and Holly. He supposed he could live with any decision she made.

"You're marrying her," she said. "Holly."

"I am."

She shook her head. "Well, we'll see how long that lasts."

He waited until he heard the sound of her car starting. He felt something building in him, like electricity. He took her mug of tea and whipped it against the wall as hard as he could.

There was no sound in his neighbourhood now. No clank of dishes being washed in another apartment, no squeal of tires as someone sped down the road, no jangle of a dog's collar, no birds. He waited to hear the familiar sound of the foghorn but it, too, was silent. The world seemed to have emptied out. He was thirty-eight years old.

He gathered the little shards in his hand and laid them softly in the trash can. He filled a bowl with soapy water, and slowly cleaned the floor. He took a piece of the white mug out of the trash and considered it one last time, then dropped it back in with the other pieces, gathered the trash bag in his hands, and walked it out to the dumpster. He had bought the mug years ago as a souvenir on a trip to Scotland's Isle of Skye. That and a white sweater, knitted locally. Would he ever go back there? It was almost at the top of the world. Now here he was, at the bottom of it.

He let himself back into his apartment, then lay on his mattress and stared at the ceiling. He felt he owed something to the woman. At the very least, he owed her an apology.

"I'm sorry," he whispered.

In the dead silence of his apartment, he told Vera Gusev that he was sorry, over and over. The ceiling fell away until there was only sky above him, the wind passing in waves over his body. High above the clouds, he imagined Vera, her hand outstretched, the light reflecting off the gemstones on her fingers, blinding him.

VERA

Overhead, the clouds were as thick and white as lambswool. She took in a deep inhalation of cold water that spread to her lungs, and then another, and this one found its way into her stomach. She sank twenty or thirty feet, past the phytoplankton and zooplankton, her body moving more and more slowly, at times moving sideways rather than downward.

She met a school of rainbow trout suspended in the water, and she moved through their bodies as though parting them with her hands. The fish regarded her with no interest, and rejoined one another as soon as she had passed. Invigorated by the movement, a few rose to the surface where there was more oxygen, and lingered there, their bodies vertical, mouths open, gasping.

The snow had dulled the colours of the landscape, and Scout was camouflaged by birch trees and low-lying shrubs. He was without his leash. He was a good dog. He was waiting. He barked at the lake. He barked again. If no one returned for him, Vera supposed he could live off rabbits and waterfowl, chickens from people's backyards. He could wander into town at night and forage in garbage cans like a raccoon, then run back into the woods when gangs of children chased him with sticks.

A sound in the distance. A whistle. Someone calling. Her dog ran through the forest, breathlessly, desperately, toward the sound, away from her, his paws kicking up snow.

A search party appeared some time later, beams criss-crossing the snow-covered forest floor. It seemed to Vera that they didn't spend enough time looking for her, were hasty, hungry, bored, cold, eager to get home. Things she thought were obvious—the thinness of the ice above her, where she had fallen through—these things were invisible to the searchers. At dawn, the search party returned and still they did not find her. The park reopened after a few days, but still some people wandered off the trail in search of her. The sound of her name in a stranger's mouth. The sound of her name in no one's mouth.

On their hands and knees, a party of six men combed through the snow, painstakingly, as though they had no other place to be in the world. She watched them for hours. Their faces reddened, their hands shook with cold. To pass the time, they told jokes. They discussed the plots of movies from their youth. And then one of the men was shouting, saying come quick, come quick, and holding something covered in snow. He shook it in the air like a revolutionary. He was an older man—in his sixties maybe—and he was triumphant. "I have found something!" he shouted. "I have found a gun!"

A week. And another.

The last thing she could remember was the boy and his father holding hands above her, the trees behind them and the bright sky overhead, before the small hole above her iced over and was covered by falling snow.

She tried to hang on to the image, but time had unfurled and lay stretched in front of her, a ribbon cut too short, too soon, and she was overwhelmed by what she could see. She watched herself be born into this world, and she saw how frightened she was, only six pounds. No one understood that she was scared. It didn't occur to anyone, not even her own mother. Whisked under hot lamps, scrubbed clean by male hands, weighed on a cold scale, the soles of her feet soaked in ink and pressed to paper. A nurse wrapped her tightly in a small blanket and pulled a cap over her head. She was not cold anymore but she was so frightened that she lay still and quiet, and soon she fell asleep. When she woke, her mother touched her nose.

More days. Another week. Still, no one found her.

A scraggly beard spread over her husband's face. Bits of skin under her nails floated upward and were eaten by the school of fish. Late at night, her husband ate with his hands by the light of the refrigerator.

She watched him struggle with the investigators. He didn't know her shoe size. He punched the bathroom wall. He held their dog. They slept together in the bed, the sheets muddy. Her husband used the toilet in the middle of the night, his urine steaming into the air, then stumbled back into the unheated bedroom and curled himself against their dog. Dead leaves collected on the bedroom floor.

In front of her house, news teams caravanned, satellite dishes on top of their vans. Coffee cups in the gutter. The smoke from a cigarette butt. Her dog's face in the picture window, tongue hanging from his mouth.

Alone, in the dark, her husband made lists of the places she might be. The policeman sat up with him late at night, drinking. Christ, Denny. Did he not realize every conversation was an interrogation in disguise? This small, unsophisticated town. Everyone thought her husband had killed her, especially her parents. It was, after all, the likeliest story. She watched the hate mail collect on the floor of her living room. Her parents stayed a week in a motel, her mother slowly pulling strands of her hair from her temple. Finally, her parents drove home without speaking.

Her body would disintegrate—all the flesh on earth, given enough time, would disappear—but her rings would remain. The metal. She thought of the rotted mummies of ancient Egypt, gnarled fingers adorned in gold. Maybe she would be found a hundred years from now, a dehydrated husk of herself, mouth twisted and torn, the alexandrite ring on her finger catching the last light of the sun.

Where were her rings? Had she lost them in the snow? In the water?

She thought of how Denny would stumble out of his studio, believing only an hour had passed, when in fact it had been five or more. No one made rings like he did; no one listened to a client with as much empathy and intensity as he did. Time slipped away from him when he was working, like it was slipping away from her now.

Her rings. They were so unusual that people stopped her on the street, in the supermarket, when they saw her hands. The rose-gold alexandrite ring was so ornate that it seemed different every time she looked at it. And indeed the gemstone did change colour—from teal green to a deep blood red, depending on the light. They had bought new cars with the inheritance from Denny's parents, but Denny had also spent ten thousand dollars on the alexandrite gemstone. He never told her, but she'd found the receipt tucked away behind his metal bench. Ten thousand dollars, Denny! What were you thinking? Did you really love me that much?

The other two rings she wore stacked on her index finger. One was traditional—an eighteen-karat yellow-gold band with three baguette diamonds. Something traditional, Denny said, to call attention to the other two.

Though the alexandrite was her favourite, the third ring was perhaps the most spectacular. The most artful. Her thirtieth-birthday present. It was made of hundreds of little criss-crossing gold wires, a moonstone hidden inside, meant to look, Denny said, like the world's most beautiful bird's nest. But to Vera it looked like a swirling galaxy—the moonstone, a tiny glowing sun.

When had Denny lost his passion for it? When had he started sleeping all day, roaming the house in sweatpants torn at the knee, complaining about his hands? Lazy depressive slob. Denny, I miss you and I am sorry. I am sorry I didn't love you as much as I should have. I'm sorry I didn't commit to you fully. Maybe that is why you were depressed. Maybe if I had given myself over to you, we could have had a better life together. But instead I drowned, my mouth full of water. The slow descent to the bottom of the lake. I am sorry, Denny. You will be okay without me. You will find someone who will love you. You will find someone who loves you exactly as you are. That was the problem, Denny. I wanted you to be more like me.

More like her: driven to the point of ruthlessness. The sign taped up in her university office—WORK HARDER THAN EVERYONE ELSE, BUT NEVER FEEL LIKE YOU'RE WORKING. The workaholic's motto. She should have told Denny that she wasn't taking the Clomid because she wanted to quit teaching and start making films again. She didn't think there was room for a child in a life like that.

Her film *Mirror* had screened at Cannes when she was twenty-eight, right after she'd met Denny. It was a remake of Andrei Tarkovsky's *The Mirror*. Told in three parts, it consisted of her childhood, adolescent, and adult memories, thoughts, and emotions, in colour, black and white, and sepia, like Tarkovsky's film. The goal was to make the viewer feel lost in terms of space and time. Where and when are we? Is the character dreaming? The film was plotless, non-chronological, and contained everything she had learned as a human being on this earth, every truth she had absorbed, everything she knew that needed to be passed along. How did she know so much at such a young age? She often wondered that herself. After it premiered at Cannes, it was sometimes shown on television.

It was airing again, now that people were searching for her body. Most people turned it off after ten minutes. That was okay. She was not offended.

What would she make a film of, if she could make one now?

How would she cut and reassemble her life, now that she was on the other side? What would be the opening shot?

Would she open it with her birth, now that she understood how terrified we are to enter this world? That we are more afraid to enter the world than we are to leave it?

Would she open it with the day she met Denny? They were the only two people in a movie theatre on a Tuesday afternoon. A lousy turnout for a foreign film playing as part of the city's annual film festival. When the movie ended, she turned to him as the lights came up, and saw that he had already been watching her.

"Well," he said and stood, a long cashmere coat folded over his forearm. "Not exactly a triumph." He was a tall man who looked to be in his early forties, his hair and skin as colourless as wild grass in winter. He had a pleasant face with blue-grey eyes and a pointed nose, a flesh-coloured mole in its centre. Not traditionally handsome, per se, and a touch overweight. But distinguished.

Within five minutes they were shoulder to shoulder, walking to an old diner, where she took out a cigarette and blew smoke rings into the air while Denny told her that he made jewellery. He produced a little gemstone from his pocket and held it up to the light while he talked. He was the son of old-fashioned Russian Orthodox parents, his father also a jeweller. He looked intensely at the gemstone when he talked of his parents; they had died only months before. He had some guilt about not having visited them more often. They had died in Manhattan, all the way across the continent, where he had been born and raised. But years ago he had traded the clusters of yellow cabs for cresting killer whales.

"I think," she said, "you're the most interesting person I've ever met."

Halfway through their meal, she discovered she could make him laugh until he cried. He was older than she was by at least a decade but she knew by the end of their meal that she was a little smarter—a little quicker. She felt like a man. She leaned across the table and asked him to go to bed with her. The most spectacular year, that year she had met him and gone to Cannes. How could so much change between two people in the two short years that had followed? The most interesting person she'd ever met in her life had become, some-how, the most predictable. The most dull. She wanted so badly to be in love again she could hardly stand it.

Something was happening above her head. A shift, a crack. A sudden rush of water. She was dislodged from her place under the ice, and the sun began to warm her body. She was moving.

Another week. Another. A month. And another.

Halley's comet entered the inner solar system and passed by the sun. The rain began. The snow melted and was gone.

The spring thaw carried her body all the way to the reservoir, where it was found by a group of children having a picnic in the April sun. The frozen water had preserved her body, though the journey downstream had shredded her clothing. The children gathered around her. They thought she was a dog or an otter caught in the tangle of bushes and twigs at the water's edge. They saw that she was face down, slick with black and gold mud, and they pulled her naked body from the water like a seal.

APRIL 1986

CHAPTER SIXTEEN

Denny

April took everyone by surprise. And now that the ceaseless win-ter was over, Lewis sat across from Denny, in Denny's living room. The hot, dry air hung between the two men.

"She drowned," Lewis said. "There's no evidence of foul play."

All this time, Denny had concocted a reality in which Vera had run off—to Berlin, maybe, or to Rome. He could imagine it: her being so angry after New Year's Eve that she had fled. Leaving him—he could fathom it, although it would have taken a heart full of hate for her to leave her dog behind. Maybe a heart full of hate was what she had for him. Even that was a better reality than the reality that she had drowned and died. Better to imagine that Vera was making films in Berlin. One day, maybe they would reconcile. He would write her a long, beautiful letter. He would get on a plane. He would roam the streets. *Haben Sie diese Frau gesehen?* Have you seen this woman? Have you seen this woman who used to be my wife?

The only secret he had kept from Vera was the ugly truth that he had loved one of his ex-girlfriends with a fiery, more intense passion. It didn't matter—the relationship had flopped and he never yearned to be back within its confines—but it was a small, polished stone of betrayal that he carried in his heart. Had Vera known? Had she known in the way that someone you don't like always knows you don't like them?

He watched a news van parking across the street. He nodded toward the stack of newspapers and hate mail he was keeping in the corner in case Vera returned. He wanted to show it to her—he wanted to show her how wrong people could be. Every time the paper ran a story about Vera's disappearance, they reprinted the same picture of him—hunched over, getting into a police car with Lewis and one of the detectives. He knew that for some people, he would forever be guilty, no matter what had happened or why.

"What do I do now?" said Denny.

"You don't have to do anything," said Lewis. "Not right now."

Denny looked at Lewis, this man who had become his caretaker. For the past four months, Lewis had come over every day to walk Scout. He called it "community policing." He said it was as much a part of his job as writing traffic tickets. At the end of January, a bottle of bourbon between them, they'd watched the *Challenger* explode.

"May I see her?" Denny asked.

Lewis hesitated. "There is very little to see," he said.

He imagined Vera in the palm of his hand, the size of a worry doll. "I'm sorry," he said to Lewis. "I'd like to be alone."

He hadn't cried yet—that would come later—but already he could feel a hollowness opening up inside of him. People would tell him he could start again. People would suggest he start dating. Though it felt impossible to him at this very moment, he had loved women before Vera, so surely it was possible to love again.

He flipped through the phone book until he came to Evelina

Lucchi's name. He had stared at it many nights, fingers poised to dial the phone. He rehearsed what he would say. Are you sure? Are you sure you didn't know my Vera? Evelina's ex-husband, Leo Lucchi, was unlisted. He imagined somehow calling him anyway. Are you sure you didn't drown my wife?

What was he supposed to do right now, standing here in his living room? How was he supposed to get through the next hour? And the next?

He wanted to gather all of Vera's things in the middle of the living room and lie down on top of them. He wanted to gather as much of her as he could in one small space, and then surround himself, as though he were building a nest. He would build a nest of her in the middle of the room and sleep in its centre until he was ready to let her go.

He walked into the kitchen and looked at the mess he had created in the months Vera had been gone. At first he'd tried to keep it clean, thinking she'd turn up at any minute. But his old habits had come back hard, and there were two weeks' worth of dishes on the countertops; the dishtowels hadn't been washed for weeks; and, he noticed, the fridge door was ajar. Vera had been on his case about that. *You have to shut it hard, Denny. Don't let it close on its own. We'll get a new one soon. Until then, please.* Standing in front of him with her arms crossed, her eyes shifting around the room to find some other transgression: a ring left on the coffee table by his icy glass of bourbon; a sock that had missed the hamper and ended up on the floor.

He should have gone with her. He poked his stomach. If he'd gone on the walk around the lake with Vera, he might still have her; he might not have this gut. The mail landed with a thud on his living room floor.

He supposed he would sell her car. Was it wrong to think of that so soon? Did it mean he didn't miss her enough? Did it mean he wasn't grieving the way a person was supposed to?

She had a life insurance policy through the university worth fifty thousand dollars—the detectives had told him this; he hadn't known. He would make a call, get the money. Donate it. Start a scholarship fund in her name. For women. For women filmmakers. Or use it to pay funeral expenses. A funeral! Who wanted to do that? Not him.

He found her address book and stared at the phone numbers. Her parents. Her colleagues at the university. Her friends from childhood, from high school, from college. The neighbours. He would have to call them all.

Would her parents want a funeral? Probably. He didn't want to have any part of it. Now that Vera was dead, he never wanted to see her parents again. They'd come to Whale Bay right after she disappeared, had spent a week in a motel glaring at him, suspecting, before the police told them to go home and try to get back to their lives.

"Okay," Denny said. He gathered her clothes in his arms and set them in a pile in the living room. It took five trips back and forth from the dresser and closet, her socks rolled into balls, the one lace thong she never wore, her bras, a few pairs of stockings, her leather jacket, so many blazers—navy-blue and black blazers—expertly tailored white button-down blouses, black pants, black patent loafers, her "power suits," as she called them, the long grey lab coat she wore when she developed film, still wrapped in its dry cleaner's plastic, ready for the new semester. Her old pairs of glasses. He put them on, looked at the living room with blurry eyes. He wished he could find something of hers that was unwashed. But the laundry basket was full of only his clothes. It was one of her habits: to do a load of laundry every day. She said she couldn't stand the smell of cigarette smoke, was ashamed of it. He searched for a sock fallen behind the dresser, a once-worn blouse put back in the closet. There was nothing but the scent of detergent. He had used her towel from *that* morning, before he'd realized it was all he would have left of her. It stank now of mould.

"Okay," he said again. He didn't feel anything until he pulled a bathing suit from the back of her dresser drawer and held it up—it was red, with a built-in bra and full skirt, the tag still on. It had cost eighty dollars. She had never worn it. There was a paper liner in the crotch. The bathing suit seemed embarrassingly feminine to him. Vera didn't even own a pair of heels. When had she bought it? They never went swimming. It seemed purchased for a special occasion—a vacation, something someone would wear on a cruise ship. It was old-fashioned—sort of sexy, he supposed, except for the full skirt. He tried to picture her in it.

What was hers and what was his? Should he gather the expensive Le Creuset cookware and set that in the living room, too? Defeated, he walked into their shared office and brought her files into the living room, her medical records, her high-school poetry, her photographs. Her cameras. All the lenses. The little brushes to clean them. The stink of the developing solution. Endless black canisters of undeveloped film. Reels and reels of experimental films she'd made on Super 8 as a college student. Then, of course, *Mirror*—the biggest moment of her career—and the fan mail she had collected in an accordion file. She had peaked. That was what she told him late at night when she couldn't sleep. It'll be downhill from here, she said, an unlit cigarette in her hand.

"Okay, okay, okay."

He slept with the red bathing suit. Slept with it wrapped around his arms, woke in the night and threaded his hands through the leg holes, then up through the straps, until his arms were bound. He twisted his limbs out of it and pressed the cool fabric against his face. In a fever dream, he walked to the bathroom, shut the door, stood naked in front of the full-length mirror, and stepped into the suit. He got it up to his thighs before the fabric wouldn't give anymore. His body was pale, slack, his penis a snail.

He found one of her hairs, snakelike, hidden in the bathtub grout, and ran it across his mouth. He wondered if she would find his actions absurd. What she would make of him in their dark bathroom, a woman's bathing suit around his thighs, threading her hair through his teeth like dental floss.

He found another strand in the drain of the bathtub. He laid the strands out, side by side. One was seventeen inches long. He wrapped them around his finger, thought he'd make a ring out of it.

Where did you want to go, Vera? Were you going with me, or were you going alone?

"Taking Scout to Squire, be back in a bit," she'd said, or maybe she hadn't—or she had and he'd slept through it. He could hear the words in his mind. She never thought twice about walking in the woods. She bristled whenever Denny showed any kind of concern. She didn't even like it when he held open a door. *For god's sake*, she would say.

I had things I wanted to talk to you about, Vera. There were things I didn't know about you. Little things. Little mysteries I wanted to clear up. I wanted to ask you but—you can never be that direct with people, you know? You can't ask people the questions you truly want to ask. Vera? Who did you wish I was? Who did you wish *you* were? What are the ways in which I disappointed you? What were the ways in which you disappointed yourself? Why did you look at me the way you did, eyes not exactly full of love?

Until this moment he had not questioned what happened after death. He had never thought about it before, not even when his parents had died.

Naked once more, the bathing suit slung over his shoulder, he lay on the pile of clothing and emptied her cosmetic bag onto the floor, pushed the circular containers of eye shadow around the carpet with his finger as though they were toy cars. Scout watched him from the doorway of the bedroom, his tail twitching like a rattlesnake.

It was three in the morning. He flipped through their record collection and pulled her favourite records from their sleeves, put them on the turntable. David Bowie, Laurie Anderson, Peter Gabriel.

He closed his eyes and remembered her dancing to Culture Club the year she'd gone as Boy George for Halloween. She was so reserved with everyone except him.

He tried to find a place inside of him where he didn't miss her. He held his hands to his chest, willing the pain in his knuckles to subside. Could he find a place within himself where he was, in fact, a tiny bit relieved that she was gone? Relieved that the fighting was over with, the guilt that the marriage was failing. Relieved that he could be himself, without judgment. He shook his head, disgusted.

Why was it so hard to cry? All he felt was hollowed out, emptied, cold. He crawled into bed, patted the space beside him until Scout curled into it, and he held his dog.

CHAPTER SEVENTEEN

Dmitri

He was not to eat inside his father's car. He was not to touch anything with his sticky hands. He was not to talk too much or too loudly. These had been the rules in Whale Bay, and these were the rules now, in San Garcia.

Holly was a wild driver. Her knuckles were white. She kept putting on the blinker, trying to change lanes, then chickening out, Leo swearing. She seemed to be terrible at shifting gears.

Dmitri pressed his back against the seat and breathed in. His father looked thin. He hadn't shaved and his face was bruised on one side. He wore light blue slacks and a short-sleeved button-down shirt with a bolo tie, his hair slicked back with gel. Black loafers that to Dmitri looked like slippers, big sunglasses like the ones policemen wore on television. The streets were lined with palm trees. Dmitri had never seen them before, except in cartoons. A whole week in San Garcia! Dmitri wanted to shout it to the world.

Holly, too, was skinnier. He could see the veins underneath the skin of her forearms, thick as earthworms. Little strands of hair poked out from her armpits like spider legs. She wore a long, pale blue dress with a thin red belt. Dmitri thought she would have worn a big white wedding dress, his father a tuxedo. His mother had packed Dmitri nothing fancy, and Leo had exploded when he searched the suitcase, finding only shorts, a pair of swim trunks, and a T-shirt with a bear on it. *He's six*, his mother had said. *I'm not buying him a suit.*

That was yesterday morning, the morning they'd left for San Garcia. His mother and father stood in front of the white beach house, arguing, his father's car idling. His mother told his father that Jesse wouldn't be coming along. Dmitri and Holly were already in the car. Dmitri could see Jesse watching it all from inside the house. *He's not going with you.*

Was it because his father hated Jesse now? Was it because his father loved only *him*?

Fine. His father had stormed away from his mother, punched the air, and then they'd driven away.

Dmitri wondered what Jesse was doing now, whether he was upset that he was at home with their mother, or whether that was the better place to be. He couldn't deny it, though: he felt better, safer, without Jesse around. If Jesse were in the back seat with him, he might reach over, quick, before anyone could see, and pinch his arm. He did things like that. A little shove, a little push, when no one was looking: the only evidence, the invisible heat of pain.

"Just trying to toughen you up," he'd say, laughing, then grip Dmitri's forearm in both his hands and twist the skin in opposite directions.

But what was worse? The burn itself or the horror of having his father rush in, after hearing Dmitri yelp. Having to watch it. Sometimes his father stuck his tongue out while it was happening, like a person concentrating hard.

Jesse never cried afterwards. He would walk stiffly back into their shared bedroom and turn his back to Dmitri, and Dmitri knew to keep quiet, to not speak until Jesse was done with whatever it was he was doing, often just staring at the wall, whispering, or rocking on his heels.

It hadn't happened since his father had left. And since that day at the lake, Jesse hadn't pinched or shoved him at all. One night he'd even heard Jesse whisper *I love you* in the night. He'd reminded their mother to pack Dmitri's bear. He'd hugged Dmitri goodbye. Dmitri didn't think those things had ever happened before.

"Take this exit," his father said to Holly, and tapped the dashboard with his finger.

Both Holly and his father were sunburnt. The back of his father's neck looked as though it were covered in bubble wrap. Dmitri wanted to pick off the dead skin and flick it out the window. A wild driver, yeah, but nervous. She didn't turn her head to look at his father when he spoke. She didn't turn her head to look at him in the back seat like his mother did when she drove.

Holly missed the exit—Leo grabbed the wheel and tried to veer them onto the ramp but at the last minute let go. "For fuck sakes," he said. Dmitri's suitcase and backpack rattled around in the trunk like dice. His father had driven for twelve hours straight yesterday, then they'd all spent the night in a smelly motel with no air conditioning. At dawn, his father and Holly had dressed in their fancy clothes, and just as the sun came up, they were on the road again.

His father took off his sunglasses and rested them on his knee. He looked back at Dmitri. He had two black eyes, in addition to the bruise on his cheek.

"A misunderstanding, that's all," his father told him. "Nothing to worry about."

Dmitri's heart was beating like a wild thing and he wet himself. His father had pissed into an empty water bottle at one point this morning, but hadn't offered Dmitri a turn.

The air was hot, so hot, inside the car.

"Do you live here now?" Dmitri's voice was so high-pitched that he winced. He'd have to toughen up a little now that he was in a real city. Maybe they'd all get murdered!

"For now," said Leo. "For now."

"I'm hungry, Daddy," said Dmitri.

They drove through a fast-food joint that Dmitri had never heard of, and his father leaned over Holly and ordered in Spanish. It sounded more natural on his lips than English. His father seemed to have adopted a new personality. Even his posture was different, more relaxed, than when he was in Whale Bay. Dmitri liked this new dad, this relaxed dad. He hoped this new dad would stick around.

"This'll fill you up," the new dad said and handed Dmitri a chocolate milkshake.

Dmitri sucked on the milkshake until his hands got cold. He wondered whether it would be okay to put the cup on the floor of the car. Likely not—even this new relaxed dad had delivered a terse lecture about keeping the car clean. Dmitri held the cold milkshake between his pee-soaked thighs.

They drove for twenty minutes before Leo announced, "One last stop," and ordered Holly to park in front of a children's clothing store.

"Come on," Leo said to Dmitri. The store was dark and smelled of dogs. It was a second-hand clothing store. A woman sat behind the till, doing a crossword puzzle. She did not speak to them. Leo walked up and down the aisles, then grabbed a couple of collared shirts and a pair of tan pants. "Take off your clothes," said Leo.

"Here?" Dmitri stammered. He scanned the store for a change room but didn't see one.

"Quit farting around," his father said, and yanked Dmitri's T-shirt over his head so that it caught on his ears. Dmitri put on one of the shirts and his father nodded and then handed him the pants. Here? He was supposed to stand in his underwear here? In front of the woman? He looked toward the entrance to see if Holly was coming, but he couldn't see her, just the front of the car. He stumbled out of his pee-soaked pants and put on the ones his father was holding, though he could see that the waistband had a suspicious stain.

"There," said Leo, kicking Dmitri's old pants underneath the rack of clothing. "Now let's go."

"Oh," Holly said as they approached the car. "Look how smart."

Dmitri couldn't remember if his father had paid the woman, and wondered if his father didn't have to pay for things in San Garcia. But more than anything, he felt relieved that his father had not noticed that he'd peed.

"I'll drive," said his father, and then they were peeling out of the parking lot.

It seemed to Dmitri that they drove for a long, long time. The landscape looked like desert. The car was hot, hotter still from his father's cigarette smoke. The big white tent appeared suddenly. Dmitri watched it grow larger and larger as they drove toward it. The road was crowded with traffic.

"You know Holly's going to become my wife today, don't you, Dmitri," his father asked.

Dmitri nodded, though he wasn't sure he did know this.

"That means she's your stepmother."

Holly turned to look at him as Leo spoke.

"You'll treat her with respect."

"I will, Daddy."

"That's my boy."

Holly continued to look at him. He was frightened of her, though he could not say for certain why.

What was it that stopped him from being able to ask why they were in a rush or where they were going? It seemed other children didn't have trouble asking their parents questions. It seemed other children didn't have the sorts of problems he had. Something had happened to his family. Too much silence in the house. He sensed he shouldn't talk to his mother or Jesse very much. He sensed he shouldn't talk much at all. He didn't like living so close to the ocean. It was too windy, inside and out.

Something bad had happened, that was all he knew. Something bad had happened between his father and Jesse. It was because of that game Jesse had played at the lake. He wondered when his father would forgive Jesse. It was a mean game, yes, but his father couldn't stay mad forever.

Dmitri looked at his father's hands tensing on the steering wheel. There was traffic. His father hated traffic.

His father took a deep breath and patted Holly's thigh. "It's all right. We knew there'd be traffic. We knew it."

"We did."

"I said there would be traffic, right?"

"You did."

"And here it is. Okay back there?" His father threw a glance at Dmitri.

"Yeah."

"You don't got anything to say?"

"Leo." Holly put her hand on the back of his father's seat. It was his old father—the old version. He was back.

"I am losing my fucking mind," his father said, throwing punches at the steering wheel in order to honk the horn. "Get the fuck out of my way, you fucks."

The white tent rose up before them. His father parked the car and then they were all standing in front of the tent, waiting in a long line, his father pacing nervously, slapping his wallet against his thigh.

"One family," said his father, and handed over a stack of limp bills to a man at the tent's entrance. Dmitri strained to see inside but he was eye level with a man's butt. There seemed to be no way of seeing around the thing. He followed the giant butt inside. Holly took his hand and he clenched it, afraid that the inside of the tent would be hotter than the car, and smokier, and more terrifying.

They were seated in flimsy blue plastic chairs arranged around a ring. The lights went down and Dmitri closed his eyes and listened to his breath, to his heart. He heard the sound of people shifting in their seats, people coughing, and then the bright click as a spotlight shone down in the middle of the ring, revealing the skinniest man Dmitri had ever seen. The man was naked except for some ratty-looking underpants. A faint drumbeat began, and the skinny man bent over and placed his hands on the floor. He raised himself into a handstand, and the audience applauded. Dmitri looked up at his father and Holly. They were holding hands, Holly's head on his father's shoulder. A circus! His father had brought him to the circus! Would they get married on top of elephants? Would they swing from a trapeze?

The man sat cross-legged in a circle of light.

"Watch," whispered Leo into Dmitri's ear, and the man began to chant.

There was an awful lot of chanting, and the man was doing nothing but sitting there.

"This is just the beginning," his father said. "Keep focused."

Two men came onstage, holding poles. They fastened the poles to the floor around the chanting man, then walked behind him and lifted him into the air. And then they let go. They left the stage. The chanting man was flying! He was flying in the air! Dmitri closed his eyes, thinking he was dreaming, but when he opened them he was still in the tent, and the man was still hovering in the air.

"Ah," said his father. "Ah."

But Dmitri wanted to scream. He wanted to stand up and shout. "He is flying! He is flying, Daddy!" he said, but his father clamped his hand over his mouth.

"Hush," his father said. "Watch."

"But how is he flying, Daddy?"

"Stop talking. Just watch."

"But—"

"Around every circle, draw a bigger circle," his father said, his voice calmer. "Around every question, there is a bigger question."

At this, a woman in front of them turned around and nodded at him. "I think it's wonderful that your parents brought you here," she whispered. Dmitri wanted to correct her, to tell her that his mother wouldn't attend something like this. He could hear the voice of his mother in his head. *This is not real. Magic is an illusion. Look, see, the coin was always in my hand.* But he couldn't see anything behind or underneath the flying man. The man was still chanting. The crowd rose to their feet, joined hands, and Leo told Dmitri to close his eyes. Leo began chanting, and Dmitri looked up at him, scared of being caught with his eyes open. The chanting sounded like *eee-ya-ya*, so Dmitri joined in, saying *eee-ya-ya* with the crowd. He felt a buzzing throughout his body, a ticklish feeling, a fullness in his heart. He was surprised when he felt tears on his face. What was happening? What kind of circus was this? Could he be a flying man one day?

His father was breathing deeply beside him, taking long embarrassing breaths, then chanting, it seemed to Dmitri, louder than anyone else around them. He wished his father would chant normally. *Eee-ya-ya.* The lights went off and somehow everyone knew to stop chanting. They stood in darkness and silence, in the heat under the big tent. At once the lights came on again. The flying man had disappeared, and a man in a robe and long white beard stood in front of a microphone. The crowd erupted with feverish applause, so much so that Dmitri felt tears again on his cheeks. It was terrifying to watch people get so worked up. He feared they would start killing one another. He hated the feeling that was welling within him, so powerful, as if at any minute he might break apart. He knew his father couldn't hear him—the chanting had started up again, and the applause was still deafening—and so he screamed into his shirt. He screamed until he had nothing left inside of him, then he wiped his face with his hands.

The man with the long beard asked them all to be seated. His voice was soft, and high, almost nasal, as though he were a cartoon character. He was a short man. Dmitri felt his father's body stiffen beside him. His father was nervous. Why?

"We have over thirty couples in the audience today," said the man with the long beard, "waiting to be blessed."

At this the crowd began to chant again, and his father looked at Holly and said, "Now, now, this is it," and took her by the hand. He grabbed Dmitri's hand as well and they sidestepped out of the aisle and walked toward the stage, where other couples were gathering around the man with the long beard. The chanting was growing unbearably loud and Dmitri felt his heart pounding. The stage was brightly lit and the audience had disappeared into blackness. The man with the beard asked the couples to bow their heads but lift their hearts. Dmitri hoped the people in the audience weren't looking at his father's bruised face and black eyes.

The man with the long white beard had both of his hands raised. The chanting had stopped and the man was speaking something that did not sound like English, but he was speaking so quietly that Dmitri could not be sure. He was a very old man and it felt to Dmitri that he spoke for a very long time.

He must have fallen asleep during the old man's long blessing, for when he woke, he was in his father's arms, and Holly was opening the door to the motel room. His father set him on a little cot in the corner of the room, then slipped him underneath the scratchy white sheet and soft blanket.

The motel had air conditioning and cable—his father had made a big point of it earlier in the hot car. The bed had a flowery coverlet that Leo yanked off and threw on the floor. He and Holly sat on the bed and Leo flipped through the channels. The little cot had the softest blanket Dmitri had ever felt. It was a pale yellow colour, thin, and soft as velvet. He wanted to wrap himself in it and stay there forever. He thought of his bear in his suitcase, waiting for him.

His father came over to him, sat on the edge of his cot.

"Today," his father said, "Holly and I were blessed by a very important man."

Dmitri closed his eyes, wanting his father to think he was asleep. He didn't want to listen to his father talk about the marriage. He didn't like the idea of it, though he couldn't say why. He wanted his bear.

He made his body very still so that his father would stop talking. His father wasn't talking about the marriage, though, he was talking about reincarnation. He told Dmitri that because he had done wrong in a previous life, he had been wronged in this life. But starting tomorrow he would do only good, even if it took him millions of lives to even out the score. Only then would he be free. Only then would he be off the wheel of reincarnation. "I'm going to sell my car," said his father. "Give the money to the Swami."

Dmitri could hear Holly calling out to his father from the bed, wanting him to be with her, but his father continued to talk. "Tomorrow, I am going to start over," his father said. "I am going to do everything right from now on, Dmitri. You'll see."

Dmitri clenched the soft blanket in his fists and looked up at his father.

"What I need now," said his father, "is a blameless life."

The motel room phone rang and it was his mother. Holly clicked off the television and sat on the bed in her pale blue dress, frowning. Dmitri watched his father watch himself in the mirror, the phone pressed to his ear. He could hear the voice of his mother through the phone.

"They found the woman."

"Vera Gusev?" his father said.

"Yeah."

"Where?"

"At the reservoir. Yesterday. Some kids found her."

His father looked at himself in the mirror, brushed his hair back from his scalp.

"You okay?" Dmitri heard his mother say.

"I am." His father looked at Dmitri through the reflection. "Yeah, I'm okay. You?"

The next morning, the city darkened with his father's mood. His father hoisted Dmitri out of the cot and closed the bathroom door behind them. Holly was a lump in the bed.

His father washed his stubbly face with a washcloth, then his hairy underarms and groin. He told Dmitri to do the same. His father peed and Dmitri watched the thick, impressive stream, the sound echoing off the hard tiles. A paper cup of coffee sat on the edge of the sink and every once in a while his father took a loud sip.

He brought the cup into the car with them, and drove with one hand while sipping the coffee, briefly taking his hand off the wheel to shift gears. The morning air was hot already but there was a breeze. His father seemed to have no difficulty getting them onto the highway; in fact, Dmitri didn't even notice his father's lane changes. It seemed as if the car were driving itself.

They exited the highway and drove down a wide four-lane street, warehouses on either side. His father gestured to one of the warehouses. "Get here early. Avoid the traffic."

His father turned into its driveway, then drove around to the back. The parking lot was empty, except for an eighteen-wheeler parked across a bunch of stalls. On the back of the warehouse, SAN GARCIA GUN CLUB was painted in big red letters.

"Thought we'd do something special," said his father. "Just the two of us."

Dmitri felt his heart lift. He couldn't wait to brag to Jesse.

"This world," his father said, "is a dangerous world. You need to know how to do certain things."

"Okay," said Dmitri but his father's face had changed. He was squinting at something in the distance.

"Oh, god damn it," his father said. He got out of the car and hurried to the entrance, then tugged at the doors. He spun and came back toward the car, and Dmitri felt the car shake as his father kicked it, again and again. He got back into the car, opened the glove compartment, and took out a little flask.

"Cocksuckers," his father said, taking a swig and then another. "Pitiful." The gun club didn't open until ten, his father said. It wasn't even nine. "Son of a bitch," his father said.

"Yeah," said Dmitri. "Shitheads."

"Be right back." His father got out of the car, walked to the entrance, and unzipped his pants. He turned back and winked at Dmitri, then soaked the front door in piss.

This didn't seem like what his father had meant last night about doing everything right, although it was kind of exciting. And surely it wasn't that bad, in the grand scheme of things, to pee on a door. In his mind, Dmitri pictured the wheel of reincarnation as a wheel of cheese, covered in orange wax. He hadn't understood much of what his father had said to him last night, but he'd nodded along, wanting his father to think that he had understood, and that he belonged here—that he belonged in his father's new, blameless life.

CHAPTER EIGHTEEN

Denny

In the morning, a knock on the door. "Good god," Denny said. He pulled on his sweatpants and threw on his robe. Scout had peed by the back door—Denny had forgotten to let him out—and was pacing, head low and ashamed.

"Okay, boy. It's okay." He let Scout into the yard and threw one of the mouldy dishtowels down over the pee. "Ah, what the hell."

It was Lewis at his front door, in uniform.

"This was found last night," said Lewis. He held out his hand and Denny saw one of the rings he had made for his wife. "Not far from where we found Vera."

"It's hers," said Denny.

"It's yours." Lewis dropped it into Denny's hand.

The ring was the alexandrite. He tightened his fist around it until he could feel the gemstone about to break his skin.

"The other ones?" Denny said. "Did you find the other ones?"

"No."

"She wore two more. One with baguette diamonds. And another

with a moonstone. They are—" He stopped himself. "They are extremely valuable, both monetarily and to me personally."

He could feel Lewis's eyes on everything. The same eyes that had judged him—and found him to be innocent—were judging the clothes on the floor, the nest he had made.

"What if someone has tried to pawn them?" said Denny. "Could we—"

"We'll continue to check the pawnshops," said Lewis. "We have your description of the rings."

He had to keep going. He couldn't totally fall apart. There was still life left. He could hear Scout pawing at the back door, wanting to see Lewis.

"Why don't I come in for a minute," said Lewis.

Denny nodded and stepped away from the door. He let Scout in as well, and the dog bounded into the living room, leaving a trail of big wet paw prints.

He watched Lewis toss a tennis ball for Scout. The dog's nails skittered on the hardwood, Vera's clothing kicked up by his paws.

It was better to have Lewis here than to be alone with all of Vera's things. Alone with that bathing suit. Should he pack up all her stuff and send it to her parents? Who had more of a right to her things? He did. He knew Vera. He was the one who really knew her.

He felt as if he were about to break open and so he poured himself and Lewis a glass of bourbon—who cared if it was ten in the morning—and they sat together, tossing the ball for the dog. He was surprised but Lewis drank heartily, despite the time of day and the fact that he was in uniform. Maybe Lewis was falling apart, too. Okay. Okay. The alcohol was warming his system.

He put the alexandrite ring on his pinky finger and twisted it. He could make any ring, no matter how intricate, in under five hours, but not this. This was his masterpiece. It had taken him twenty hours. He had cut the alexandrite in what was called a cushion cut—a slightly rounded square—then surrounded it in a double halo of diamonds, and set it in an eighteen-karat rose-gold band. He might wear it for a while, on his pinky finger, or on a chain around his neck. He hated the idea of putting it back in its velvet box, in a drawer somewhere, where it would gather dust and be forgotten. His own wedding ring was a plain rose-gold band, meant to match the alexandrite. Should he take it off and put it in its velvet box, too? What he wanted to do, though he couldn't articulate why, was swallow them both. He wanted the rings lodged inside him somewhere, visible only via X-ray, extracted only via autopsy. He hoped someone would find the other rings. He wanted to swallow them as well. The little bird's nest ring with the hidden moonstone was his favourite. It was the first time he had not simply taken a strand of gold wire and bent it to his will—it was the first time he had asked the wire, *Where do you want to go?* And he had ended up with this sort of bird's nest, without meaning to, without intending to. He had never told anyone this, not even Vera. He told Vera that he had meant it to look that way, but in truth the ring had made itself.

He took another sip of bourbon. He cupped his hand around the alexandrite and watched the green gemstone slowly turn red, adjusting to the light. There was a place he could get to—not all the time, just sometimes, alone in his studio—where he could feel the consciousness of the metal he was working with, of the gemstones. But he hadn't felt that in so very long.

Where was the moonstone ring now? At the bottom of the lake? In the belly of some prehistoric-looking fish?

The year he'd met Vera had been the strangest year of his life until now. It had begun with his parents' death and ended with his marriage. From the heaviness of grief to the sweetness of new love. Vera's sharp observations, her perfect hands, the way she always had an unlit cigarette in her mouth when she was reading. "This is where I want to be," she'd said, the afternoon they'd driven around Whale Bay and found themselves looking at a little bungalow with a FOR SALE sign in the yard. Elevated, so that one could see the ocean but not have to bear the brunt of its merciless winds. A part of town where university professors lived, known as The Hill. An outbuilding in the back— this would be his studio. In those early days he could feel her against him, even when she was in another room. When he saw her, he'd run his hands through her long black hair until he reached her waist. The way she paced their living room, clicking her lighter, while she rehearsed her lectures.

Even their first fight—he had been short with her in the grocery store after she'd chided him for buying bottled salad dressing instead of making it himself—had ended with them doubled over in the parking lot, howling with laughter. "We'll never go back," Denny said. "We'll never go grocery shopping again."

And then, of course, the day they'd gone to the pound and returned home with Scout.

He put the alexandrite ring in his mouth and looked at Lewis, who was still throwing the ball for his dog. He tried to swallow the ring but feared it would lodge in his throat.

Lewis took the ball from Scout and told him to sit, then lie down, then roll over, before he threw it. "He's amazing," he said to Denny. "Did you train him?"

"Vera," said Denny, out the side of his mouth. He took the ring from under his tongue, stuck it in his pocket. He hoped Lewis hadn't noticed.

"What else?" asked Lewis. "What else can he do?"

"He'll play dead," said Denny, a sudden surge of alcohol like a blast through his consciousness, and he shot Scout with an imaginary gun. "Bang," he said. The dog rolled onto his back, his tail wagging. Lewis erupted in applause.

"He'll do almost anything," said Denny, and topped up his and Lewis's glasses. "Scout, walk!" And the dog went up on his haunches, crept across the living room. "Scout, under arrest!" And the dog leapt up on the wall, his paws up, as if he were about to be frisked.

"Yes," said Lewis. "Yes!"

The bourbon rushed through his veins and Denny saw it, clear in his mind—Scout leaping from Vera's car, after a squirrel perhaps, running onto the frozen lake, and Vera running after him. Their footfalls kicking up snow. The snow balling in clumps on Scout's legs. Then: skidding onto the ice, paws splayed. Looking back at Vera.

Why not call him back from the lake's edge?

Why not whistle?

He was a very good dog. Even if he were on the scent of something, Vera could have gotten him to come back to her. She wouldn't have needed to run after him. She wouldn't have needed to run out onto the lake.

"Scout," said Denny. "Come." And the dog came immediately, sat by his feet, and looked up at him.

Had Scout fallen through a patch of thin ice? Had she saved him and then fallen in herself? Maybe. But could he live with the uncertainty? No.

"Was—" he started. "Was Scout wet when you found him?"

"What's that?"

"New Year's Day. When you went out to Squire Point. When you found Scout, was his fur wet?"

Lewis looked at him, then up at the ceiling. He shook his head. "No. I mean, it was snowing but I don't think so, no."

"She wouldn't have walked onto the ice. She wasn't stupid—why would she walk out onto a frozen lake?"

"I don't know."

"She wouldn't have done that," said Denny. "And the little boy—his fingerprints were in her car. Why won't you listen to me?"

"I am listening to you."

"I don't mean you. I mean—why aren't they investigating the boy more thoroughly? Why isn't anyone doing anything?"

"We questioned him. Thoroughly."

"And it still doesn't make sense. Why did she suddenly drop the phone?"

"The boy says Scout jumped out of the car—look—listen, I do believe they did everything—"

"No," said Denny. "You don't believe that. I can tell. I want to talk to him. I want to talk to the boy."

"Denny, stop," said Lewis. "She drowned."

Did she? Is that what had happened? Denny thought of the things Lewis had told him about Leo Lucchi, the boy's father: *Such a loser, really. As far as I can tell, guy's never had a real job. Lives over by the factory—yeah, over there.* Lewis had told him how Leo had bruised up his youngest son's face. He'd even shown him an old mug shot of Leo, even though he wasn't supposed to.

"You told me you wanted to be a detective," he said to Lewis. "Well, be one."

"What do you want me to do?" Lewis looked at Denny. He lobbed the ball to Scout again and the dog went shooting after it.

"Let me talk to the boy."

"I can't do that," said Lewis. He took another sip of his bourbon. "I mean, for so many reasons I wouldn't even know where to start."

"Then let me talk to Leo. Get him in a corner."

"He left town, Denny," said Lewis. "Look, I get it, but you're drunk. You're not thinking straight."

He squinted at Lewis. "You're also drunk."

"I am," said Lewis. "I am and I shouldn't be." He looked down at his uniform. "I'll be back tomorrow to walk Scout. Get some rest."

Denny took another swig of bourbon, and another, until he felt maniacal with power and possibility. Scout was at his feet, tongue out, waiting for him to throw the ball again. Fine, he thought, his chest rising in great heaves, I will find a way to talk to the boy myself. I will find Evelina's son and I will talk to him. I will ask him what Scout was running after. I will ask why Vera didn't call his name.

CHAPTER NINETEEN

Lewis

Lewis watched Scout noodle around in the backyard, the sky a perfect blue above his head, the sun hot on his skin. He whistled, then pulled a dog biscuit from his pocket and placed it in Scout's warm mouth. He tried to stop himself from feeling slightly joyful that Denny had asked him to look after Scout for the whole day. He'd told Lewis that his arthritis was so bad that he couldn't get out of bed, but Lewis suspected he was horribly hung over from yesterday's bourbon binge. He wondered if he should do more for his friend, beyond looking after his dog. Get him in a support group of some kind. On the other hand, it wasn't as if Denny was *dying*—all he needed was better medication for his arthritis, some counselling for his grief and depression, and physical therapy. The body responded physically to emotional pain, Lewis knew that was true.

For the most part, their friendship was without tension, although yesterday Denny had started sputtering about wanting to track down Leo and his son. Lewis wanted to shake his friend. Snap out of it! Go outside! Get out of bed! Walk your dog! Let's go! Come on,

Denny! Wake up! You didn't drive your wife to suicide! And no one killed her either!

The past four months had been some of the most disappointing and frustrating in Lewis's career. They'd had Leo. They'd had him! They had the rifle. But it hadn't been fired. And there was no bullet wound in Vera's body. Her death was ruled a drowning. A tragic accident—her running onto the ice after her dog, perhaps. No connection between Leo and Vera. Bad luck: the death blamed on the harsh winter, which was over. There was no reason why Leo—or Jesse, for that matter—would want to kill the woman. There was no evidence of anything. The detectives had moved on to other cases, other crimes.

And it was likely she *had* drowned. Her body had been found, autopsied, and then buried. There were no signs of foul play. The dog could well have run onto the lake. She could have gone after him. Scout *had* wanted Lewis to go out onto the lake that day. He must have known. If Lewis had ventured out, could he have saved her? He wondered how far under the ice she'd been, as he'd stood and watched from the shore. He wondered how long it took to die.

It had been so satisfying, for a time, to have a villain, if only for Denny's sake. Lewis had spent four months hating Leo, praying for justice. Leo had become the devil in Lewis's mind, especially after Lewis had seen those little boys—the look of terror in their eyes. But now Leo was just some man, some falsely accused man, who had gotten remarried and moved away.

Now it was back to business as usual. Weeks without a single interesting call. He hadn't become a police officer to change the world—he wasn't that naive—but he did believe in his ability to change things on a small scale. For instance, what he was doing now—helping Denny look after Scout, being there for a grieving man. It counted for something.

He would apply to be a detective this year. His reports were good and thorough—he even carefully filled out reports for throwaway stuff like public urination. He was detail-oriented. He was dependable. Of course, there were other options. Canine unit. He looked down at Scout and smiled. That might be okay. Bomb squad. Or he could get into administration. Sergeant, lieutenant, captain, deputy chief. His whole life stretched out in front of him. It would be a good life.

"Okay then, boy," Lewis said to Scout. He tapped his thigh and Scout heeled beside him, pausing to sniff something and then to look up at Lewis. Lewis felt so happy walking the dog down the hill to downtown Whale Bay that he found himself skipping a bit, and Scout picked up his pace in response. They passed the movie theatre, Billy's Burgers, the grocery store, Marco Polo's Pizza, a Chinese restaurant, a corner store. The two arrived at Lewis's apartment so quickly that Lewis decided to walk all the way to the beach, to prolong the feeling. He'd forgotten how wonderful it was to have a dog. His little border terrier had died when Lewis was a teenager, and if he thought about him long enough, his eyes welled with tears.

"Look at what a great dog this is!" He couldn't help it—he said it loudly to a woman sitting on a park bench and she looked up at him and laughed. He'd never felt so delighted. He was always a little tired on his days off, after a long stretch of tedious shifts, but today was different. He wouldn't spend the whole day watching TV, like he usually did.

"I love you," he said to the dog, within earshot of the woman still, and heard her laugh behind him. "I love you and I miss you." He was talking to Scout and his boyhood dog; he could almost see them both, past and present together.

It was some kind of day. Late afternoon now, and the sky every shade of pink. The light spread out over the ocean. Lewis and Scout walked to the edge of the water and he unclipped the leash and let the dog wade in. Would Scout swim? He would! The wonderful dog paddled toward the pink light, then spun and paddled back to the shore. He did this for some time before Lewis realized the dog wanted him to throw a stick. "Fetch!" he yelped, too loudly, too boisterously, wanting to jump in the air, to run into the waves and splash around with the dog. "Yah, yah, yah!" He threw his hands into the air and spun around. "Yah, yah, yah!" A few people were staring at him, including the woman on the bench, who was walking toward him. "Yah, yah, yah!"

He felt more alive than he had felt at any other time since moving to Whale Bay. A small place. A place that threatened to make him small. He did not want to be a small person. He had big plans for himself. He would move to the city. He would be a detective. He outstretched his arms, felt the April sun on his face. What a winter! So much snow, followed by so much rain. And now this sudden heat. He wanted to do a handstand, right there, on the beach, and be met with thunderous applause.

The only being who was as happy as he was in that moment was Scout, who had pulled himself out of the water and was smiling, panting, tail wagging, waiting for the stick to yet again be thrown. "Yah!" Lewis tossed the stick into the ocean and Scout plunged in after it, and Lewis ran in as well—why not?—it was hot as hell out here! Live! He waded up to his knees before he felt the cold and stopped.

It was too cold. Even such joy couldn't mask how cold the ocean was. Okay then. He backed out, sorry that he had done such a thing, for his shoes and socks and most of his pants were sopping wet, and it felt as though he were wading through quicksand. Hilarious, though, not a tragedy! He laughed and pulled off his shoes and socks, and rolled his pant legs and sat on the hot sand. The sun was as bright and strange as a nuclear bomb. The world was some sort of fantastical creation, at this moment existing only to delight him and the wonderful dog. "Scout!" he cried and the dog ran toward him and sat by his side. He ran his hands through the dog's wet fur. He closed his eyes and wished that he and Scout were not in front of the frigid Pacific Ocean, but rather the tepid water of one of the lakes back home. Full of weeds, sure, and speedboats, but he and Scout could swim together, the sun on their backs. He imagined his father waving to them from the shore, his baseball cap resting on his knee. His father would have liked Scout. His father loved dogs, had loved his little border terrier with the same intensity as Lewis. He could still hear his father's voice in his head. What his father would be saying at this very moment—what his father would have said as Lewis ran into the sea. He could feel his father's spirit—or something, he wasn't sure—so strongly, as if the air around him was charged.

When he opened his eyes, the woman from the park bench was standing above him, a big straw hat obscuring her face.

"I want to be you," she said. "I want to be as happy as you so badly right now."

"Okay," said Lewis. "Do it. Be me."

The woman laughed. She patted the dog's head. "I love you!" she said to Scout. She laughed again and sat next to Lewis on the sand. "I'm not as convincing."

"You just met him," said Lewis. "Give it another few minutes. It was love at first sight for me."

They had thrown sticks into the water for Scout for ten minutes before she took off her hat, and Lewis stopped and stared. There she was, standing in front of him, it was definitely her, and why hadn't he noticed until now? And why hadn't she?

"Oh," Lewis said. "Oh."

"What?" said Evelina.

"It's you," he said.

Evelina shook her head, not knowing, not recognizing.

"No one ever recognizes me in my plainclothes."

He watched Evelina think on this a moment. "Like Superman," she said.

"A bit like him, yes," said Lewis.

"Oh, god, you're the cop," she said. "I mean, the officer. Officer Côté." She took a step back, as if he might lunge and arrest her.

"Hey," he said. "It's okay. I'm actually a nice person."

"I'm sorry," she said. "Of course you are. It's—the last time I saw you—are you—did they—the woman, I mean—"

"No," he said. "I mean, we found her."

"Oh, thank god," said Evelina. "Is she alive?"

"She drowned." He watched her face, waiting for something—relief, or happiness, or sorrow—anything. He didn't want to admit it, but he was so attracted to her that it took everything he had not to take her in his arms. "Where are your boys?" he said.

"Dmitri—my youngest," she said, "is spending spring break with his father."

"And you're not altogether happy about it," he said, looking at her face.

"He's getting remarried," she said. She looked at her hands. She was wearing a wedding ring, and she saw him looking at it. "I—"

"What about Jesse?" he asked.

"He's—" She gestured over her shoulder, at the little white beach house behind her. "You can see him, actually, from here."

"Oh yeah," said Lewis. He hadn't realized he was so close to her house. He waved, and the boy waved. He thought of Denny, drunk and drooling, almost rabid. Desperate to have someone to blame. Desperate to talk to the boy.

"I'm sorry," she said. "Listen, I should get back."

"Of course," he said, "though—" He paused, trying to figure out a way to prolong their interaction. He knew if his fellow officers saw him with Evelina they would look at him disapprovingly. But the case was closed. There was nothing more to solve. She was a beautiful woman standing in front of him on a beautiful day. He smiled and pointed at his soaking socks and shoes. "I mean, I'm going to be here for a while, until these dry out."

"Do you want—" she said, and nodded her head toward her house.

"I do," he said. "Yeah, I do."

CHAPTER TWENTY

Evelina

They hosed the sand off Scout together, and she put Lewis's socks in her dryer and his shoes on her back porch, where they would dry in the last of the evening sun. Jesse was playing with Scout in the yard. She drank a glass of beer and felt something swell within her. She excused herself from the kitchen table, and walked to the bathroom. She wanted another beer, desperately. She wanted to get a little bit drunk. Lewis had found another beer in her fridge and the bottle sat sweating on the table when she returned. She drank it quickly, eager for the euphoric feeling. Would Jesse recognize the policeman? The moment felt dangerous: the lie she and Jesse had told, forever in the air. Wouldn't it be easier to end things now, before they even got started? Tell him she had something to do and get him to leave? Or would that make her seem guilty of something? Maybe this was the right thing to do—pretend that she and Jesse had nothing to hide. Act normal, act natural. She'd have to find a way to whisper something in Jesse's ear.

Lewis leaned toward her, and she felt the heat from his body. He put his hand on her arm.

"Is it okay that you're here?" she asked.

"Is it okay that I'm socializing with you, is that what you're asking?"

"Yes. Is it okay?"

"She drowned," he said. "The case is closed."

It was the closest she had been to another person, aside from her sons, in so long that she ached. Her flirtation with the clerk had fizzled and she bought her lottery tickets at the grocery store now. She couldn't bear to face the clerk. She hated that she kept having this thought: maybe he's a nice enough man, a Christian-enough man, to want me even as I am now. It was confusing to her, too, that how she felt inside did not correspond to what she saw in the mirror. She looked fine! Lovely, even. Where was the madwoman she imagined herself to be, hair matted, obese and slobbering, limping, moaning, her ankles swollen and bruised, clawing her body along the street with overgrown fingernails? Vera had drowned. That was what the news said; that was what Lewis said. A casualty of the blizzard. A tragic accident. All kinds of safety warnings were issued about the dangers of frozen lakes. The thinness of the ice. There was talk of installing a safety railing, or at the very least putting up a warning sign.

Still, Evelina looked for something in the eyes of the policeman standing across from her, his hand on her arm—some note of suspicion, but he was only smiling, hungry, she could tell, for her.

She wanted to take the policeman into her bedroom.

Her children were her most magical creations; she couldn't deny it. But here she was, in her kitchen with this strange and handsome man, slightly drunk—on the cusp of the night *going somewhere*—and the look in his eyes took her back to her former life and that ache for greater possibility. She would never rein in her children, she vowed. She would encourage them to do everything. Everything. She'd hated being young to a certain extent. But but but. How had she become a person who derived pleasure from scratch-and-win cards? No more fucking cards. She wanted to ram her head into the table until it cracked open, then lob her brain across the room like a softball. No more fucking cards. It was time to start over. It was time to get past the failure of her marriage to Leo and begin again. Maybe she could be an artist of some kind. Fine. Tomorrow she would go out and buy a sketchbook. She would take an art class. No more fucking cards!

"My apartment has a roof deck," Lewis said, breaking away from her, though still so close that she could feel his breath on her lips. "We could get Chinese food? Watch the sun go down over the water?"

"Yes," said Evelina. "Yes."

She found enough batteries to get her little boom box working, and she and Lewis went through her shoeboxes of cassette tapes, trying to agree on what to take to his apartment. She missed this kind of silliness—changing her taste in music to suit Lewis's, flipping past any embarrassing cassettes and lingering on the ones that made her seem like a person worth knowing (Marvin Gaye, Dr. Buzzard's Original Savannah Band, Anita Baker), blaming any truly ridiculous cassettes (the soundtrack to *Cats*!) on her sons.

He lived only a few blocks from her, and so they walked together, Jesse trailing behind, holding the dog's leash. Jesse seemed to not recognize the policeman. Maybe she would see where the night went before she told him. Told him what? To lie forever? She shook her head. Couldn't she enjoy herself for one night?

Lewis was her height, maybe even an inch shorter. Leo had been so much taller than she was—but it was pleasant to walk with a man and be at eye level. Broad-shouldered—more so than Leo, in fact— long purposeful strides and beautiful hands. Such nice straight white teeth. Never a smoker probably. Tanned skin. Smooth. God, he was young. How much younger? She would have to find a way to ask.

"How long have you been a police officer?" she asked.

"Three years," he said.

"You look young," she said, hoping she didn't sound like someone's mother.

The air was warm and pleasant on her skin. She had slicked her hair behind her ears and put on the peacock feather earrings, changed into a long summer dress under the guise of having sand on her clothes from their time at the beach with the dog. She was on a date. Her shoulder brushed against his as they walked. She glanced at Jesse, hoping that what she was doing wasn't a sort of cruelty.

CHAPTER TWENTY-ONE

Lewis

Lewis liked Buddy Miles and so it was Evelina's copy of *Them Changes* that shot out of the boom box as they sat on the roof of Lewis's apartment building, Scout sprawled out behind them, Jesse watching television in Lewis's living room. Lewis rooted through his container with chopsticks and tossed Scout mouthfuls of beef. He wanted to ask Evelina about Leo.

It was complicated, what he was feeling: an undeniable desire for Evelina, but also his loyalty to Denny, and a gnawing sensation that whatever he was doing with Evelina might be wrong—morally, ethically, professionally—in every way. He reached for another beer, desperate to dull the feeling and enjoy the evening. They had forgotten to bring up a bottle opener and he felt his heart lift a little at the opportunity to show off for Evelina. He took another bottle in his hand and used it as leverage against the first. The top popped off dramatically and Evelina clapped her hands.

"That's fantastic," she said. "Leo used to do it with his teeth. Your method is much more civilized."

"I care too much about my teeth," he said. He offered her the opened beer. He was pleased she had brought up Leo. He could ask her about him. He could be on a date and still pry a bit, yes? For Denny's sake? For his own curiosity?

But Evelina was curious about the thing everyone was curious about. What was it like to do his job?

"I mean," he said, "on a busy day I go from call to call. I don't even have time to eat." The truth was, he'd only had a handful of days like this.

"Calls for what?" she asked.

He paused a second. "Trespassing to assault to death," he said. He watched her for a reaction but she only nodded. "You clear your calls, you write your reports."

She leaned toward him and looked at his waist. He wasn't sure what she was looking for. "Do you have a gun on you right now?"

"Oh," he laughed. "Yeah. Look, what if I run into someone I've arrested before? Someone who has a grudge? In the grocery store or something? I'm not taking that chance."

"I guess that makes sense," she said, but she looked perplexed. He guessed she had never held a gun before.

"Look," he said. "It's like being a hunter."

He felt someone's eyes on him and looked over his shoulder to see Jesse, hands scrunched in his pockets. The sun had disappeared and the air was cooling, the sky deepening blue.

"Hey there," he said.

The boy blinked at him, then asked in a nervous voice whether he could do the trick with the beer bottle again. Lewis felt a pang in his stomach. He wondered whether the boy recognized him. He couldn't tell. He hadn't seen Jesse since January, and Lewis had been in uniform then.

"Of course," said Lewis. "Here, I'll show you how." He glanced at

Evelina to make sure this was okay, then placed a beer bottle in Jesse's hands. "Now hold this tight, and don't let it move." The boy gripped the bottle with intensity. "Now what I'm going to do is put the cap of my bottle under the cap of your bottle," Lewis said, and then, in one fluid motion, as if by magic, the cap flew off and landed by Scout's paw.

"Holy shit!" the boy said, and Lewis looked to Evelina to see if she would scold him for swearing, but she only laughed.

"Still hungry?" Lewis held out his container of chow mein, and Jesse took it, sat cross-legged by Scout.

"What is this?" he said.

"Chow mein," said Lewis. "Noodles."

"Never had it before," Jesse said. He looked at the chopsticks, frowned, then started shovelling the noodles into his mouth with his hands.

"Manners, Jesse," said Evelina, but the boy ignored her. Now that it was dusk, a few mosquitoes began to buzz around them. Evelina slapped the back of Lewis's head and he slapped her ankle, and Jesse flicked one off Scout's ear. Lewis told Evelina to close her eyes and he ran his hand softly over her face. "There was one on your cheek," he lied. "It keeps moving."

"Where are you from?" Evelina asked. She had beautiful arms. The muscles of her forearms tensed as she reached for her bottle of beer. A long, elegant neck. He watched her throat as she drank from her beer. Her collarbone. Her jaw. She must be a decade older than him, but she was a masterpiece.

"Wisconsin," he said. How dull that sounded. How uninteresting— how normal—he must seem to her. A young, baby-faced cop from the Midwest. She probably thought nothing bad had ever happened to him.

"Your parents?" she asked. "Are they still there?"

It had been so long since he'd been on a date—if that's what this was—that he'd forgotten about this part. The part where he had to explain the inexplicable—why he was who he was, and how he'd ended up that way.

"My mother," he started, for this was the relatively easy part, "died when I was young."

"I'm sorry," she said.

Only in his worst moments did he let himself go down the dark path of what his life would have been like if he had been raised by both his mother and father. He had hidden the pain of his mother's death in the deepest part of himself, where it was impossible to reach. A freak car accident. No one's fault. No one to be angry with. His father had climbed into bed after the accident, pulled the red plaid blanket over his body, turned his back to Lewis. The unbearable silence that had followed.

"Your dad?" she asked.

Lewis looked at Jesse to see if he was listening, but the boy was focused on his food. "He died three years ago."

"Oh," she said.

"A month after I moved to Whale Bay," he said.

"I don't know what to say."

"It's better not to say anything," he said. "I mean, there isn't anything to say." He reached for her hand, and she took it.

"Are you close to your parents?" he asked.

"Not really," she said. "They moved to the city, to be closer to my sister and her children." She paused and looked at him. "None of them approved of Leo."

He knew he was supposed to ask her more about her own family now—or maybe even Leo—but his throat felt stuffed with sand. He hoped she wasn't offended. He would ask her, eventually.

The boy set the empty container of food down and stretched out, using Scout for a pillow. The dog licked Jesse's forehead and his ears, and Jesse laughed. Evelina said she needed to use the bathroom, then disappeared down the ladder to Lewis's apartment.

"How did you get the dog up here?" Jesse asked, watching his mother negotiate the ladder.

"It was high comedy," said Lewis, thinking of his hands on Evelina's, how they had lifted the dog together, her body against his.

Lewis stacked the containers and gathered the chopsticks, napkins, and empty bottles of beer into a plastic bag. Scout's tail was wagging idly. Jesse rolled to his side so that he was facing the dog and ran his hands through his fur.

"Oh," said Jesse. The boy took his hands off the dog and became very still.

The boy didn't say anything. It occurred to Lewis that if Jesse had met Vera in the woods that day—and had been in her car—he would have also met Scout. It was important to be delicate. He didn't know whether to say anything or not. Did the boy recognize the dog? Did the boy recognize *him*?

The boy's eyes filled with tears and Lewis couldn't ignore it. It must be horrible for Jesse to have been the last person to see Vera alive. And then to have to see her face everywhere, in the newspaper, on the news. Lewis hadn't considered it until now—he had thought only of Denny. Sometimes Lewis thought of himself as the most perceptive, empathetic person in the world—because of his father—but in moments like this, when he hadn't considered something as obvious as the little boy's relationship to the dead woman, he realized he was still so young and unwise.

"Are you okay?" he asked Jesse. He thought of the day in Evelina's house, when he had asked the boy the same thing.

"Fine." Jesse rubbed at his eyes. The boy was a funny-looking little thing. Big brown eyes. A delicate face. Sharp features. A sweet little puppet version of his father. He couldn't tell whether Jesse was okay or not. There was an intensity to him that Lewis hadn't seen in a child before. It reminded him of his own childhood, the constant tension in his shoulders, the way he felt that if someone bumped into him, he would shatter.

"You doing all right?" he asked again. "I know this year has been hard for you."

The boy looked at the sky, to stop his tears from falling. "Yes," he said. "Yes, I am okay."

"If you need to talk—I—" His heart was pounding. What was he supposed to say? Should he let the boy know that he knew who he was? Should he let the boy know he could tell he was in pain? That *he* had felt pain as a boy, too?

"I'm okay," said the boy. "I remember this dog, that's all. I met this dog before."

"I know," said Lewis.

"You do?"

"I'm a police officer," Lewis said. "I've spoken to you before."

The boy looked at him. He was trying to place him, figure it out. Finally, he nodded, remembering. He started to back away from Lewis, as though he were going to run.

"It's okay," said Lewis. "I'm just asking if you're all right."

"I'm okay."

"We found her, Jesse, you probably heard that already. She drowned."

"We watched it on the news, my mom and me."

"You don't need to be afraid of me."

"Okay," said the boy. He reached for the dog and petted him again. "I like this dog."

"I do too."

"I'm happy to see him again," the boy said.

They sat for a while, petting the dog. Lewis showed Jesse that Scout liked his belly rubbed, and the backs of his ears, and under his chin. He did not like to have his tail touched, or his paws. A couple of stars were now visible, and Jesse pointed them out to Scout.

"How's your little brother?" Lewis asked. He remembered the bruises on the little boy's face. The shock of it. How awful it was to see.

"He's with our dad."

"You see your dad much these days?"

Jesse gave Lewis a cold, hard stare. "No."

"Okay, okay." Lewis laughed, but Jesse was stone-faced, petting the dog in long rhythmic strokes.

"Jesse?" It was Evelina, back on the roof. "You okay?"

"I'm getting cold," said Jesse. He stood and grabbed the plastic bag of trash and disappeared down the small opening where his mother had just been.

When the boy was out of earshot, Evelina fixed Lewis with an inquisitive look.

"It's the dog," he said to her. "He recognized Scout."

"Oh," said Evelina. "I didn't think about that."

"I told him who I was. Listen, maybe this wasn't a good idea."

"You're probably right," she said.

Still, he went to her, took her in his arms.

"No," she said. "I want to do this," and then she was kissing him, kissing him in a way that made him think she wanted him to make love to her, right now, on this rooftop. He ran his hands down her back and started to hitch up her dress. But, no, that was too much, that was taking it too far.

"Stop," she said. "Let's be reasonable."

"Evelina. If it's too much, with Jesse—"

"No," she said. "I want to see you again."

———

And then she was gone. He stayed on the rooftop until the sky was dark, Scout by his side. He hoped it was okay what he had done. He wanted to see her again. How else was he supposed to exist in this small town, with only Denny for a friend?

In a parallel universe, he would be calling his father right now, telling him he'd met a woman named Evelina and that was why he was calling so late. Describing her to his father, describing the boy, describing the evening. His father had the raspy voice of an old man, even though he was only in his fifties. Lewis had called his father every day after he moved to Whale Bay. He didn't know anyone else his age who did that, and although he couldn't articulate precisely why, it seemed like something to hide. Maybe this would be the year he would work up the courage to call his uncle, his father's brother, and finally crack the code, solve the mystery, of why his father had been the way he was.

His father walked three miles a day. He lived in a little rancher outside town, with access to a forest trail. Lewis had explored every inch of that surrounding forest as a child. In the summer it buzzed with cicadas. His father walked with a net over his face, swatting his arms, his knee socks pulled up so mosquitoes wouldn't bite his ankles. It seemed to Lewis that there was a huge swath of the population like his father: retired, widowed men or women living alone, with hardly any friends to speak of, who did things like roam the woods. Introverted, strange human beings. His father was a birdwatcher. A twig of a man in a button-down shirt and ill-fitting shorts, a baseball cap that had long ago faded from red to pink. Not much of a talker.

Why hadn't anyone ever spoken to him about his father when he was a boy? Surely his teachers would have noticed the strange man who lived alone in the woods with his son—surely they would have known about Lewis's mother's death. Didn't it occur to anyone to check on the family? To make sure everything was okay? Didn't anyone notice that Lewis had packed his own lunches from the age of six? A handful of crackers stuffed into his backpack, or sometimes nothing at all? Didn't anyone notice the look of strain on Lewis's face? Didn't anyone notice that a child should not be so nervous, so quiet?

But what was anyone supposed to do? His father was not abusive. If someone had come to the house, they might have found it a little downtrodden, a little depressing. Nothing extraordinary. It would have taken someone spying on his family—bugging the house—to see his father waking Lewis up in the night, turning on the bedside lamp and saying, *I can't go on, I'm sorry, Lewis, but I can't do this anymore, it's too hard, I'm so sorry that I have failed you*. Biting his fingernails as he spoke. It would have taken someone spying on them to hear the little boy beg his father in the middle of the night to live a little longer, to stay a little while, *come on, we'll go birding tomorrow, I'll stay home from school*.

How to articulate the panic he felt when his father didn't pick up the phone on those initial nights after he had moved to Whale Bay? His hands shook, his pulse quickened, he found himself on his hands and knees, scrubbing the grout of the linoleum floor, anything to pass the time. An hour passed and then he would call again.

"Lewis," his father said, "I was out walking."

The relief that washed over him like a wave. They talked about the things they always talked about. The last time they talked, they talked for an hour.

"Okay, then," Lewis said, something forming in the pit of his stomach, his foot tapping anxiously on the floor.

"Yes, okay then, Lewis," said his father.

"It's getting late."

"It is, yeah."

"Okay, then," said Lewis.

"Okay," said his father.

"So, I'll call you tomorrow."

And then the sound of his father saying goodbye, goodbye, my son, goodbye, quieter and quieter, as Lewis took the phone away from his ear and set it in its cradle. Now, on the roof of his apartment, he wondered how long his father might have stood there, on that last evening, the phone still in his hand though the line had gone dead, saying goodbye.

CHAPTER TWENTY-TWO

Denny

A freak heat wave in April. There was no wind. His calves itched and he ran his nails over his pale dry skin until his legs were covered in angry red lines. Really, who was he kidding. If he was honest, really honest, he hated Vera a little bit. All her perfect, prim achievement. Her efficiency. Her healthfulness. Practicality. Snobbery. Superiority. Sometimes he wanted to buy a rotisserie chicken and eat the whole thing on the floor with his hands. And so he would! He hobbled to the car, gracelessly steered it to the grocery store, the gas light blinking frantically, bought a herbed chicken, a carton of milk, and a box of Corn Pops—Corn Pops!—returned home, sat on the floor, and sucked clean the bones. He poured the contents of the cereal box into a mixing bowl, drowned them in milk, and sat in the middle of his unmade bed, the lights off. He ate until he felt his bowels about to move, then took the cereal with him into the bathroom. He was reverting to a Neanderthal! He would gut a boar and wear its pelt. He stuck his fingers down his throat until he brought the whole wretched mess up, then stood there sputtering, drool and vomit on his shirt, and prayed that Lewis would return soon with his dog.

"You doing okay?" said Lewis.

"Yes, yes, I'm fine," Denny said. Scout was on his belly, wiggling and licking Denny's hands. The dog nosed around, then hopped up on the couch and sat staring at the men, his tongue hanging out of his mouth.

"You sure, Denny?" said Lewis.

"I am well! I am fabulous!" He threw out his arms and spun around the room. "Never been better!"

"I'm sorry," said Lewis. "I meant—"

"There's one moment," Denny said, "when I first wake up but before I'm really awake—when I feel fine, rested. Sometimes it lasts long enough that I can fall asleep again, get another two or three hours."

"Okay," said Lewis. He sat on the couch and began to pet Scout.

"There's the whiteness of the room, the whiteness of the sheets."

"Okay—"

"I'm not sure my eyes are even open. I could still be dreaming. And sometimes my body isn't there at all. But then I remember. I remember that she is dead. I get nothing but that small moment now."

"I—"

"It is the only good part of the day."

"I'm sorry," said Lewis. "I don't think any of us know what to make of death."

"All I want," Denny said, "is one more moment with her. I want to close my eyes and when I open them, I want her here."

"I know you do," said Lewis.

"If we'd had a child, maybe—"

Denny closed his eyes and the men were silent. How could he possibly tell his friend how bad he felt? Should he say it? Should he collapse on the floor and ask for help? He could taste the bile in his mouth, but also the sweetness of the Corn Pops, and bits of rose-mary stuck in his teeth. His friends had mostly deserted him. Who would want to be around him anyway? He was so deeply, so hid-eously sad. Surely no one else could carry around such sadness; surely people did.

Lewis was stroking Scout. He watched Lewis get up and walk into the kitchen, refill the water dish, and scoop a cupful of kibble into Scout's bowl. He was such a good person—Lewis. Well, not entirely good. Lewis had broken the news to him that he had gone on a date with Evelina. It hadn't been a pleasant conversation at first. But he had to accept it, didn't he, even though it felt like a betrayal. He needed Lewis in his life. And didn't everyone have the right to move on and be happy?

I'm happy for you, Denny had said, but he wasn't.

Now, Denny watched Lewis as he moved the coffee mugs and plates and cutlery from the countertops into the sink, and filled it with soapy water. If Lewis didn't come by, would he even remember to feed Scout?

"You know," said Denny, the sadness inside of him threatening to open up and consume him, a kind he had never felt before, "it is getting awfully hard for me to be a dog dad."

"Don't say that," said Lewis. "Scout loves you. You're a team."

Lewis walked back into the living room and started straightening it up, too—magazines put back on the coffee table, plates and glasses removed and set into the soapy water of the kitchen sink.

"I can't even walk him," Denny called out, Lewis invisible to him. He heard the sound of a trash bag being heaved out the back door.

"I'm happy to keep doing this, Denny," Lewis said, reappearing in the doorway. "It's no trouble."

"It'd be less trouble if Scout lived with you. Think about it." Denny bent down, his hands curled into claws because they were hurting him, and with a grunt he eased himself on the floor beside Scout. "That isn't to say I don't love you," Denny said to Scout. "I love you with all my heart."

"He knows," said Lewis. "Now, stop."

Good god, he was really blubbery, drooling even, from sorrow. He looked up at Lewis. He wanted Lewis to see it—to see what grief could do to a person. To see that he was undone. Denny felt the tears coming strong now, but he fought them this time. His sorrow was turning into anger, self-pity, and shame. "We have a connection," said Denny. "Me and that boy."

"What are you talking about? What connection?"

"He was the last person to see her alive."

"It will get better," said Lewis.

"Stop saying that. I'm sick of you saying that."

"I don't know what else to say," said Lewis. "I'm sorry."

"I want to talk to him. I have no one left. I want to talk to him about Vera."

"Denny."

"What?"

"I don't think that's a good idea."

"Look, this is destroying me," he said to Lewis.

"Denny, what could the boy possibly have to say?"

"I need to know. I need to know what Scout ran after. I need to know why Vera didn't call him back to her."

"What if he can't answer that? What if he's already told us everything he has to tell?"

"If he had," said Denny, "you wouldn't still suspect Leo. I know you do. I know a part of you wants to let me talk to the boy. Let me talk to him."

"I can't do it officially. You know that."

"Then—I don't know—bring him over to the house or something. We're friends. Bring him over."

"Denny, I don't know."

"I don't want to scare him. I want him to get to know me. And then—once he feels comfortable, comfortable enough to talk, comfortable enough to know that I'm not a monster—I want to ask him about that day. I want to know what he knows."

"I don't know," said Lewis. "I don't want to upset him. And Evelina—"

"I am dying," said Denny. "I am dying here."

"I can get you help."

"I don't want help. I want to talk to the boy."

"I think—"

"Bring him over, please." He was on his hands and knees, bearlike, and he could feel the weight of his stomach reaching the floor. He knew he looked pathetic, frightening. He did not care. He looked at Lewis. He stared him down. He let his tears fall this time, he didn't wipe them from his face, he let them fall, and he let his dog lick the salt from his hands, and he stayed this way, on all fours, until Lewis was saying, "Okay, okay, give me some time though, this can't happen right away, give me some time to figure this out, but, okay, yes, okay, eventually, when I feel the time is right, I'll let you talk to the boy."

CHAPTER TWENTY-THREE

Jesse

The nights were merciless, the air still and heavy. Jesse felt the blood slow in his veins. His feet swelled. His crotch itched terribly. Some sort of scaly looking thing was growing in the space between his right testicle and thigh. He locked himself in the bathroom, poked at it with tweezers, tried to cut it off with his mother's tiny sewing scissors, poured Listerine over the wound and covered it with a paper towel.

The woman's face was all over the news since her body had been found. Photos of the woman's husband, too, a large-bellied man. He was as pale as a zombie. Jesse dreamed that the man was going to hunt him down in the night and eat his body. He dreamed that the man was a great white whale with five hundred teeth. Some nights he hoped that the man would come and eat him, and he left his window open. He waited and waited but nobody came.

It was a good story, the one he and his mother had made up. *The dog jumped out of the car and the woman ran after him, into the woods. I never saw her again. My father never saw her either. He found me in the parking lot and then we drove home.* Dmitri was too young to contradict the story—he hadn't seen the woman anyway, so it didn't matter what he said. And it had worked. And so what if her body had been found? It wasn't like his father had shot her.

Still, he dreamed of the woman at night, dreamed that they were swimming together but then she would start sinking and he would look down and see that her legs were encased in blocks of concrete. Or he dreamed he was in line to get tickets for a movie and when he stepped up to the cashier's window, it was her, and she would reach for him with cold, black limbs. He woke crying so hard from these dreams that his pillowcase was wet and he was so congested he could barely breathe.

His brother came home from San Garcia. Holly was the one who dropped him off—who knows where his father was. Maybe still down there. His mother was on the beach with the policeman, so Jesse put his hands on Dmitri's shoulders and examined his brother. His brother needed a bath, a change of clothes, and a good night's sleep, but seemed all right. "Was it okay?" he whispered in his brother's ear. He wasn't sure whether he was sad that he had not come along, or relieved.

"Yeah," said Dmitri. "We saw some flying people."

"What are you talking about? How's Dad?"

"Dunno. Fine."

He led Dmitri into the bathroom and they watched as the tub filled with water. His brother took off his dirty clothes and Jesse looked over his body, the backs of his thighs, his butt. His brother's skin was smooth and untouched.

"Hop in," Jesse said, testing the water. His brother moved slowly into the tub, heavy with fatigue, and Jesse handed him a washcloth to hold over his eyes while he shampooed his hair. He made two small tufts like devil horns, then handed Dmitri one of his mother's compact mirrors so he could see what he'd done.

"Give me a mohawk," Dmitri said. And so Jesse gathered his hair into the centre of his head and spiked it. "Good," said Dmitri. His eyes were blinking rapidly, trying to stay open, and so Jesse moved the washcloth once again over his eyes, tipped his brother's head back toward the faucet, and rinsed his hair. He ran the slippery bar of soap over Dmitri quickly, not skipping over his brother's private parts like he used to but washing everything with a businesslike efficiency. He felt no urge to pinch his brother, or to pull his hair. No urge to make his eyes sting with soap or shampoo. He pulled the stopper and wrapped his brother in a big red towel. They both liked to watch the water spiral down the drain and so they stood a moment, staring into the bathtub, waiting for the final loud glug as the tub swallowed the last of the water.

"Brush your teeth," Jesse said to Dmitri and passed him his toothbrush.

"That's your toothbrush."

"I don't know where yours is. Use mine." While Dmitri brushed his teeth, Jesse searched Dmitri's drawers for clean pyjamas. But the laundry hadn't been done and there was nothing clean for his brother to wear. Dmitri's bed was made, thank heavens, and so Jesse found a pair of sweatpants and held them out for his brother and then tucked him into the bed. He lowered the blinds and turned on their night light. Somewhere outside, a car drove by.

"Who's that," whispered Dmitri.

"Shh," said Jesse. "It's no one." For the first time in weeks, the wind picked up and rattled the windows.

"Where's Mom?"

"At the beach. She thought you were coming home later."

He wished his brother were older, so he could tell him that his mother was on a date with the policeman who had been in their house. He didn't know how he felt about it. He wished someone else, someone older, were there to tell him how to feel. He liked the policeman. He liked him a lot. And he could tell his mother liked him, too. And yet. Would they have to keep the secret forever? His mother told him to forget about it, to act natural. She told him that he would have a happy life. And that she wanted to be happy, too.

Dmitri's eyelids fluttered and he reached for his bear, but it wasn't in the bed. "Where's Brownie?"

Jesse glanced around, then darted into the living room, where he found the bear in the bottom of Dmitri's little suitcase.

"He almost suffocated," said Jesse, and tucked him in with Dmitri but his little brother was already asleep. He watched him for a very long time.

When he was sure Dmitri wouldn't wake, he walked into the bathroom. He kept a stash of birthday candles, an empty jam jar, and a pack of matches in a plastic bag taped under the sink. Three or four lit candles, dropped into the jar, were best. It was a special, secret task reserved for nights like this, when he couldn't sleep and couldn't stand to listen to his brother's innocent breathing.

He had seen a movie once that talked about damaged people, and that adjective—*damaged*—had surprised him. What did you have to do to damage a person? Was he already a damaged person?

He lit the candles. He stared at his face in the mirror. Every part of it. And then he narrowed in on his eyes. It took a while—a few minutes—but gradually his face disappeared. The space around his eyes grew black. It was as if he were descending into himself, as though a sinkhole had opened up on the other side of the mirror.

His father said there was a deeper place within him, within his thoughts, and it was a quiet place. A silent place. Jesse wanted so badly to go there. He searched the blackness behind his eyes for that quiet place. He searched for a long time. He dove down through his spinal cord and exited somewhere around his heart, floated around in his lungs, tunnelled through his veins. He tried to search his thoughts for the quiet place, but the inside of his skull was hollow, and because it was round there were no corners or shadows. Nowhere for him to hide.

He went back into the bedroom and put his hand on the back of his brother's neck. It wasn't Dmitri's fault the woman had died. None of this was Dmitri's fault.

He laid his head on his brother's back and smelled the soap, the laundry detergent on the sheets.

"Are you scared of me?" Jesse whispered. He wished he could take back all the times he had been cruel to Dmitri. All the times he had pinched him, dragged him around their bedroom by his ear, threatened to rip Brownie into a million little pieces.

He wasn't sure whether he wanted Dmitri to wake up or not, and he wasn't sure he wanted to know the answer to his question. Still, he asked again: "Dmitri, are you scared of me?"

His brother turned to him. "Sometimes," Dmitri said.

"Okay. Go back to sleep," he said. "I love you. I do."

Jesse felt it so strongly he couldn't bear it. He wanted to tell his brother about the woman at the lake. He wanted to tell someone, anyone. It was so horrible that he didn't like to think of it. It made him feel sick inside.

Someday he'd tell someone, but that day was not now.

He looked up at the glow-in-the-dark stars on the ceiling, then down at his brother.

He stood and rocked back and forth on his heels. His face was red and streaked with tears. He waited for a feeling of relief now that he was crying—but he felt nothing. A dullness perhaps. A sort of hollow sound echoing around in his brain. His hands were shaking. From this moment forward, he would do everything right. There was no room for new guilt of any kind.

The phone rang and he ran for it, desperate for it to be his father. *Tell me what to do.*

But there was no one on the other end. Silence, then someone breathing heavily, a click. He replaced the receiver and looked at the kitchen table, which was covered in sketches. His mother had started drawing. She drew court jesters, women in gowns, men in tuxedos. The drawings were beautiful—done in pencil and filled in with faint watercolours. He stared at the pictures, which at that moment were so lifelike he closed his eyes, terrified that they would start speaking.

The house was dark, silent except for the sound of the refrigerator and the wind over the water. He prayed that his mother would come home. She had said she'd only be gone an hour—she and the policeman wanted to watch the sunset—but it felt like longer. He prayed to hear her key in the door. When he was alone, he could feel the woman everywhere. She was in the corner. She was in the walls. She was in the closet. She was in the shadows. She was waiting for him in his bed.

His father had told him that when he died he would find a way to tell Jesse about the afterlife. They had made a pact. It would not be scary. It would not be a haunting. It would be a verification that his soul had not disintegrated, that life was not totally meaningless. That even after death, he was still there, here, there.

He had not seen his father since New Year's Day. He wondered when they would see each other again. And what they would say to each other. It had been Jesse's idea not to go to San Garcia. It didn't seem possible to be in the same room as his father with what had happened hanging in the air between them.

Should he call the police, get it over with? He picked up the phone, then put it down. He picked up the phone again. *Tell me what to do.*

The sound of his mother's key. The sound of the door opening. He hid in the dark of the hallway and watched his mother and the policeman in the doorway, the policeman's hands on her lower back, sand falling like rain from their bodies. He had watched his mother and father kiss before, but this was a different sort of kissing, animal-like. If his mother and father had ever kissed like this, he had never seen it. The policeman guided his mother through the doorway and shut the door with his foot. He locked eyes with Jesse and they both froze.

"Hey," the policeman said. He broke away from Jesse's mother and ran his hands through his hair. "Hey, man."

"Hey," said Jesse. He hoped the policeman couldn't see his tears.

"Just saying goodnight." The policeman opened the door and stepped into the night air. "I'll call you," he said, and then he was gone.

Jesse ran to his mother, let her cup his face and kiss his wet cheeks. "What's the matter, baby?" she whispered, taking him in her arms.

"She's here," he told his mother. "She's here in the house with me."

"Who is?" said his mother.

He could smell the policeman's cologne on his mother's dress. He let himself go limp in his mother's arms.

"Vera is," said Jesse. "She's everywhere."

VERA

She is not a man, and she is not a woman. Skin has grown over her eyes, over her mouth, her ears. Her body streamlines into something pale and cylindrical, cool to the touch. She stays in the troposphere for what might be minutes or years—decades, perhaps, eons maybe—the clouds in her way, the rain soaking her, the sun's heat on her back, the earth five miles below. She feels the pull of time and gravity and love and sorrow. A part of her is still human. She is Denny's wife, and her parents' daughter. She is mother to no one but her dog, nosing through the leaves in their backyard. She searches her body for her hands, and finds them where they've always been, at the ends of her arms. She can swim through the air. She breaks free of her cylindrical form and her hair streams out in all directions, unbound by gravity.

"Denny, Denny," she calls. But no one is up here. Up here she can see the earth's horizon, the sun and moon, the stars so bright she has to squint. She rolls on her back and stares at the underside of a cloud. It is not how she imagined. It looks nothing like cotton candy. There is nothing soft about it. It is made up of a million jagged particles. She grazes it with her foot, and it is as sharp as glass.

Although the earth is five miles below her, she can—somehow— outstretch her hand and touch Scout's back. Her touch is too light for him to sense or feel, but she is there, ruffling his fur—and she can feel his undercoat, the warmth of his skin. She can feel Denny's breath on her fingertips, feels the force of his breath on her skin when he cries. She wants to climb inside his mouth, but there are limits to what she can do, even now. She presses her face to his face nonetheless, tries to pry apart his lips. I am here. Denny, I am here. Open your mouth, Denny, so I can slide down your throat.

She has left no will, no instructions. She was thirty years old. She hadn't expected to die. It's okay, Denny. I am up here. It doesn't matter what you do to my body. It isn't me. I am all the way up here. I will not feel it if you burn me. I will not suffocate if you bury me.

Relief, not panic. This is what she feels now. To have the anxiety of the moment—the fight for another breath—the anxiety of the days, the weeks, the months, the years, taken from her as gently as her mother would have removed a splinter from her hand. It is a pleasant feeling.

She is relieved not to feel bitter, rigid, locked into her routine, as she did before she died. Scared. Worried she had trapped herself into a life that was not meant for her (teaching, academia, a hot office with a flushed-face eighteen-year-old sitting across from her, trying to talk about *Persona*). So often she wanted to take her students by the shoulders and shout: Do you have any idea how hard I worked to get where I am? And you sit across from me, smugly thinking one day you'll be more successful?

She dulled the feeling with exercise and an early bedtime, waking at 6 A.M., walking Scout at Squire Point before she taught for the day.

The night before she died, she dreamed of a man she had never slept with but wanted to—she dreamed he cut the wedding ring off her finger, slipped it into his own hand. What overt symbolism! She was no genius, and certainly not in sleep.

Leave me alone.

Denny's last words to her. She had come out into the night air, heavy with smoke from the fireworks, and found him fumbling in his pockets for the key to his studio. Come to bed, please. Denny, come to bed. Softly, at first. So pathetic-sounding were her pleas that she began to shout it—come to bed, come to bed, come to bed—until her voice sounded ridiculous to her, a caricature of an angry woman. She wanted to go to sleep. Was it such a crime? Was it so awful to ask her husband to come to bed at a reasonable hour, even this night, New Year's Eve? She imagined a baby wailing in a crib somewhere in the house, and Denny out in his studio, drinking. Denny, come to bed right now. I need you to come to bed.

Leave me alone.

She should never have started teaching. She should have pursued a career in film as some dogged man would, assured of his own genius.

So many doppelgängers. Daily calls from people all over the country to the police station, claiming to have seen her, even long after her body has been found.

One lazy afternoon, in a low-ceilinged room on the third floor of an abandoned office building, a group of men discuss various conspiracy theories about her death. There are six of them and they sit in the dark so as not to draw attention to themselves. A few cigarettes glow in the dimness. They are the same men who searched for her. The same men who found the rifle in the snow.

"Oh, well, I don't think the missing boy is an alien," says one man, much older than the others. "I'm not sure how you've arrived at that."

"We'll take a vote."

"Why would he be an alien?" The old man shifts uncomfortably in his seat, the cigarette smoke burning his eyes.

"Okay, then," says a man in a bowler hat. "Hands up for the theory of the child prostitution ring."

No one tells her to do anything, but she knows that what she is meant to do is float. To stop dipping back down to the surface of the earth.

To stop caring. To float. She feels she could float all the way to the edge of the universe, if she wanted to.

Her body decomposes, and it is the opposite of being born. No hips open to accommodate the passing through of her head; instead, it's a narrowing, a narrowing of all feeling, and of light. Her body disintegrates; she blinks and she is no longer there. A single fragment of bone remains for a very long time, then it, too, is reabsorbed.

It's okay, Denny. I am up here. I am up here. We did the best we could. We loved each other so deeply at first. Think of that. Think of how hard we laughed. She feels the absence of her own eyes and her own tears, and the absence of her own mouth and her own voice, and the absence of her own arms and the absence of the warmth of another person's arms around her.

Again, the sensation of being pulled upward, as if by puppet strings. But there is no one working her. It is the pull of the exosphere, which she gives in to, letting herself float up like a helium balloon. So, this is death, she thinks. This is my heart breaking. This is me leaving you.

SEPTEMBER 1986

CHAPTER TWENTY-FOUR

Evelina

It wasn't only Lewis who moved in, of course. She said that Scout could live with them for what she called a trial period. She wasn't sure why she kept it vague—perhaps so that if Denny changed his mind there could be an out. Perhaps so he wouldn't break her children's hearts. Perhaps so that it was clear to Lewis that it was a trial period for the two of them, too. *Bring your stuff over. Put the rest in storage until we get a bigger place. Do you want me to redecorate? I want you to have a say. I want you to feel like this is your home, too.*

It was the end of September, the sky full of twirling leaves. Lewis had put an envelope of hundred-dollar bills on the table this morning—*October Rent and Other Stuff,* it said, in his careful cursive. She studied the *R,* the *S,* the flourishes of the two lower-case *f* 's. She was often surprised by a person's handwriting—disappointed in its sloppiness, in the way it seemed to belie intelligence. Leo's, for instance. Chicken scratch, less legible than Jesse's. Hard to take seriously. He held a pen as if he were frightened of it. Each letter differed in size. When their relationship started to fall apart, she found herself more and more hostile to Leo's penmanship, believing it to be an outward manifestation of his brutishness, lack of sophistication. Lewis's script, however, was elegant, feminine.

Scout lay under the kitchen table. Evelina crouched and petted the dog's head. The window was open and she could hear the surf. Maybe later they'd go for a walk on the beach. Jesse and Lewis were growing closer. She watched Jesse absorb Lewis's goodness like a sponge. Whatever nervousness she had felt about Vera was dissipating. It all seemed like some distant dream.

She couldn't tell if she was healing Jesse by not talking about what had happened, or damaging him further. And now this romance. This lust she felt for Lewis. Was it at the expense of her son? She knew that a truly good person would ask themselves that difficult question. But she couldn't quite bring herself to.

She picked up her drawing pencil and started to sketch the dog. She hadn't drawn an animal before—only people, and clothing. Maybe she should become a fashion designer. She had an eye for it, despite growing up in a place where people wore rubber boots all year round.

"Oh," said Evelina, rubbing her ankle furiously. "Oh for heaven's sake." She pinched the flea between her fingers and carried it to the toilet. She added *flea shampoo* to her grocery list.

"Fleas," she said when Lewis got home from his shift and the boys were back from school. She pointed at Scout and then at her ankle, in a mock angry voice. There it was: they were playing house together. Here she was, in the role of angry wife.

"Okay," Lewis said, though he was obviously enjoying himself, too. "We'll give him a bath. Jesse can help."

Evelina patted the dog's head. "You stay off my bed now," she said, wagging her finger at Scout. All of them—they were laughing.

———

Her bedroom was cool in the morning now that it was fall, and she turned to face Lewis. His skin was smooth, no moles or pimples or weird tufts of hair. He squeezed her upper arms as though he were working icing out of a pastry bag. He was a decade younger than she was. She felt ashamed of this but couldn't say exactly why. She wanted to be his age, she supposed. The young, innocent one. She liked older people. She liked being the baby. Well, nothing was perfect. Choose happiness. Love didn't have to be thrilling.

"You're my baby," she said to Lewis.

He fiddled with her pyjama top and, finding her skin, put his hand on the small of her back. His face was heavy with sleep and he closed his eyes. She could smell the beer on his breath from the night before. He'd only had two, even though he didn't have to work today, and she made a mental note of it: when Leo started drinking, he didn't stop until there was no more alcohol around for miles.

"What do you think about," Evelina said after a time, "when you drink?"

Lewis opened his eyes and stretched his arms above his head, groaning a little. "I think," he said. "I think about my life. I think about what Denny's doing. He sleeps on the floor. I think about that."

"How is he going to manage?" said Evelina. "I mean, financially."

"He'll be okay. His doctor thinks the arthritis will get better." Lewis looked at her. "He also—well—he inherited a shit ton of money when his parents died."

"Must be nice," she said. She thought of her own family suddenly, how her parents had moved away to be with her sister. She felt so alone in the world, even with Lewis right beside her and her sons asleep in their bedroom on this lazy Saturday morning. "What else do you think about?" she said.

"My father," said Lewis.

"What was he like?"

"I don't know," he said. "He was a really difficult person, Evelina. I don't know how to sum him up in a few words."

"Do you ever think you'd like to do something else? I mean, for work."

"Like what?" asked Lewis.

"Something less upsetting."

"Oh," said Lewis. "You're worried about me?"

She nodded. To some extent, she was. His stories about his job haunted her, especially when they involved children. She worried she was too absorbent, that his stories would get into her bones and become her own.

He'd told her once that if a child committed a crime by age twelve, he could help that child turn things around. He could have a huge impact on that child's life. But if that child was fifteen? Forget about it.

She had thought of Jesse, of course. He was eleven now, ten when it had happened. Why was fifteen the cut-off for redemption? The point of no return?

"I like my job," he said to her now. "I have the constitution for it. I believe in people. I believe people are good."

"I don't know if I do," she said, and they looked at each other. "I believe my sons are good. I believe you and I are good."

Already she could feel Lewis's desire to tell her he loved her. It wasn't that she didn't want to hear it. He was lovely. Kind to Jesse. Gentle. But also no-nonsense, like the night he'd sat Jesse down and asked him matter-of-factly if the kids he hung around with were good people, who did good things, who wanted good things for their lives. The best intentions in the world, Lewis said, can be so easily under-mined by the decisions of others. It seemed to her that Jesse had a reverence for Lewis. She noticed he was better behaved, more polite, sweeter, now that Lewis was around. And so much nicer to Dmitri. It was good for both of her boys to have a man around whom they could trust. Lewis had come to her a few nights ago, smiling and shaking his head, and told her that he was going to take Jesse to the drugstore the next day for some antifungal cream. "He's got a wicked case of jock itch, Evelina," he said, "and he's too embarrassed to tell you. He says he had it earlier this year and cured it with Listerine! Listen, don't tell him you know." Leo, of course, would have swatted the back of Jesse's head. *Get your filthy hands out of your pants.*

She wanted to love Lewis, to let herself fall into his arms and let him say what he wanted to say. What was stopping her? She hoped, desperately, that she didn't still have feelings for Leo. She hoped she wasn't taking up drawing as a weird way to be more like Holly.

"Listen," Lewis said. "I'm going to go check on Denny. I'll take Jesse. He can walk Scout around while I talk to him."

"Okay," she said, her pulse quickening. It made her nervous to think about Jesse and Denny in the same room, but of course she couldn't tell Lewis that. She wished Lewis would stop seeing Denny. He seemed like the last real threat to their happiness.

She listened to the sound of Lewis and Jesse getting ready. She wished they would come in and kiss her goodbye.

"Back in an hour," he said to her from the doorway.

"Okay," said Evelina. "We'll probably be down at the beach. Dmitri's been asking to go."

"Don't freeze out there," he said, and then he was gone.

She swung her legs over the side of the bed. She could *choose* happiness. She didn't have to be alone. Still, wasn't there something weak about attaching herself to another man so quickly? She hung her head and watched her stupid tears land on her stupid thighs, then finished her cry in the shower where she could ignore it, where she could pretend it was water on her face. But she wasn't sated, even after she'd shampooed and conditioned her hair. She stepped out of the shower and into her housecoat, then slipped into Jesse and

Dmitri's bedroom. She lay on Dmitri's bed and smelled the sweet smell of her still-sleeping boy. Jesse's side of the bedroom was a disaster. He had balled his sheets in the night, kicked off the comforter, thrown his clothing on the floor and then stepped on it, so that it looked as though it had been dropped from a great height. For some reason two or three pennies were always on the floor. Evelina had convinced herself that the boys were being haunted by a ghost, who left them pennies like breadcrumbs. She scooped the pennies into her hand, slid them into her pocket. She kicked Jesse's clothing toward the laundry hamper then dropped it inside. She did not feel like doing laundry today, even though Jesse's sheets were crusty with filth. If she could get him to stop blowing his nose on his pillowcase this year, she would feel victorious.

She shut the door to the boys' bedroom and slipped back into her own. She took out her photo album—the one with pictures of her and Leo. The one from before the boys were born. She found herself in a waking dream—reliving her past. She saw it play out in front of her, her nineteen-year-old self walking the docks toward the fishing boats, asking to speak with the captain, asking if she could be a cook. That's how it worked back then—you hung around, talked to people, said you were seaworthy, and got hired.

The sound of seagulls and the heavy clunk of a crab trap being offloaded. The slosh of a bucketful of octopus parts. The stench. Men who'd eat the head right off a herring. Raw shrimp and roe. A seal bobbing its head in the water, waiting for her to throw him a fish.

It wasn't Leo she missed; it was her old self. That old, dangerous self. Her old self could never keep such a secret. Could she really live with Lewis, when he was the only one who didn't know what had happened that day at the lake?

———

An hour passed and still Lewis and Jesse had not returned from Denny's house. She felt a vague sense of panic, or fear, but told herself no harm could come to them. Maybe they had stopped at the park. Maybe they were throwing sticks into the ocean, and watching Scout run into the waves. But there wasn't time to worry: she could hear the sound of Dmitri calling out for her, wanting cereal and then a day of playing in the sand.

The phone rang and she held the receiver a minute before putting it to her ear. Please, she prayed, don't do this. Don't be someone calling to tell me awful news. Be some telemarketer. But who did she really want it to be? Did she want it to be Leo? She wished there were some way of knowing where he was and what he was doing. And whether he was okay. She took a deep breath and put the phone to her ear.

"Is this Evelina?" the voice said.

"It is."

"This is Denny Gusev."

"Hi, Denny," she said. "Is Lewis with you?"

"No," he said. "He left already. But—something happened."

"Go on," she said.

"It's about Jesse," he said, "and I think you should know."

CHAPTER TWENTY-FIVE

Jesse

The curtains were drawn in Denny Gusev's house, but a single ray of light spilled into the living room, illuminating the mess on the floor. It was a mountain of women's clothing and makeup, things Jesse didn't know the names of but had seen in his mother's cosmetic bag at home. It was a newer house, and the floor didn't creak when he walked across it. Lewis told Jesse to wait a minute, then disappeared into Denny's bedroom with Scout. Jesse looked around the dark, dirty living room. The furniture looked expensive, like something out of a magazine. Everything was grey or white or black. At the centre of the pile of women's clothes was a big indent, and Jesse wondered if that was where Scout used to sleep. Dogs loved sleeping on piles of laundry; he knew that now that he had a dog.

On top of a bookshelf were photos of Denny and the woman from the lake. Jesse held his breath and closed his eyes. Her ghost was here, ready to drag him down to hell. "I'm sorry," he whispered into the dark air. "I'm sorry. Please." He tried to avoid her but the woman was watching him from the photographs, with a hundred pairs of eyes. It seemed to Jesse that photos of her were everywhere—on the walls, the coffee table, the bookshelf, in the hallway.

"I'm a good person," he whispered to the photographs. "I promise you. I'm good. I know I am." He knelt next to the piles of clothes and cosmetics. "I promise you I am a good person." He gripped one of her tubes of lipstick and then one of her shoes and tried to feel her spirit radiating from the objects. "I want you to know that I am good."

He put down the lipstick and the shoe and walked to the bedroom, where Denny was sitting up in the bed with his legs straight out in front of him and a folded newspaper on his lap. Scout was on his back on the bed, his paws curled, his eyes closed tightly in sleep. Lewis sat in a chair by the window, flipping through a stack of unopened mail. Both Lewis and Denny looked angry, as if they'd been arguing. Lewis looked up and saw Jesse and put his hand out to Denny, as if to tell him, *Stop whatever you're about to say*.

It was stuffy in the bedroom, even though it was the end of September and the air was cool. A red bathing suit was hanging from one of the knobs on the chest of drawers, the price tag still on. There were pictures of the woman in here, too, and more mountains of clothes, though on second glance Jesse realized that they belonged to Denny.

Scout flopped over and curled into a snail. Jesse sat on the end of the bed and ran his hands through the dog's thick fur. He tried to think of something else, something that wasn't the dead woman. But the bedroom smelled like Scout did, like mildew and old, dead leaves. Maybe Vera had smelled like this, too.

Jesse could see a small mountain of Scout's dried poop in the corner of Denny's bedroom. It looked like it had been there for a very long time.

Denny was rifling through the newspaper. "Here," he said, and with a great deal of effort passed the funnies over to Jesse. The big man winced even as he turned the pages of the newspaper. His hands were so stiff they looked like they were made of clay. Jesse read the funnies quickly, then began folding and unfolding the newspaper.

Denny looked as though he were going to cry. "Have you ever had a dog before?" he asked.

"No," said Jesse. "I asked for one every year." He tore a piece of newspaper free and folded it over, made a crease.

"What was the holdup?" Denny said.

Jesse smirked. He would use that expression sometime. *The holdup.* "Dunno."

"You have a way with animals," said Denny. "Anyone can see that."

"Really?"

"You both do." Denny nodded at Lewis.

"Who wouldn't love this dog?" said Lewis.

"People are assholes," said Denny, then covered his mouth. "Oops."

"I can handle it," said Jesse, folding the newspaper again.

"Okay then, pal," said Lewis.

Jesse folded the newspaper over and over onto itself, then handed it to Denny.

"What's this?" said Denny.

"It's a boat," said Jesse. "For good luck."

Denny took the boat and examined it. "I could wear it as a hat," he said. He put the newspaper hat on his head and he looked at Jesse.

After a long time, Denny spoke. "You were the last person to see her alive," he said. He took the hat off and put it on his lap. "Could you—could you tell me what happened that day? I am trying so hard, still, to understand."

Jesse looked at Lewis—would he save him from this moment he did not want to have? But Lewis was looking at the floor.

Jesse thought of his father. *This did not happen.* And his mother. *You can't tell anyone what you've told me.* But he also thought about the woman, and now, Denny. He thought of Lewis. He wanted Lewis to love him. He wanted Lewis to love him so very much. In the presence of Lewis, Jesse felt he was his true self—an honest, kind, good boy. But that didn't matter if he continued to lie. He looked at Scout, who was at the foot of the bed. Scout was staring at him with his big grey-blue eyes. Scout knew what had happened that day. Scout knew. Jesse felt he could continue to lie to Lewis and even to Denny right now, but not to Scout.

"Do you think she killed herself?" Denny said.

"No," said Jesse. "No." He looked at his hands.

"Jesus, Denny," said Lewis. He got up from the chair, walked to Jesse and put his hands softly on his shoulders. "We can go home if you want."

"I miss her," said Denny. "I miss her so much."

"It's okay," Jesse said to Lewis. It wasn't. It wasn't okay, nothing was okay, but maybe if he just said a few nice things about Vera, it would all be over and he could go home. "She was a very nice woman," he said. Lewis sat back down, and Jesse looked at Denny. "She was very nice to me."

Denny closed his eyes and put his hands in the air. Jesse wasn't sure what he was doing. What he was reaching for. "I know. Vera was kind. Yes, she was. Yes. Thank you."

"We should probably get back," said Lewis. But Denny shook his head, his face suddenly annoyed. He turned to Jesse.

"Maybe," said Denny, "if it's okay, you could tell me a little more about your time with her."

"What do you want to know?" Jesse said. He could feel his bladder, full and pressing against his abdomen.

"Anything," said Denny. "Anything you remember."

"She thought I was lost," said Jesse. "She was worried that I was cold."

"Were you?" said Denny.

"I was. I was really cold." It was true. His bones had ached with cold.

Denny and Lewis were looking at each other. The silence was unbearable after a while, and so Jesse continued. "She gave me a ride to look for my dad."

"And then?" Denny said.

He took a breath. This part he had rehearsed with his mother so many times. "Scout jumped out of the car." Jesse hesitated, thinking it through. The woman had called the police, then Scout had jumped out of the car. Right? No, not right. "I mean, I opened the door and Scout jumped out of the car." Yes, that was it. The reason she dropped the phone. His teeth had started to chatter, even though the room wasn't cold. His bladder felt as though it were inflating. What would happen if he ran—ran out of the house and didn't stop running? Could he survive, on his own, on the streets? Should he go?

"Okay," said Denny. "And why didn't she call Scout back to her?"

"She called for him," said Jesse. "She did. But he ran into the woods."

"And she ran after him?" said Denny.

"She did."

Jesse tried to picture it, as if it had really happened. He could see her running after the dog in his mind, her jacket streaming out behind her, Scout's paws kicking up snow. He closed his eyes for a minute, seeing it, then opened them again. It wasn't too much of a stretch to imagine it—although it had been him she'd been running after, not the dog.

"And what did you do?" said Denny.

"I stood there, by her car. I waited for my dad."

"What was Scout running after?" said Denny.

"I don't know. A mouse maybe."

"A mouse?" said Denny.

"A squirrel. I don't know," said Jesse. The detectives had not asked him this. He and his mother had not talked about what kind of animal Scout was after, or even if it was an animal at all. "I didn't see what it was."

"And she ran into the woods, onto the trail? Into the forest?"

Jesse looked at Lewis. He could see that he was failing the test. Denny and Lewis and Scout were all looking at him, and seeing that he was a liar.

Lewis had been mostly silent this whole time but now he leaned forward in his chair, an expression on his face that Jesse had never seen before. "Try to see it in your mind from the very beginning," said Lewis. "Can you describe the parking lot to me? What you looked at while you waited for your dad?"

There were two parking lots at Squire Point, Jesse knew that much. He remembered that his father had parked in the first lot. That was where they always parked. The other lot was for people who wanted to go camping. They never parked there. "It was the first one," he said.

"The first parking lot," said Lewis.

"Where we always park. It was snowing." But still the men looked disappointed in him. The detail he should have been able to provide was what Scout was running after. *That* was what he had to invent.

Lewis got up from the chair, sat next to Jesse on the bed, and put a hand on his shoulder. Jesse felt the heat from Lewis's hand, the weight of it, the pressure.

"Scout was—Scout was running after—" But he couldn't think of anything. A cat? Why would there be a cat in the woods? It was a good thing he didn't say it was a cat. A mouse was stupid enough.

He should have said a fox. A fox or a rabbit. A rabbit—that seemed more likely. "A rabbit," he said, but Lewis was already asking him another question—

"So you stood there until your father came?" said Lewis.

"Yes," said Jesse. He could feel a kind of exhaustion creeping in behind his eyes. He wanted to lie down.

"You didn't move," said Lewis.

"No."

"You stayed in the first parking lot, waiting for your dad."

"Yes."

He was crying, though the two men didn't seem to notice. Denny was staring at him. Jesse thought Denny might open his mouth to reveal those five hundred teeth. His mouth might open like a great white whale, and he might eat him.

Lewis turned to face the window. He seemed to be whispering to himself.

"I'm sorry," Jesse said to Denny. "I'm so very sorry."

"Oh," said Lewis, turning to face Jesse. "Oh no."

Jesse looked up at Lewis, then realized that Lewis was staring at his legs. He had peed himself. His pants were growing dark with it.

"This isn't right," said Lewis. "Let's stop this."

"What do you mean?" said Denny. "We're only talking."

"Denny, please," said Lewis. "This is wrong. The boy is scared to death."

"I have waited for such a long time," said Denny. "Are you my friend, Lewis?" Denny was saying, "Are you my real—"

"Will you be quiet?" said Lewis. "Be quiet. He doesn't know anything. It's over."

"But it doesn't make sense to me—my god, it makes no sense at all—"

"I told you to shut up," said Lewis, and Jesse winced. He had never heard Lewis speak sharply before. He wondered if Lewis had another side, a violent side, a bad side, and if he would have to be frightened of him now, too. Maybe all this time Lewis had been tricking him. Maybe Lewis had known all along. And if Lewis knew, would he kill him now?

But instead Lewis put his arms around Jesse and whispered in his ear, drowning out the sounds of Denny's pleading. Lewis whispered that it was going to be okay, that he loved him, that he was here to protect him, and that he would take him home.

It had been so cold in the back of his father's car on the long drive back into town from Squire Point, his brother periodically turning to look at him. The sound of his own breath. His chest heaving. Running his nails over the upholstery, concentrating on the feeling of the fabric, and watching the snow falling in clumps outside the car.

"Jesse," whispered Lewis. "Jesse. You don't need to do this anymore. I'm sorry. It's okay." He stood and turned to Denny. "I'm taking him home. I'm taking the boy home."

CHAPTER TWENTY-SIX

Lewis

"It's over, it's over. I'm taking you home," Lewis said. He searched his patrol car for a tissue but there was only a napkin from his lunch days ago. Should he stop and get the boy a chocolate bar? What good would that do? He drove around for a long time, thinking, then pulled up in front of Evelina's house and walked with his arm around Jesse, whose shoulders were still heaving. The boy wiped his tears and looked up at him. Lewis unlocked the door, and Scout ran into the house.

He needed to watch over this boy. Children with this much pain inside of them turned into monsters. Children with this much pain ended up in jail. They hurt people. They had to hurt someone as much as they had been hurt.

"You don't have to lie to your mom," Lewis said. "I'm the one who made a mistake. I scared you half to death. I was the one who was supposed to be in charge."

Was that the kind of thing a good parent would say? Lewis couldn't remember a single time that his own father had apologized for his behaviour. Lewis was the one who had to apologize; Lewis was the one who had to make everything okay. He wanted to be a good parent to the boy. He wanted to be. Was it okay to reverse the roles like that? For a parent to apologize to a child? Would the sky rip open? Would the ground fall out from underneath his feet?

"Hey," said Lewis. "I'll tell your mom what happened, all right? You go on and watch some TV. You've been through enough today."

His heart was pounding and his palms were slick with sweat. Once Jesse was absorbed in the television, Lewis took the phone from the kitchen wall and walked with the long cord until he was in the bathroom. Evelina had indeed taken Dmitri to the beach—she'd left a note for him, a cryptic one, saying they needed to talk. Still, he hid in the bathroom in case Jesse heard him. He shut the door and dialled the phone quickly, his fingers trembling.

"Need to talk to you," he said, his hand cupped around the phone.

"Lewis? What's going on?" the detective said. "Why are you whispering?"

"Can you look at the Gusev file for me," said Lewis. "Leo's statement from his arrest."

"Okay," said the detective. "What do you want to know?"

"Can you get the file?"

The detective told Lewis to hold on. It seemed like he sat in that small pink bathroom for a very long time. He stared at the tile floor, at Evelina's hairs curled around the base of the sink. He broke off a piece of toilet paper and fiddled with it. He prayed Evelina wouldn't come home.

"You there?"

"I'm here," said Lewis. He could hear the sound of the detective flipping through the pages, then taking a loud sip of coffee. His foot tapped uncontrollably on the bathroom floor.

"Okay," said the detective. "I've got Leo's statement in front of me. What do you want to know?"

"What parking lot did Leo say he picked his son up from?"

Finally, after what felt like an interminable amount of time, the detective spoke. "Statement says it was the first parking lot."

"The first one?"

"Yeah."

"Okay," said Lewis. "Okay, one more favour. Get Jesse's statement for me."

"Got it right here," said the detective.

"Okay. What parking lot did he say his father picked him up at?"

"All right, hold on," said the detective, and once more Lewis waited. "It doesn't say. I mean, we didn't ask him."

"Read me his statement."

"It says, quote, 'I got scared and opened the door, and her dog jumped out and ran into the woods. She ran after the dog and I never saw her again after that. My father came back and he drove us home.' End quote."

Lewis took a deep breath and stood, pacing the small bathroom. He didn't care anymore whether Evelina came home while he was on the phone. All he cared about was why Leo had said he'd picked up Jesse from the first parking lot, and why Jesse was saying the same thing.

They were lying.

For one thing, the first parking lot had no pay phone.

And he had found Vera's car at the second parking lot.

"You there?" said the detective.

"Yeah," said Lewis.

"Well?" said the detective.

Could Jesse and Leo have gotten the parking lots mixed up in their minds? Jesse surely could have. But Leo?

"Thanks, man," said Lewis. "That's it. That's all I need."

"Uh-huh," said the detective.

Lewis hurried to the kitchen and found a piece of scrap paper. He drew a big circle. That was the lake. He drew a line to the left—that was the trail leading from the lake to the first parking lot. He drew a line to the right—that was the trail that cut through the campground that led to the second parking lot, the one with the pay phone. He drew little circles to represent the two parking lots.

Jesse had said that Vera found him in the woods and took him to her car to get warmed up, then she drove him to the other parking lot to look for his father, called the police, then the dog jumped out of her car and she went after him into the woods, then his father came back for him and they drove home.

So for that to make sense Vera must have originally parked in the first parking lot, then driven Jesse to the second parking lot, where she had made the call.

Jesse had said he hadn't moved when Vera had gone after Scout. That he'd waited for his father to pick him up.

But if that were true, his father would have picked him up from the second parking lot.

It was a small inconsistency. Could be an error of memory. Leo had been drinking, after all. And the boy could have gotten confused.

Or they were lying. Both of them. A boy who was covering for his father. A boy who was telling his father's lie.

He waited for Evelina at the kitchen table. He heard her key in the door, then the sound of her and Dmitri taking off their shoes, thumping them against the side of the house to shake out the sand. Their footfalls as they walked down the hall.

"Hello?" Evelina called out. "You guys home?"

Dmitri reached the kitchen first and ran to Lewis, his arms out-stretched. "You're back!" he cried and crawled into Lewis's lap. Lewis stroked the boy's hair, tucked it behind his ears and kissed the top of his head. He wished he could prolong this moment forever—this sweet moment, holding this little boy, his sandy hair—instead of the inevitable future that awaited them. He could still be wrong, couldn't he? It could all be a misunderstanding.

"Hey," he said to Evelina. "Hey. I need to talk to you."

"Okay," she said. She was wearing a long sweater and shorts, her legs covered in goosebumps. Her feet were tanned, sand between her toes. The window was open and a cool breeze blew into the room. "Why don't you go watch TV with your brother," she said to Dmitri and he sprang up, ran into the living room, and was gone.

"You look like you've seen a ghost," she said. He could see a kind of steeliness in her eyes.

"There's a problem," he said.

"I know," she said. "Denny called before we went to the beach. He told me what you did to Jesse—"

"Evelina," Lewis said. "Evelina, wait—"

"You should have talked to me," she said. "You shouldn't have made him go over there—"

"I know, look, you're right—I—you're right, Evelina—"

"Denny feels terrible," said Evelina. "He told me he was so sorry. He told me it was his idea but as far as I'm concerned you're the one responsible."

"I know, look, I'm sorry—but this isn't about that," he said. He rose to his feet and took her by the shoulders.

"What's it about then," she said. He could see that she had already hardened herself against him. "So," she spat and shrugged his hands off her, "what's it about then?"

"It's about Leo and Jesse," he said.

She reached for the countertop, as if to anchor herself.

"Listen," he began. "Listen to me. I think they might both be lying—"

"What are you talking about?" she said.

"Vera Gusev's death," Lewis said. His hands tingled and went numb. His ears rang. He felt the sweat run down his back. Was he doing the right thing? There was a part of him that wanted to forget it. To move on and forget. But Jesse. He had to do this for Jesse. His face—he couldn't forget the look on the boy's face. As if his father were going to hunt him down and shoot him on the spot. He understood why he had felt such a kinship with the boy. They shared a secret. They were boys with a secret. They were boys who had to bear a terrible secret about their fathers, and who were utterly alone. But Jesse wasn't alone. Jesse had him. And so he had to save the little boy, even at the expense of what he had with Evelina.

"I think Leo lied to us," he said. "And I think Jesse is covering for him. I need to talk to Leo again."

"I don't think that's a good idea," said Evelina.

"Why? I can't ignore this. If Leo was involved and Jesse is covering for him—well, that's too much to ask a child to bear. Evelina, as his mother—"

"Lewis," she said, her voice quiet.

"I need to talk to Leo. Get him to tell us what really happened. Evelina, there's something he's not telling us. And it's killing your son."

"No, Lewis." She reached for his hand. "Don't do this."

"Why not?"

"Because Leo didn't kill that woman," she said and took a breath. "Jesse did."

VERA

Once in the exosphere she is no longer human. The cylindrical mass that she felt herself to be has dissipated, and she emits nothing but a soft buzzing sound.

What effect did she have on the earth? Her death caused six people great pain—Denny, her mother and father, Jesse, Leo, and Evelina—and she can see the energy from that sorrow rise from the earth like water from a geyser. Smaller, imperceptible streams rise from a number of friends and acquaintances, but they dissipate so quickly that it astonishes her.

She watches herself be born, and then she watches her mother's birth, and her grandmother's, all the way back until the woman she is watching is covered in coarse hair, alone under a dark sky.

She can see the blue halo that rings the earth, and she can see the satellites orbiting. Up here, there is nothing for her to use as a visual reference, though she knows she is moving. There isn't a ripple of anything against her, like her shirt would ripple if she jumped out of a plane. The earth appears to be covered in snow, but it is just the clouds. If she reached out her hand, she could use the handle of the Big Dipper to pull herself higher, higher, even higher.

Did her death matter, in the grand scheme of things? Which actions matter, and which actions don't? The only thing she knows definitively is that acts of kindness go unnoticed, but acts of cruelty do not.

Knowing what she knows now, she could have been a good mother.

She understands, now, why people have children.

It is because we fail as ourselves, all of us fail. But we have a secret plan, a subconscious desire within us to become something astonishing, like the caterpillar that unwittingly becomes a butterfly. And, so, knowing that we will fail as ourselves, what we do instead is make something astonishing. We make our children in an effort to remake ourselves.

Before she floated all the way up here, Vera watched Jesse, as though he were her son. His mother doesn't understand how damaged he is, although she is a good woman and Vera has some affection for her. But Vera knows his heart is broken in a way that he will never recover from. When you break a child's heart, their heart is broken forever.

Remember that, she thinks. Remember that you cannot be a good parent—or even a good person—if you have forgotten what it was to be a child. If you remember, keep remembering. Do what you have to do so that you don't forget.

She hopes he isn't as damaged as she thinks he is. Maybe all little boys dream of killing their fathers.

Long ago, her husband gave away their dog. He cried in the living room after Lewis picked up Scout and drove away.

Scout slept with Jesse instead of her husband. Her old wonderful dog slept at the foot of the boy's single bed so that Jesse had to curl his legs to accommodate him.

Long ago, Jesse cried in the night. She doesn't think anyone should cry like that.

What ultimately concerns her is time. Time looks like a record—a flat black disc, with the earth in its centre. Not unlike the rings of Saturn. When she wants to, she puts the needle down, and she can see whatever it is she wishes to see. She can watch a trilobite move through the waters of Siberia, over five million years ago, and so she does. He emits a kind of clicking sound from his spine.

But all of that is so many miles below her. Long ago, she left the atmosphere. Long ago, she traversed the solar wind and braved the heat of the sun. Long ago, she passed the planets and all of their moons. The universe expands as she moves through it, expands faster than she is travelling, and so her journey is infinite, and she will never reach its end. She feels as though she is floating on the surface of the ocean, buoyed occasionally by the blip of a galaxy, as if going over a wave.

She has been dead for such a long time. She is dead and gone.

In the end, all that remains is her work. She held a mirror up to the world, and still it did not change.

And what is there to say about death?

It hurts physically. It hurts to drown.

The ice shattered beneath her, like the shards of a mirror, and she plunged into the water, black as ink, cold as the edge of the universe. Her lungs filled. She could feel the water behind her eyes.

It took about four minutes for her body to die. As her consciousness faded, it was not unlike being put under anaesthesia. She had no sense of time passing, and indeed she felt as though she had been dying for thousands of years, enough time to float all the way to the edge of the universe, although her death happened in the time it took for the ice to re-form above her head. Once she was gone, she had no sense of self, no sense of her body, no sensations of any kind. There was only nothingness. It was peaceful. As it is in the deepest of sleeps, devoid of dreams.

Above the frozen lake, the clouds were thick and white as lambs-wool. Above the clouds, the black sky was lit with stars, the moon visible only to a pilot and his passengers on their westbound flight across the ocean, travelling back in time.

JANUARY 1986

CHAPTER TWENTY-SEVEN

Jesse

"He told me to stand here."

"Who did?"

"My dad."

"Where is your dad now?"

"Dunno."

"How long have you been out here?"

"Dunno."

"All alone?"

"Yes."

The woman had on a huge green parka with a fur-rimmed hood, black corduroy pants, and hiking boots. She wore glasses with thick black circular frames that made her look like an owl, and had impossibly long black hair. She did not look like anyone Jesse knew. She looked like a city person. Someone who would smoke long cigarettes. Maybe a spy.

Her dog—a white and grey dog, a fluffy and wonderful-looking dog—ran through the woods behind her, looking up every once in a while to make sure she was still in sight. He wanted to pet the dog more than anything.

"And you don't know where your dad is?"

"No, ma'am."

She put her fingers to her mouth and whistled for her dog, and he ran to her side, nosed her pocket for a treat. She patted his head and clipped on his leash. The woman looked about Jesse's mother's age, but seemed more confident, more adventurous. He couldn't imagine his mother going for a walk in the woods alone, with a big dog, though apparently she used to work on fishing boats.

"I think I better call someone," the woman said.

"He said he'd be back soon," said Jesse. "Please don't make me move." He tilted his head upward so no tears would run down his face. It was snowing harder, and he opened his mouth and let the flakes land on his tongue.

"A little boy shouldn't be alone out here. It's freezing. Why don't you come back to my car and we'll get you warmed up. Then we can come up with a plan."

She spoke in the same tone his mother used when she was frustrated with him. He didn't understand why the woman wanted him to move. His father would be right back. He had told him to stay here, face this tree, and think about what he had done.

"We were supposed to stay right here, on the trail," he said to the woman.

"Who was?"

"Me and my brother. We were supposed to stay here."

"Okay, honey." Her voice was even more impatient. "Where is your brother?"

"With my dad."

"But you don't know where your dad is?"

"No." He wanted to tell her that it was only meant to be a joke, a mean joke, sure, but only a joke. He wanted to tell her that he knew he had done a bad thing. That he should never have pretended that Dmitri had fallen through the ice.

Her dog was whining, pulling at the leash, wanting to continue. She hushed her dog, then turned to Jesse. She seemed to be rolling something over in her mind. "There weren't any cars in the parking lot when I got here, love."

Jesse shrugged. What could he say to get this woman to leave him alone? He didn't want to tell the truth—that his father had threatened him with a beating if he moved.

"I need to stay by this tree," he told the woman.

"You know," she said, "there's another parking lot about a half mile from here. I wonder if he's there."

"Please," Jesse started, but the woman had decided that she had solved the mystery.

"That makes sense," she was saying. "Come on. Let's get you warm. I don't think he meant to leave you out in the cold. You must have gotten separated, yes? He's probably somewhere on the trails looking for you."

Jesse considered this alternative reality for a moment—one in which his father was calling his name, Dmitri perched on his shoulders. *Jesse! Where are you?*

"My dad said he'd be back soon," he told the woman.

"We'll wait a bit in the car, get you warmed up. Then we'll try the other parking lot, okay? Let's. Come on now."

The woman's dog was whining more forcefully, and Jesse saw that the woman was getting impatient, both with her dog and with him.

He didn't want her to be angry. He was so tired of people being angry.

But he also didn't want his father to hurt him. He felt certain that the guilt of what he had done was punishment enough. But he didn't know what his father was capable of. His father did not seem like anyone else he knew. And now Jesse had broken a rule—a law, it seemed—by pretending his brother had fallen through the ice. Everything else he had ever done—every little cruelty—seemed so small now. He wondered if his father might kill him this time. He had felt before that his father hated him, but—after what he had done—he knew if it hadn't been true before, it was now.

"I can't leave a little boy alone in the woods, do you understand?" she said. Her voice was sharp, and Jesse winced.

"Okay," he said, stepping away from the tree cautiously, as though his father were around the corner, keeping watch. He took another hesitant step. And another. Finally, he walked to the woman and petted her dog. It was a nice dog, with thick fur. The dog licked Jesse's hand, and he smiled.

"My name is Vera," the woman said. Her voice was softer, and sweeter.

"I'm Jesse." He felt better now that he wasn't facing the tree, his face bright red from the cold.

"Okay, Jesse, my car's up here a hundred yards or so," said Vera. "Come along now."

"We were going to learn how to shoot today."

"Oh?"

"My dad said he'd teach us."

"We'll find him." She put her hand on the top of Jesse's head and they walked along the trail that way, as though he were a little puppet. "How old are you, honey?"

"Ten," Jesse said.

"Just about all grown up."

"Yeah." Jesse felt his heart lift a bit.

"Here we are. Come along now."

They reached the parking lot and she unlocked the car, held the door open for Jesse. "Hop on in. That's it. Okay. Let's get the heat on." It was a much nicer car than the one his father had. It was a nicer car than his mother's. He had to step onto a running board to get into the passenger seat. He was high up, way up off the ground, in this woman's beautiful car. The seat was leather, slippery and cold, and he watched his breath leave his body in a narrow jet. In his father's car, the gearshift said "Toyota," right on the knob. There wasn't a gearshift in this car. The woman had a fuzzy black steering-wheel cover and the car was spotless.

The woman shooed her dog into the back seat and got into the driver's seat. She took off her gloves and Jesse saw that her fingers were covered in beautiful rings. He had never seen rings like that before; they looked heavy, expensive, unusual. One had a giant gem-stone on it and the woman caught him looking at it.

"Look," she said, waving her hand in front of his face. The gem-stone glowed a blue-green colour. "Now look again." She put her hand down by his feet, out of the light. The gemstone was dark red, almost purple.

"How does it do that?" he asked. His mother wore a thin gold wedding band and that was all.

"I don't know," she said. "But it's my favourite thing in the world."

The woman unzipped her jacket, turned on the car, and blasted the heat. Freezing air blew out of the vents, and Jesse moved his face away from it, dug his chin into his chest. The stereo had come on and weird music was playing now, too loudly, violin and piano music, people moaning in the background. It took the woman a long time to turn it off. She kept pressing the volume button instead of the power button. It made Jesse want to scream.

"I'm sorry," she said to him. "I'm just so nervous." She looked at him, then shook her head. "Look," she said, "let's drive to the other parking lot, see if your dad's there."

Jesse sat on his hands, which were raw and red from the cold, and stared out the window of the woman's car. His breath fogged the glass and he fought the urge to draw a picture with his finger—his father scolded him when he did that. But he couldn't resist. Quickly, hoping Vera wouldn't see, he drew three vertical lines. He pretended they were bars, and that he was being taken to prison. Vera offered him a butterscotch candy and he sucked it slowly, let it clang around in his mouth. He drew two more lines on the window. He listened to Vera tell him what a brave boy he was being, how she would help him find his father, how the trails should be more clearly marked. In the back seat, her dog panted out stale breath. He was whining again, and the woman kept hushing him in a stern voice.

"The good news is that there's plenty of daylight left," she said. "We'll find your dad and your brother, Jesse."

"Okay," Jesse said. He had an urge to wrench open the car door and hurl himself out, then run into the woods. He felt strong and self-sufficient. He felt as though he could be a boy who lived in the woods—he knew he could survive it. There was nothing more beautiful than snow falling in the forest. There was nothing more beautiful than the lack of sound—so quiet it was as if his ears were stuffed with cotton—and nothing more beautiful than the smell of damp earth.

Down a little road, and then they were at the second parking lot. There was no one in sight. The woman looked at Jesse. "No," she said. "Well, all right."

Her face looked suddenly exhausted, and she turned away from him, looked out the window.

"Oh, I'm a fool," she said, laughing as she turned back to him. "What we ought to do is call your mother. Do you know your phone number?"

He nodded.

"Good," she said. "I'll find a quarter."

She turned off the car and hopped out, dug through her pockets and then looked under the seat. Jesse could see a quarter on the floor by his feet but didn't say anything. He did things like that sometimes—didn't speak up, didn't help people—but couldn't say why, or what pleasure it gave him.

"If I had kids, I'd never let them out of my sight," she was saying. "Can't imagine it." Her face was flushed. "Damn it," she said.

Jesse watched her as she tried to figure out what to do. She kept twisting one of her rings off her finger—the one that changed colours—then sliding it back on. She asked whether she had left her change purse at home. How would he know? He watched her rummage through her jacket and produce a pack of cigarettes. She brought one to her mouth but did not light it.

"There," she said, finally spotting the quarter. She asked for his phone number, then shut the car door and walked to the pay phone, so that Jesse could hear only the sound of the dog panting behind him.

"Good boy," Jesse told the dog. "Such a good, brave boy."

He reached behind him and stroked the dog's ears, which were thick and soft and slightly damp from the snow. He let his hand rest on the dog's head. The dog kept trying to lick Jesse's hand and finally Jesse let him. He held out his hand, and the dog's big rough tongue ran over his palm. "Good boy," he said again. He tried to imagine what would happen next: his mother would arrive in her car, take him into her arms. She would be mad about him pretending Dmitri had fallen through the ice, but she would get over it. He took a deep breath and let himself relax for the first time that day.

The woman tapped on the driver's side window and Jesse looked up. She was shaking her head and gesturing back at the pay phone, the unlit cigarette in her hand. She opened the car door and told him his mother hadn't picked up. She walked again to the pay phone. Jesse felt his body tense. He leaned toward the open car door, so he could hear her. She asked to speak to the police, and he knew suddenly that his father was back at the other parking lot, walking toward the tree, Dmitri behind him. He felt it in his bones. If he ran fast enough, he could reach the tree. If he ran fast enough, he could catch up with his father and he wouldn't be beaten. He knew the trails well enough. In an instant, he was out of the car, the woman shrieking behind him, the snow falling faster now, until he was invisible.

Jesse had watched the Olympics on TV: he knew how to run. He kicked up his legs, imagined there was a windmill beneath his waist, a circular motion, both feet off the ground, his arms at ninety-degree angles, all the power coming from his shoulders, his feet flexed up and then down each time they struck the ground; he imagined he was moving the earth, kicking up a huge cloud of dirt and snow to wipe out whoever was behind him. He would be a great athlete one day, he was sure of it. He ran deep into the woods, past the campground, until he reached the lake. He had a good sense of direction and knew if he crossed the lake at this point he would meet up with the trail that led to the place where he had been standing. If he ran fast enough, he could reach it before his father and he wouldn't be punished.

His heart was beating so hard that it seemed to be outside his body. He stopped at the edge of the lake and wrapped his arms around himself, sides heaving. He spat into the snow. He heard something behind him and spun to face the dog, the woman's nice dog, wide-mouthed, its tongue hanging out, snow balled onto its legs so that it looked as if it were wearing white leg warmers.

"Go on," he said, waving his arm in the direction of the trail. "Get." The dog stayed put, its mouth hanging open so that it seemed to be laughing. Jesse heard the woman whistling for the dog. He felt a heaviness in his chest that he was not the runner he thought he was; surely he should be farther away, out of reach.

"For crying out loud," he could hear the woman saying. "Slow down." He stared at the icy expanse of lake ahead of him. If he crossed it, he'd be on the other side in a matter of minutes—and back to where his father had told him to wait. He could even see the hole where his father had broken through the ice, in search of Dmitri. He could run around it. Surely the woman wouldn't come after him.

"Good, brave boy," he whispered as he slid one of his boots and then the other out onto the frozen lake. His legs were shaking and he clenched his fists, determined to make it to the other side.

"Jesse."

He could hear the woman close behind him and the loud panting of the dog.

"Stop that. Come back here."

He shook his head, not looking at her, and continued his journey across the lake, back to his life with his father and brother. He reached the spot where his father had broken through the ice. A thin layer had formed over the hole, and snow fell softly on it; soon it would be covered. The paper boats were nowhere in sight. Underwater probably, or pecked apart by birds.

"Everything is going to be okay, Jesse," she called out. "I need you to turn around and walk back to me." Her voice was shrill, hysterical even. He hated the sound of it.

His father would be so angry, not only that he wasn't waiting by the tree but also that the woman had called the police. Jesse would have to tell the police the awful truth: that he had pretended Dmitri had fallen through the ice. They would ask why. Because I was angry with my father. Because I wanted to make him suffer. He would have to say these words to the police in front of his father. His father hated the police. The police would see the bruises on Dmitri's face and take his father away. And then, once his father was out of jail? Well, his father—his father would kill him.

"Leave me alone," he shouted back at the woman. "Please, I'm fine," he said. "Go away."

He slipped and felt the toe of his boot plunge into the cold water. He scrambled to his feet and stared at the long stretch of ice ahead of him. He couldn't see the hole in the ice. It was snowing hard and he was turned around, couldn't tell which direction would lead him back to the tree where his father had told him to wait. "Go away," he said to the woman. He could not make his legs move in any direction. "Leave me alone," he said. "Please."

"Stay right where you are," she said. "Don't move. I'm coming, honey. You're going to be okay."

He watched as the woman charged onto the lake toward him, her dog behind her.

He put out his arms as if to stop her, but she kept coming for him. "No," he said.

Despite all the exciting stuff Jesse saw on TV or read about in books, nothing exciting had ever happened to him. He would get sick but it never turned into pneumonia. His mother complained of a headache but it never turned out to be a brain tumour. She took a corner too fast but they never crashed into another car, or ran anybody over. The black backpack left at the bus stop in front of their house never exploded; the knock at the door never ended in a home invasion, everyone gagged and tied to chairs. The phone rang but nobody had ever died.

The woman was one step away from him, and Jesse watched as she put her foot down and the ice below shattered. Oh god, he heard her say. She came crashing down, unsteady on one knee, teetering at the edge of the hole in the ice, and she reached for him. She had him by his coat. He wrestled away from her grasp, terrified of being pulled into the water. One push. All it would take was one push. He closed his eyes and pushed her as hard as he could.

"Don't," she said, but he leapt away from her, and then she was underwater.

In an instant his father was beside him, shoving him out of the way. Leo reached into the water and grabbed the woman's arms, and dug his knees into the ice.

"I've got you, don't worry," his father was saying. "Hang on, hang on," he said.

"Don't let go," the woman yelled at his father. "Please," she said, but her voice was unsteady and Jesse could barely make out her words, her mouth full of cold water. His father had the hood of her parka wadded in one hand and her arm in his other. He slipped forward and the woman's head went under again.

When she came back up, as if by a feat of incredible strength she lunged toward Leo and grabbed his shoulders. "Please," she said. "Please." Her glasses had fallen off and Jesse could see her eyes, which were deep-set and wild, almost bulging. It was too much and he looked away, wished she were still wearing her glasses so he wouldn't have to see those frightening eyes.

"I've got you. I've got you," Leo said. He was kneeling at the edge of the hole, embracing the woman. Her legs were kicking frantically. She was trying to use Leo as leverage, trying to get one of her legs back onto the surface of the lake.

"What the hell is wrong with you," Leo yelled at Jesse. "Help me. Grab on to her."

Jesse could see his father's eyes darkening. His father's face morphing into that other face. The other face, the other one Jesse knew so well.

"I didn't mean it," Jesse said. "She wouldn't leave me alone." But his voice was nowhere to be found, and it came out only as a whisper. He couldn't make himself move.

"I've got you," Leo said to the woman. "Stop fighting me. Relax a minute."

"Help me," said the woman, "help me."

Leo whipped his head around to look at Jesse. "Grab her! Come on!"

The woman was crying, scrambling to keep her hands clasped around Leo's shoulders. "My hands, my hands," she said. She began to wail. "I can't hold on."

"God damn it," said Leo. "What the hell is wrong with you?" He was looking at the woman but Jesse knew the words were meant for him.

"My hands," she said. "My hands are too cold."

"Don't let go," said Leo.

His father's legs were slipping. He tried different positions but there was no traction—everywhere he placed his feet, they shot out from under him. There was nothing to hold onto. No rope to throw. The woman was thrashing in the water, and she was screaming.

"God damn it. God damn it," his father was saying, over and over.

"Don't let go of me," the woman said. "Help," she said again. "Please help me."

She was clawing at his jacket and Jesse saw that his father was going to be pulled down with her, down into the water. His father gasped, struggled to secure his footing again. He braced himself to lift the woman onto the ice, but soaked with ice-cold water, she out-weighed him.

"Dad! Dad!" Jesse said. "Let go!"

His father was making a horrible wailing sound and Jesse knew he wouldn't stop trying to save her. The woman's lips were turning blue and her teeth were chattering. His father's clothing was wet and plastered to his body. Jesse grabbed his father's shoulders and tried to pull him away from the hole in the ice. He tried to wrench open his father's hands. He began to hit his father as hard as he could, but he saw it was making no difference and so he took hold of his father for balance and kicked the woman's arms and hands, anything he could reach of her, until she let go and plunged into the water.

"Don't," the woman was screaming, and his father threw Jesse onto the ice with a strength that was almost superhuman, and scrambled to grab her again.

"Grab my jacket, grab my hands," his father yelled. But it didn't matter. The woman's face had changed and she had stopped screaming. Her mouth opened and a gush of water spilled out. She raised her arms and tipped her head up. She broke through the surface of the water with her hands one last time, as if she were trying to lift herself out of the lake and fly into the open sky. She opened her mouth once more, and seconds later she was underwater.

"No," said his father, and he grabbed for her but she was unresponsive, staring up at him from below the surface. Her arms floated down to her sides and then she was sinking.

A bubble, then another, then nothing.

Jesse could see her. He could see her face. The woman's expression softened. His father backed away from the hole in the ice and together they watched her go.

Jesse and his father knelt at the edge, peering down. At some point, Jesse realized his father was holding his hand. He waited for the black water to bubble with life and for the woman's hand to shoot out and grasp the ice. His father seemed to be waiting, too.

The ice cracked beneath them, and the next thing Jesse knew, he was in his father's arms, and his father was carrying him to the lake's edge. The snow had stopped and for the first time that day Jesse did not feel cold. His father set him on the ground.

All he could hear was the sound of his father breathing.

"Listen," his father said, bending to Jesse's level and taking him by the shoulders. His eyes were bloodshot and wild with something that looked like anger but might have been sorrow. He scanned the lake— as if the woman might reappear somehow, as if by magic—then looked back into Jesse's eyes. "You have your whole life ahead of you. Do you understand this?"

His father's voice was unlike any other voice he knew. Jesse struggled not to be affected by it. The very air around his father seemed to shimmer as though it were charged. In the distance, he could see the woman's dog by the edge of the lake, but the dog was silent, unmoving, not even panting. Hidden by the birch trees, out of sight.

"None of this happened," his father was saying. "This did not happen, do you hear me? Do you understand this now?"

"I understand," said Jesse. "I understand."

"You did not meet this woman. You have never seen her. This did not happen."

For a moment, Jesse wondered whether he had misremembered his childhood—had he imagined his father was an out-of-control, angry monster? No. He could remember his father's face turning purple if the phone rang at the wrong time. What had happened to *that* man? Who was this person, tears in his eyes, clothes soaking wet, looking at his aging hands?

They were in the parking lot now, though Jesse could not remember walking there. Had his father carried him up the trail? Had he closed his eyes, let his head slump against his father's shoulder as he was carried to the car?

"No one will ever know."

His father held the car door open for him. He waited for Jesse to get in, then leaned over gently and fastened the seat belt, tugging it a little afterwards to make sure it was secure.

His brother was in the front seat, waiting. The snow was falling around the car in heavy clumps. His father was digging in the snow outside the car, looking for something, and it took him some time before he climbed into the driver's seat.

Even from the back seat, Jesse could smell the tequila on his father's breath. He could hear his father breathing in ragged, choking gasps. He leaned closer to his father because he thought his father might be speaking—and as he leaned closer he heard that, yes, his father was saying something. Over and over his father was telling them, in a voice not much louder than a whisper, that this day had never happened, that this day had never been.

When they pulled up to his mother's house, Jesse could see his mother watching from the window. She was holding the phone receiver in her hand.

They walked toward the house, and he listened to his father tell his mother that Dmitri had fallen on the ice. Jesse nodded as his father told her the story, his mother's eyes on him as he did so.

His mother took Dmitri into the house, and for a moment Jesse was alone with his father.

His father's clothes were wet, and he was looking past Jesse into the house. Jesse could hear his mother asking Dmitri whether his face hurt, and then the sound of her searching the freezer for an ice pack, telling Dmitri to hold it to his face.

The snow had stopped and the sky cleared above their heads, the stars finally visible after weeks above the clouds. His father's car was idling, a plume of exhaust rising from the tailpipe into the night air.

"Dad," Jesse said. But he couldn't make himself ask the question.

He waited for his father to hold him. To take him in his arms and tell him that he loved him. That they would recover from this. That everything had an end, even the bad times.

"So long," his father said to him, and Jesse felt something move within him, some familiar old ache of disappointment.

JANUARY 1987

CHAPTER TWENTY-EIGHT

Lewis

Lewis parked his patrol car and let himself into Denny's house and stood in the living room. Scout bolted in and out of the rooms, searching for Denny. The dog nudged at Lewis's legs, poked the backs of his knees with his muzzle.

It was the one-year anniversary of Vera's disappearance. He felt he had to stop by. He felt he had to say something, to commemorate it. He didn't see as much of Denny these days. What he had done—letting Denny talk to Jesse, no matter that it had led to the truth—had fractured the friendship for both of them.

He had told Denny what had happened to Vera. The whole truth, not a half-truth, or nothing at all, as he could have done. He went through the entire story, start to finish.

Denny, he's a little boy.

A little boy who was terrified of his father.

He has his whole life ahead of him.

The lights were off in the living room and it was so quiet Lewis could hear the hum of the refrigerator. Scout circled toward the bedroom then back to Lewis, his tail low and moving back and forth.

Lewis flicked on the lights. He saw vacuum tracks across the carpet and a once-overflowing wastepaper basket that was now empty. In the kitchen, the floor sparkled and the counters shone. Lewis opened the fridge but it had been emptied of its contents and wiped clean. No dishes in the sink; all were drying on the rack, the sponge back in its holder. Gone were the piles of newspapers and junk mail and crusty glasses of orange juice. Gone was the smell of rot and mildew. He opened the cupboards and saw that all the food had been thrown out. Only the dishes remained, gleaming.

"Looks great in here!" Lewis called out. The windows washed; the sills free of dust. Scout's water dish, often empty, was full of clean, cold water, as if Denny had been expecting them.

At first, Denny had wanted to prosecute Leo. And it was still a possibility. But was it worth it? Wouldn't it do more damage to the boy in the long run—more damage than had already been done? One long night, they had argued until four in the morning. Denny had even raised his fist to Lewis.

They left her there.

"Hey, man! You home?"

Maybe Denny had hired a cleaning service. Or maybe he had cleaned the place himself. He was on new medication for his arthritis, and it seemed to be working. Perhaps he was coming around. Finally! Maybe he was going on a diet. Maybe he'd thrown out all his stale food so he could start over. Maybe he'd finally donated Vera's things to Goodwill or the Salvation Army, or driven them to the dump.

Whatever the case, Lewis surveyed the clean house with a feeling of pleasure. Denny was finally moving on, and here was the first sign of it.

Denny! It's over! Move on with your life! Get up from off the floor and let us live again! Let us drink and dance! It is over, my friend! Not your grief, not your grief, but the doubt! You are free! We could even be friends again—true friends, nothing between us! It is over! It is finished! It is the first day of the year! Hooray! *Callooh! Callay!*

"Where are you, man?"

He stood in Denny's immaculate kitchen, opened the back door and let Scout into the yard but the dog was crouched low and didn't want to go outside. His police radio crackling was the only sound.

He put his hand on the door frame and called out again. He scanned the yard but there was no sign of him. The mower had been returned to its place beside the garage, the electrical cord coiled into a perfect figure eight. Denny had raked, too, and gathered the leaves in a black garbage bag, which he had leaned against the house. The yard cleared of its leaves, Lewis saw that there were flowerbeds, neglected but for a few hostas that would bloom in the spring, and some blue ornamental grass that was doing quite well. "You back here?" he called.

Maybe he was in his studio. Lewis had never been in Denny's studio, although he had always wanted to see it. What went on back there? He walked to the little outbuilding—it looked like a shed—and opened the door. The lights were off and he imagined when he flicked them on he would finally see all the equipment Denny had told him about—the kiln, the centrifuge, the thing Denny called a quench tank, where a ring finally broke free of its plaster cast and exploded into being. But when he flicked on the lights, the studio was empty. A long rectangular-shaped room lined with workbenches, a couple of stools on wheels. He knelt and ran his hands over the rough cork floor, in search of something left behind. A little diamond? He wasn't sure what he was looking for. Nothing but a sliver of some kind of metal. The place swept clean. The way Denny described his studio, it must have taken days, weeks maybe. What had he done with all the equipment?

Scout crawled over to Lewis and lay by his feet, panting heavily. "Okay, boy." He patted Scout's head, then scooted his feet out from

under the dog. He walked outside again and scanned the lawn. A pair
of pruning shears had been left out to rust—Denny must not have
noticed them—and Lewis picked them up and walked toward the
garage.

He put one hand on the door, his other hand on his gun.

"Denny, you in here?" he called out.

He imagined Denny hanging from a rope. He imagined him in
his fancy car, the engine on, his head rolled to one side.

Lewis was rarely nostalgic for his difficult childhood, but he wanted
to tell Denny about it now. He wanted to explain why his hands were
shaking and his body had gone numb.

He wanted to tell Denny about the last conversation he'd had with
his father. That long goodbye, a month after he'd moved to Whale Bay.

He wanted to explain to Denny that his father's craziness had
fractured him, so that he felt his own personality was a glass that
had been dropped from a great height onto a hard floor. He wanted
to explain that the child of a crazy parent spends his whole life trying to fix the world. But that, faced with Denny, who *did* need fixing,
Lewis had felt a kind of calm, a remove, a move toward *sanity*. He felt
how he was supposed to feel. A lightness.

He didn't need to fix Denny. And so he had performed only the
manageable duties of friendship: walked Scout, occasionally tidied
the house. He hadn't, as he had done for his father when he was a
child, teenager, and young man, sat up with him all night, or called in
sick so he could spend the day with him when he knew he was particularly sad. For the first time in his life, Lewis had put himself and
his own needs before Denny's.

But maybe that had been a mistake. Maybe Denny had driven to
the ocean and waded in, wanting to drown like Vera. Perhaps he had
leapt in front of a train. Perhaps he was in a motel room somewhere,
washing his pain medication down with a bottle of cheap vodka.

Cutting his wrists. Affixing a rope to the ceiling fan, taking a step off the back of a chair.

It was one of his father's neighbours who found his father's birding binoculars on a clifftop, a few miles from the house. The neighbour looked down. He called out but got no response.

His father must have fallen about a hundred feet.

It was a lie—it didn't get easier. There was no help when you lost someone you loved. And there was no help for someone like his father, nothing that could have made it better, nothing Lewis or anyone could have done or said to prevent his father from killing himself.

It was important to be honest about this. It was important to see the world as it really was, and to understand its limitations and his own.

These were not conclusions he had reached on his own. They were the words of his uncle, whom Lewis had called one night at Evelina's urging. *It's good to know the truth*, she said. But there wasn't much truth to be known. His uncle told him his father had always been odd, even when they were children. He didn't wish to mine the past any further. He wasn't unkind, but he was gruff, and Lewis knew he wouldn't call again.

Now, his hand on his gun, he opened the garage door and flicked on the light.

Nothing, not even the car. The floor had been swept clean.

"Okay," he said to the empty garage. "Good. Okay, then."

He walked back into the empty house.

Nothing but the clean rooms and the name of Scout's vet pinned to the fridge with a magnet and Vera's red bathing suit hanging from the dresser.

The carpet had been vacuumed in the bedroom as well, the sheets washed and the bed made. The closets were empty save for their hangers. He took Vera's bathing suit in his hand.

He had a sudden, overwhelming desire to see an orca breach in the bay, an eagle soaring, a heron at the shoreline. He wanted birds, lots of birds. He wanted to lie in the water and have the salt of the sea clean his body. He thought of Denny's face after he had told him that Vera was dead: an expression of wonder, like a child's, as if he were seeing something no one had ever seen before.

Lewis sat on the bed, where Scout was waiting for him. He took the dog in his arms and buried his head in his fur. He didn't say much of anything. This wasn't how he had pictured it. In his mind, he and Denny were clinking glasses. In his mind, they were toasting Vera. In his mind, he was a great police officer, on his way to becoming a great detective. He had solved the mystery, after all. He had done it.

He sat on the bedroom floor, his legs out in front of him, and breathed in the clean scent of the house. He stayed that way for over an hour, thinking at any moment he might hear Denny's car in the driveway. Or the phone ringing. Something. Someone. Anything. Nothing but the distant sound of the foghorn, the ever-present sound of Whale Bay.

He wanted to tell Denny how profoundly meaningful he had found their friendship to be. That Denny had taught him how to be a friend. That Denny had taught him to be a normal person. A normal man. And that, armed with his new knowledge, he knew he could be a good husband to Evelina.

"A husband." He said it out loud. That's what he would do: he would marry Evelina. He would be a father to her boys, and one day to a child of his own. He would never let anything bad happen to any of them.

He hoped Denny was on an airplane, bus, or train, heading off to start a new life, and would soon send Lewis a letter or postcard, letting him know where he was. Or maybe Denny had fled because the truth about Vera's death was too much to bear. Maybe he would never hear from him again.

Maybe his disappearance was some kind of terrible gift. Some way of letting Lewis carry on with Evelina and the boys.

He lay on the bed and put his head on Denny's pillow.

"Okay," he said. "Okay."

He felt that it was the right decision not to have arrested Leo. He felt it was the right thing not to have sought legal justice, in whatever form it would have taken, for what had happened to Vera Gusev. A terrible thing had happened to her, but he understood why it had happened. He understood that a little boy's pain could blossom into rage. Although his own relationship with his father was different from Jesse's relationship with Leo, he understood Jesse with a deepness and intensity that surprised him.

And he understood that now he, too, had to keep the secret. For so long, he had been the only one who didn't know what had happened. Jesse, Evelina, and Leo. They'd all known. Only he and Dmitri, too young to comprehend it anyway, didn't know the truth. But now that he knew, it was better to keep quiet. Not to act. Not to disturb the universe. He would carry the secret forever. He would do it for the boy.

He opened the bedroom window and let the cold wind into the room, to clear out the ghosts. He understood something else, too: he did not feel young anymore.

He hoisted himself from the bed, left the house, and stood in the front yard, regarding the big picture window. He had grown so used to seeing Denny through the window, slightly warped from the glass, that he could see him now, clear as anything, sitting on his fancy velvet couch, a glass of bourbon in his hand. Denny raised the glass to Lewis, and Lewis nodded back.

Well, wherever you are, Lewis thought, goodbye. Goodbye, Denny. Goodbye, my friend.

CHAPTER TWENTY-NINE

Leo

A quick trip to Whale Bay to get some things out of storage, including the Remington. He hadn't meant to see anyone. Meant to dip into Whale Bay, then dip out again. But instead he found himself on the block where Evelina and the boys lived, staring at the little white beach house, imagining himself walking up the steps and letting himself inside. He hadn't seen Dmitri in eight months. Even longer since he'd seen Jesse. He'd sent them a few postcards. Talked to them a few times on the phone. He'd talked to Evelina, too. About what had happened with Jesse. And he had talked to Lewis. And they had made a deal. This was not part of the deal. He was not supposed to be anywhere near the boys.

It was late on a Sunday morning. Leo figured the boys and Evelina would never know he'd been there. But just as he began to turn away, Lewis emerged from the front door in uniform. The two men looked at each other.

"Thought you were staying down south," said Lewis, walking toward him, rubbing his hands together, his breath fogging the air.

Leo braced himself for something. A fist? A bullet? What did this police officer feel toward him? The Remington was useless, unloaded, locked inside his suitcase.

He felt ashamed of his sweater, which he'd retrieved from the storage locker last night. It was the one he'd got in Scotland, a white cable-knit sweater, like the kind fishermen wore. He thought it made him look worldly. But now, standing in front of Lewis in that perfectly pressed uniform, Leo thought he looked shabby, like a person who couldn't afford a nice winter coat. This is why he hated being around people—all they did was remind him of what he didn't have. He didn't even want it—money, things, a house with a lawn to mow. He didn't want any of that stuff at all. He'd given whatever he could—his car—to the Swami. The Remington would be next. Only worth a few hundred dollars, probably, but every penny counted for something.

"Just up for a few days," said Leo. He gestured to the suitcase at his feet. "Had to get some things."

Lewis continued to walk toward him, and Leo found himself stepping behind the suitcase, as if somehow the little piece of luggage—the Remington swaddled within—could act as a shield.

"Don't mean any harm," Leo said and put up his hands. "I don't even know why I'm here." He looked away from Lewis and found himself inspecting the sidewalk with intensity. He supposed Evelina had gotten everything she wanted.

"It's okay," said Lewis. He gestured up and down the block. "Where's your car?"

"Took the bus. In fact"—he looked at his wrist as if there were a watch there—"I should be going."

"I'll drive you," said Lewis. He nodded toward the white beach house, where Leo could see the faces of Jesse and Dmitri in the front window. "We'll go together."

———

He sat with his oldest son in the bus station, a cup of coffee between his knees, waiting for the bus to arrive and take him back to San Garcia. It was the end of January; Jesse was eleven years old. The new year stretched out in front of them.

Leo raised his eyebrows, drummed his feet on the floor, and checked the big wall clock. He knew he was supposed to say something to Jesse before boarding the bus to San Garcia and disappearing once again from his life, but he didn't know what. He hadn't meant to see the boy again until he was older and more time had passed between them. He prayed for Evelina and Dmitri to come back from getting their hot dogs.

The bus's engine started, and so he rose to his feet, and finally Evelina and Dmitri returned. Dmitri was eating his hot dog with both hands, mustard in the corners of his mouth. Evelina wiped his face with a napkin.

He eyed the engagement ring on Evelina's finger. Not too expensive-looking: a simple band. He couldn't help feeling as if he had been robbed of something, even though he would never want to live with Evelina again. But shouldn't a life like this be available to him? Why wasn't it?

The sound of the bus's pneumatic door opening. The conductor announcing it was time to board.

Evelina smelled like lavender. In her heeled boots, she came up to his chin. They looked at each other, but there was nothing to say.

Jesse and Dmitri stood beside her.

"Take care, my sons," he said and bent to their level.

He took Jesse and Dmitri in his arms. He remembered when they were babies and their heads smelled like baby powder and milk. "Goodbye," he said.

He moved away from them and joined the long line of people waiting to board the bus. He stood a moment looking for Lewis before he spotted him, hanging back, almost out of sight, at the entrance to the bus station. He wondered if Lewis was hanging around in case Leo decided to bolt. But he wouldn't bolt. He would go back to San Garcia and stay out of the boys' lives. That had been his deal with Lewis. The deal they'd made, late one night on the phone.

But Leo felt certain he would resurface—he would see his boys again one day. Not immediately. Maybe not for years. And he would never speak of Vera Gusev or what had happened that day at the lake to anyone, not even Holly, who he hoped would be waiting up for him when he arrived.

"Dad," Jesse called out. "What kind of car you drive?"

"I don't," said Leo.

The line wasn't moving, and Leo imagined breaking out of it and going back to Evelina's house for Chinese food. In his mind, he set the table, asked where she kept the placemats, napkins, and cutlery, and whether they should eat in the kitchen or dining room. He thought of the mismatched plates, the cheap knives and forks he and Evelina had gotten at a thrift store before they were married. He imagined that she now had chopsticks inlaid with abalone shells, and special dishes for dipping sauces, and a large rectangular platter that she would put in her oven's warming drawer. He imagined himself inspecting the little sauce dishes, taking a liking to one shaped like an oyster shell, and turning it over in his hand. Bringing it to his ear as if it were a conch. *Is this thing on?* he imagined himself saying, waiting for laughter.

"Dad," Jesse said. "You coming back anytime soon?"

"We'll see," said Leo.

His suitcase was like a dead weight in his hand.

2020

CHAPTER THIRTY

Evelina

"You're listed as next of kin," the woman on the phone says to Evelina, who sits up in bed and fumbles to turn on the little bedside lamp. The room shoots into light, and she sees that it is almost seven. Lewis is snoring beside her. There isn't any point in showering. She presses a hot washcloth to her face, brushes her teeth, steps into a pair of black stretch pants and slides a grey sweater over her shoulders, wiggles her feet into her driving moccasins. Her hair is completely white and cropped to the chin, and she combs it out with her fingers, checks her purse for her keys, and leaves a quick note for Lewis on the counter. It is shocking to leave the house before the sun is up. She feels like a fugitive. Her vision is poor and so she pushes the seat as far forward as it will go and drives with desperate, squinting eyes. The hospital is twenty minutes away. She clenches the wheel. She turns on the radio, hoping the music will comfort her. Her hands are shaking. The car cost a small fortune. She turns on the heated seats, lets herself sink into the soft warm leather. There is no one on the road at this hour, no reason to be nervous, no reason not to trust

herself to get there, but still she scans the side of the road, waiting for
something to leap out in front of her.

"Will I recognize him?" she asks.

"I don't know," the coroner's officer says. "He looks different than
he does in his driver's licence photo."

"He has a scar on his left ankle," Evelina tells the coroner's officer.
"He was born with a club foot. His left leg—if you measure it—is
smaller than his right."

"That's helpful, thanks," says the coroner's officer.

The coroner's officer is a woman. The nurses hurrying through
the halls are women. The janitor pushing the big custodial cart is a
woman. Two doctors in white lab coats. The front-desk receptionist.
Evelina can't see another man in the cold white hospital except for the
photograph of her ex-husband that the coroner's officer places in her
hand. Dead as he is, she thinks he still might burst through the double
doors at any minute and ask her what the hell took her so long.

She takes a breath and unlocks the door to Leo's apartment. He had
been living two miles from her and Lewis's house in Whale Bay. The
television is on, muted, showing the news. She watches for a moment,
then shuts it off. The apartment is in a low-income housing co-op, the
units squished together, a small concrete courtyard in the back with a
basketball hoop. Some graffiti. When did he move back here? Why
didn't he live in San Garcia still? Did her sons know he was here? She
waits while the sun rises, waits for it to illuminate the living room.
Someone (Leo?) had painted the walls varying shades of blue. Either
that or the light is playing tricks on her old, tired eyes. She studies the
walls, but can't figure it out. It is possible she is going blind. She will

do it tomorrow: make the long-procrastinated appointment with the ophthalmologist, have Lewis take her in their stupid fancy car.

There is a keyboard in the middle of the room with sheet music to "The Joint Is Jumpin'" spread out over the music stand. A beat-up leather couch, probably bought second-hand, with a pillow and balled-up blanket. She guesses that he spent his nights here, and fell asleep with the television on. It is an old-fashioned living room—so unlike her and Lewis's, everything digital, blinking, so minimalistic that she still can't figure out how to turn on the overhead lights. Leo would hate her new car. She hates it, too. But these things bring Lewis so much happiness, and she wants Lewis to be happy, for now that she is growing old, she is aware that she will die many years before her husband.

She finds the pamphlets on the kitchen counter. Leo had attended a timeshare seminar. That seems right. Mexico. He seemed like the type of man who would spend a lot of time down there, then relocate entirely. He should have died there. He should have died in a palapa, a margarita in his hand. A man alone on a beach.

His bedroom is also painted blue, even the ceiling. He had striped sheets. She smells the pillow but it smells like any old man's pillow. The coroner's officer has given her a bag of Leo's clothes and she removes the heavy scuffed boots from the bag and sets them inside the closet, takes the T-shirt and the jeans with a torn knee and places them on the bed. She sets the pair of white tube socks and the ratty boxer shorts on top of the T-shirt. In the bottom of the bag is Leo's old military jacket. She remembers the day he found it in a thrift store, how proudly he hefted it onto his shoulders and sauntered around, searching for a mirror. Tore off the tag with his teeth, threw his arm around her, guided her out of the store and into the street. It is threadbare now, the neck stained from sweat. She can't believe he still wore it. She breathes in, and there it is—the faint scent of his cologne.

"You big idiot," she says to the room.

On the bedside table are two pictures in silver frames: Jesse on his wedding day (Jesse must have sent Leo the picture—Leo did not attend), wearing a lilac shirt and a black tie, his hair slicked back with gel. He looks so thin in the picture that she finds it shocking. He became a vegan as a teenager, and was always too skinny after that, crow's feet and laugh lines in his face. In the picture, he wears a tiepin in the shape of a dog.

"You should have been there," she says to the empty blue room. "It was such a nice day."

She knows there are things, of course—ways in which Jesse has hidden his damage from her. Drugs, she is certain, when he was younger. But something else, too. A sense she had when Jesse was a teenager. Out-of-control promiscuity. What he actually got up to remains a mystery, though she saw glimpses of it: kids showing up at the house in the middle of the night; empty bottles of antibiotics from a walk-in clinic; even something Dmitri said once—that Jesse needed to always be touching someone.

Evelina sets the frame down and picks up the one behind it. It is a photo of Dmitri and one of his dogs, a dramatic mountain landscape in the background. He, too, has chiselled his body down to what looks like stone.

Jesse and Dmitri don't speak anymore, though neither will articulate why. They didn't have a falling-out. There was no argument. No screaming match; nothing came to blows. She thinks she knows why, though. She thinks it is because Jesse finally told him what happened.

Now, Dmitri lives in a loft five hundred miles away. He has three dogs.

He isn't lonely, he says.

He has found a life that works for him.

She will call Jesse and Dmitri when she gets home. She will tell them that Leo had a massive heart attack in his sleep, did not suffer, did not leave them anything, never updated his medical records to list anyone but her as next of kin, was living two miles away from her and Lewis for years.

She searches for a photo album, or more pictures in frames, a Polaroid on the refrigerator door, but finds nothing. She guesses that he was the type of man who didn't spend much time at home. She might wander into the neighbourhood bar. That's where she will find out about Leo, not in this stale, cramped apartment, with its empty refrigerator and its never-slept-in bed. Some guy in a newsboy cap will tell her about Leo. Some guy with a beer in his hand.

In the back of a dresser drawer, she finds a Moleskine with a bunch of pencil sketches. He must have been teaching himself how to draw—or maybe Holly taught him before they split up. Gradually, the sketches become less abstract and start to look more like people. Mostly, the drawings are of old men—no, these are self-portraits. He managed to capture his signature hangdog look. He figured out how to draw his own eyes. She stares at him, staring back at her. When she comes to the portraits of her, she puts her hand on the dresser. This isn't, of course, what she looks like now. No, these are drawings of her when they first met. Hair down to her waist; her face so much fuller. The portraits are so startlingly good that he must have drawn them from a photograph. But where is the photograph? She would like to have it. She would like to look at her young self. Her eyes flood with tears. She would do anything to go back in time, to take her young self by the shoulders.

She rifles through the dresser, searching for the photograph of herself, but finds instead a small sealed envelope. It is affixed with insufficient postage, and thus the letter is not recent. She bites her lip and unseals it, carefully, as though the dead man will return at any minute and she will have to quickly press it closed.

The letter is folded in thirds, two rings weighing it down. One is a simple gold band with three rectangular-shaped diamonds, but the other is an incredible feat of goldsmithing. The band is made of what looks like hundreds of tiny entwined gold wires, a small milky gemstone tucked in the centre, meant, Evelina presumes, to resemble a bird's nest with a little egg hidden inside. Or maybe the gem is meant to be Saturn, and the gold wires are its rings. She turns the ring over, studying it, but it is an optical illusion: she blinks and it is a bird's nest; she blinks again and it is Saturn.

The letter consists of only two sentences, written in cursive so shaky and tentative that it looks like a child's.

They slipped off her fingers and into my hands.

She puts her fingers to her mouth. What was his name? Denny. Denny, that's it. She is holding a letter meant for Denny Gusev.

Why didn't Leo mail it, or throw it away? Why has he kept it all these years?

Is it too late to say I'm sorry?

The rings must be worth thousands of dollars. She could be holding thousands of dollars in her hand.

She wonders if she should try to find Denny. To give him back the rings. Yes, that is the right thing to do. Though he is probably dead by now. Either that or eighty years old. He might not be alive, but he might have children. Or other family. Or Vera might have family who would want them. She will do it when she gets home: search for Denny's name, figure out a way to get in touch.

She slides the Moleskine back into the dresser drawer, the rings still in her hand. She thinks she might drive all the way to Squire Point and spend the morning out there. She roots around in Leo's closet, finds an old, moth-eaten overcoat. She tucks Vera Gusev's rings into one of the overcoat's secret pockets, so there will be no chance of losing them.

"Goodbye, Leo," she says, and locks the door.

It is nine o'clock when she reaches the first parking lot. The sky is bright with morning sunlight, and she finds herself alone on the trail that leads to the lake, the wind lapping violently around her as she walks.

Years ago, city council voted to install a railing. You used to be able to walk straight across the lake in winter, nothing but a sheet of ice between you and the water. You can't do that now. She supposes it is safer, but you can't install safety bars and railings all over the wonderful, dangerous parts of the world. It is good for the world to remain a little bit dangerous, she thinks, though she isn't sure where the thought comes from, or where it leads to. It seems like something Leo would have said to her in the early days. Maybe he once said those very words, and now the thought is implanted in her mind as her own. Anyway, it doesn't matter. The lake hasn't frozen over in years. In fact, she can't remember the last time it snowed in Whale Bay. But today the wind is vicious and so she draws the old coat around her, tucks her chin into her chest. Ahead of her, she sees a bronze plaque. MIRROR LAKE, it says. She is sure the lake didn't have a name before. When did this happen, and who decided on the name? "Mirror Lake," she says aloud. The name isn't altogether displeasing.

She walks quickly to the edge of the lake, where there is a bench for people to sit and look out over the water. She is surprised to see a woman sitting there, a woman all in grey. For a moment, Evelina thinks she is a statue. But instead the woman turns her head as Evelina approaches and offers her a cigarette.

"Why not?" says Evelina, who hasn't smoked since her fishing-boat days. She sits next to the woman, and the woman holds out a lighter. Evelina lights the cigarette, sheltering the flame from the wind with Leo's coat. "My ex-husband was a smoker," Evelina says. "The smell—it brings me back."

The woman looks about as old as Evelina, and wears a grey coat that has seen better days, and thick, black-rimmed glasses.

"He died," says Evelina. "Last night."

"Just like that," says the woman. "Like a bolt of lightning." She scans the lake while she speaks.

"Like that, I suppose," says Evelina. "We hadn't talked in years."

"Will you have a funeral?" the woman asks.

Evelina shrugs. "No."

"Oh, I'm sorry," the woman says. "I didn't mean to upset you." She passes Evelina a tissue, and when Evelina presses it to her cheek she finds that indeed she is crying.

"You didn't upset me," says Evelina. "I'm just tired."

Sitting here, on the little bench at the edge of the lake, she wishes she could tell the woman how unhappy she was for most of her life, how she spent her twenties and thirties trying to stop herself from backing into a corner and screaming until the blood vessels burst in her eyes—but how nothing is wrong anymore, not really, and how every day she has to remind herself of this, and some nights she has to repeat to herself that everything is okay now, and some nights she can't believe how many times she has to say it before she begins to believe it herself.

She has a wonderful group of girlfriends now, and they are even planning a beach holiday this summer, their husbands left at home. And Lewis. She has Lewis. That is something—to have loved someone for so long and so deeply—though in truth they are more like old friends. He was so muscular when they first met that she laughed the first time he took off his shirt. You're like an action hero, she said, running her hands over his biceps, his chest, pulling him toward her.

And yet when was the last time she kissed his lips? She still finds him handsome, though he doesn't tend to himself like he used to.

In all their years of marriage, they had only one awful fight—decades ago, when he told her he wanted to have a child. She said no. Anyway, that is his life's regret, not hers. And they have money. Lewis's pension is not insignificant. And she isn't a bookkeeper anymore for the Whale Bay Operatic Society—she has become their costume designer. For years, she kept a sketchbook filled with court jesters, people in gowns, men in tuxedos. She took it to work with her one day, and the director saw them, offered her a job. She has held the position since her early forties, thinks she'll retire when her eyes finally give out. Even still, she has to remind herself that she doesn't have to use rags instead of paper towels. She still buys only the cheapest four-pack of toilet paper. You never know. The wind could shift and you could find yourself, alone and homeless, at the edge of the world.

The truth is, not everything in her life is all right. She wants to explain to the woman in grey why she hardly sees Dmitri. Why they never speak, save for an obligatory Christmas phone call once a year. And why lately she feels such a coldness from Jesse, a coldness that seemed to start the day his daughter was born. But how can she explain such things? Where would she begin? She understands they are busy now, attending to their families and careers. Still, she suspects that it is more than their busy lives. She suspects they share too many memories that none of them want to revisit. The past is not buried. The past is right there, like a coin in a shallow pool, and all she has to do is reach.

In the last moments of the day, right before she falls asleep, she feels what all of them must feel—a small sliver of toxic bile running through her blood, the weight of what happened.

Maybe it is easier, then, to drift apart. To forget.

Still, on the rare occasions that she is invited to Jesse's house, she finds herself watching him closely when he holds his daughter. Studying his hands. How tightly they grip the baby's little thighs, her little arms.

Or did he get all the violence out of him that day at the lake?

She remembers the last time she saw Leo, right after Holly left him, and how he described to them over dinner, in detail, his ascetic lifestyle. He looked to her in that moment more like a small woman than a man. Something about the hips. The flesh having been winnowed. Punishing himself, that was the obvious answer. Searching for redemption. He barely touched his plate of food that night, though he drank plenty of their beer.

"A woman died here, years and years ago," Evelina says, and takes a deep drag from the cigarette.

"I remember," says the woman in grey. "We're sitting on her bench." She gestures behind her, where indeed Vera's name is engraved.

"I wonder who donated it," says Evelina.

"Her husband did," says the woman in grey.

"My son," Evelina begins. "My son—"

"Yes?" says the woman in grey.

"My son pushed her into the water."

Evelina turns to see the woman's reaction, but the woman has stood up and is a few paces away. The woman doesn't respond, and Evelina wonders whether she has heard her. It is a bold thing: to tell a stranger the secret she has carried in her heart since she was thirty-five years old. She wants to shove the words back in her mouth.

The woman whistles, and then whistles again, and Evelina hears the dog's footfalls before she sees him emerge from the woods, his fur slick with morning dew. The dog makes his way to the two women, and Evelina lets him run his warm tongue over her cold hands. "Hi, sweetie, hi," she says to the dog, petting his head and scratching his ears. He reminds her so much of Scout she can hardly bear it. "Hi, sweetheart. Yes, sweetheart."

"Come on, boy," the woman says.

"I used to—" Evelina begins to say, but the woman and dog are already walking up the path. She feels her pulse quicken, her heart pounding in her chest. You're dreaming. You're dreaming. Wake up. Wake up. Wake up now.

"Wait," Evelina calls out. "Wait." She stumbles up the path but catches her moccasin on a root, and then she is on all fours, pine needles stuck to the palm of her hand.

"Please," she says. "Come back."

The sun is rising through the trees and the trail is backlit, but Evelina thinks she can make out the image of the woman and her dog. She blinks and there is nothing. What was she thinking? She shakes her head. She has come down hard on her wrist and she sits a minute, worrying it with her other hand. She feels a deep pressure building in her chest. She isn't sure she has ever let herself feel anything for Vera, but now, her hand wrapped around her wrist, she feels a great pain. What wouldn't she give to be able to tell Vera she is sorry? She feels, in this moment, that she would give almost anything.

"Come back," she calls again, but there is no one on the path except her.

Evelina rises to her feet and walks back to the lake. The cigarette has made her dizzy and she opens the coat a little, lets the cold breeze off the water enter and wrap around her chest. She cranes her neck and lifts her face to the sky. Her cellphone is ringing, and she knows it is Lewis, newly awake and having discovered her note, calling to make sure she is okay and to ask why she didn't wake him. But certain things in life you have to go through alone.

The wind picks up and Evelina watches it move over the surface of the lake. Now that the sun has fully risen, the water is a deep, rich gold colour, and she relaxes for the first time that morning, lets the coat fall open a little more, does not shield herself from the cold.

"I'm sorry," she says to the lake, "I'm sorry." She stands at the water's edge, and fishes Vera Gusev's rings out of the coat pocket and holds them in front of her. "You have no idea how sorry I am."

She thinks of her own desperation as a young woman, furiously scratching away at a lottery card in the hope of winning a million dollars. In the hope that happiness could be that simple.

As though she is skipping stones, she sends one of Vera Gusev's rings, and then the other, over the surface of the lake until they reach its centre, then waits until she feels certain they have sunk to its depths.

At the morgue, she had held the photograph of Leo away from her body and stared at his face. It could've been any old man in the photograph. The morgue was as cold as she had imagined it to be, and she was grateful that she had worn a sweater. Still, someone—one of the assistants, maybe—should've wrapped a blanket around her. There should've been some gesture of kindness, of comfort, of warmth.

In the photograph, the old man's face was thin, drawn, his head entirely bald. But it *was* Leo, yes, in the photograph. Yes. She could identify him, yes. That is Leo. That is Galileo Dmitrius Lucchi.

She hadn't said his name aloud in so very long.

"How did he die?" Evelina asked the coroner's officer.

"Technically?" said the coroner's officer. "A heart attack. But if you want my opinion, your husband drank himself to death."

Now, staring into the lake at Squire Point, she thinks of Leo when they first met. The sudden red rock and desert sprawl of San Garcia.

A wormhole has opened and on one end, she stands at the edge of the lake in her black stretch pants and moccasins, her hair as white as crushed ice; and on the other, she stands on the deck of an old wooden seiner, throwing a silver fish into the sea for a harbour seal.

Well, she wants to say to the dead man, were you reincarnated? Are you flying around currently as some little bird? Are you an earthworm, nosing your way through black soil? Are you coming out of your chrysalis, wings spread in the gold-coloured light? Are you a great white whale, breaking through the waves, while I watch alone from the shore? Are you a sea anemone, slowly moving along the ocean floor? Are you being born? Did you hear music when you died? Did you feel happy? Were you ready to go? Have you risen above it all and are you looking down on me? Are you watching me watching you? Am I the only one you ever loved? Do you care what happens to your body? Where are you now?

ACKNOWLEDGMENTS

WITH IMMENSE GRATITUDE to my agent, Claudia Ballard, and to my editors, Nicole Winstanley and Sarah Savitt, who transformed this book (and my life). To Lara Hinchberger, Deborah Sun de la Cruz, and to everyone at Hamish Hamilton/Penguin Random House Canada; Virago/Little, Brown UK; Malpaso Ediciones; and William Morris Endeavor. To Brian Trapp and Jeanne Shoemaker, especially. To E., my greatest creation. To Patrick O'Keeffe, Tania Hershman, Kate Soles, Leah Stewart, Sara Peters, Mika Tanner, and all I'm forgetting whose eyes moved over the pages of this book. To Gary Dawson, Roger Denley, Michael Harvey, Jim Hewes, Officer J., and the late Jennifer Schmidt. To the Center for the Study of Women in Society, the Office of the Vice President for Research and Innovation, and the College of Arts and Sciences at the University of Oregon; the Canada Council for the Arts; the Ohio Arts Council; the Mineral School; the Writers OMI at Ledig House; and the Iowa Writers' Workshop, where this book began. My title comes from Jia Tolentino's essay, "How a Woman Becomes a Lake," published in *The New Yorker* in November, 2018. (Thank you for your blessing.) Always and forever to Lorna Jackson, the inciting incident of my writing life. And to Brian Hendricks, somewhere out there and dearly missed.